*A Tale of lies, deception, friendship,
love and murder*

DANGEROUS ATTRACTION

D1478162

BY PEGGY CHERNOW

Also by Peggy Chernow

Despicable Lies

Second Chances

Trapped

To my sister, Kay Blossom
who has been a source of great support
and a valued, loving critic.

And as always, to my wonderfully patient husband,
Bart, who is always by my side.
His wise advice and kind suggestions
are greatly appreciated.

AUGUST

Savannah stood outside the Fort Lauderdale court-house and watched in dismay as a deputy from the Sheriff's department led her best friend Marci away. Marci turned and gave her a forlorn smile, trying not to cry, but her quivering lower lip betrayed her emotions. Only hours before, the two inseparable friends had been planning a celebratory late summer vacation trip to Paris; but now, deemed a flight risk with her passport confiscated, the only place Marci would be visiting was a 6-by-8 foot holding cell in the local Broward County jail until she could clear her name or await her trial in confinement.

CHAPTER 1

Savannah Wright, all five foot five inches of her, rose gracefully from her position on an upholstered stool behind one of the twelve display cases in her father's shop. *Wrights* was a prestigious jewelry store located on the famous Ft. Lauderdale shopping street, Las Olas Boulevard. The attractive avenue was designed to attract cars, foot traffic and tourists, much like Worth Avenue in Palm Beach or Rodeo Drive in Beverly Hills. The airy, sun-filled showroom catered to both foreign visitors and a wealthy local clientele. Rent on Las Olas was exceptionally high, and the merchandise in the stores lining the street was commensurately expensive. *Wrights* was one of the largest jewelers in the southern part of the United States and had earned a reputation for excellence. The store was a mini-Tiffany & Co. or Harry Winston.

Savannah smiled as a new customer entered the showroom and began to look around at the exquisite merchandise. "Welcome to *Wrights*. How may I help you?"

"I'm looking for a pair of gold and silver earrings. Nothing too fancy or super expensive. I'm treating myself, so keeping the price down is important."

"I understand." Savannah swiped a strand of long blond hair off her face. "Do you have anything special in mind? We have a full range of inventory here, if you don't mind my bragging. I'm Savannah Wright and my Dad began this establishment. I admit I may be biased, but I think our jewelry collection is outstanding."

"It's nice to meet you, Savannah. I'm Marci Morgan. I'm new in town and – as of yesterday – newly divorced. I decided to treat myself to a "'happy to be out of that awful marriage'" present. I hope that doesn't sound too weird." She grimaced thinking she probably sounded foolish. "But I deserve it. Our marriage and divorce were equally unpleasant. I'm looking forward to starting a new life."

Marci looked a little embarrassed for having so unguardedly blurting out her feelings to a stranger. She was normally shy, but for some reason she felt the need to explain the reason for buying jewelry for herself. "I was thinking maybe something by David Yurman. I already have a gold and silver braided cable bracelet from his earlier collection, and I get a lot of complements on it. Do you carry that designer?"

"Yes, we do and your reason for coming in doesn't sound weird at all. Folks come up with all kinds of excuses to pamper themselves with jewelry, and a divorce – no, actually a chance for a fresh start--is as good as any. I've even known men and women to give themselves elaborate divorce parties. To many, who have felt trapped in bad marriages, their divorce is a time for celebration. One girlfriend of mine actually gave herself a theme party, and asked all her guests to wear black and white stripes to represent her escape from prison. It was pretty hilarious."

Marci laughed. "Well then, I guess my reaction is rather mild in comparison."

Savannah led Marci to a glass display case and pulled out two sets of Yurman earrings. "This first pair is priced at $1375 and the second is $2775, because its workmanship is more complicated. Both are lovely and would match the bracelet you described. Why don't you try them on? See which you like better."

Marci picked up both pairs and held them up to her ears in front of the large oval mirror sitting on the display counter. She examined both sets closely and decided she would be thrilled to own either one. She was clearly torn, but finally handed the least expensive pair back to Savannah. "I'll take these. Both sets are gorgeous, but I can definitely use the extra $1400 I'll be saving. Money is a little tight for me right now. My ex fought me for every penny of our settlement. He was generous while we were married, but as soon as he walked out, and with a new mrs. waiting in the wings, he became Mr. Scrooge."

Marci appeared angry for a moment, but then her expression softened. She knew she should not take her frustration out on Savannah. "The judge ordered Stan to give me half the value of our house and seven years of alimony," she explained. "It was a fair settlement but not generous. Before I married my ex, I was studying fashion design and yearned for a career in that field. But because I married so young, at barely twenty, I never finished college, and instead I devoted myself to being the perfect corporate wife and doing volunteer work. I'm seriously regretting that decision and plan to resume my studies in night school here."

She shook her head at her predicament. "I need a job and to make a new life for myself." She forced an awkward smile. "Meanwhile, my ex is off in Europe wining and dining the woman he left me for." Marci shrugged her shoulders in defeat. "I realize life's not fair, but I certainly never expected at the ripe old age of thirty-six to end up like this...single, alone, and having to worry about how long my money will last."

Savannah studied the woman carefully. Marci was super-model attractive, with short brunette hair and dazzling green eyes. She was clearly athletic, and probably had worked out often as evidenced by the toned, muscular appearance of her arms and legs. She exuded a sweet vulnerability. Savannah gathered Marci's ex had hurt her badly, and that the scars of her failed marriage would hang over her until she could begin to forge a new path.

She liked Marci and instantly felt a strong kinship, understanding exactly how difficult it was to survive and regain personal esteem after a bad marriage. She had endured the same thing herself ten years ago. She had recovered from her divorce trauma and wanted no part of being tied legally to another man. She was popular and open to new relationships, as long as they were casual, but she sensed Marci would not be, at least not yet.

"Sounds like you've had a rough time." Savannah commiserated. "I've been there too and I promise, there are better days ahead." She picked up both sets of earrings. "Please excuse me, Marci. I'll be right back." She went into the office at the back of the store to speak with her dad.

While she was waiting, Marci strolled casually around the charming shop examining other pieces in various cases. She recognized jewelry by Gucci, Ippolita, Kendra Scott and Roberto Coin. *Wrights* truly deserved its reputation as an elegant store, and it had a beautiful selection of fine jewelry.

She gazed around the impressive shop with its multiple, high-polished mahogany and glass display cases, sparkling crystal chandeliers and colorful paintings showing scenes of old Fort Lauderdale. It was a warm and inviting place, and she couldn't help but envy Savannah for working here.

Savannah returned from the office carrying a small white bag with a *Wrights* green ribbon tied to the handle. "Here are your earrings, Marci. I hope you enjoy them and wear them in good health."

"Thanks. How much do I owe you?"

Savannah gave her a figure and Marci looked surprised. "That can't be. It's less than the original price you quoted me only a few minutes ago? I think you've made a mistake. Maybe you'd better recalculate." She handed the bag back.

"No, that's the correct amount. However, I appreciate your honesty. There's no mistake. I spoke to my dad and he agreed to give you the *Wrights* friends and family discount. After all, we divorced gals have to stick together," Savannah grinned. She could see from Marci's smile that she was thrilled and appreciated the gesture. Marci wore her emotions on her face.

"I don't know what to say. That's so kind of you both." She looked to the back of the store were Savannah's father stood looking on. He was a handsome man, probably in his late fifties with a gorgeous suntan and silver hair. He looked more like a man who spent his days relaxing on a boat than working in a store, even if he was the owner of the business. She exaggerated the words "thank you" so he could read her lips. He smiled back and gave her a thumbs up.

"My dad's a truly nice man," Savannah said, watching the sweet exchange. "I told him a little bit about your story and he immediately wanted to do this for you." She looked back at her dad and smiled. "I've got an idea. Would you like to come back here around 5:30 tonight? That's when we close. You and I could go across the street to Cages for a drink. It's a lively place and we can celebrate your divorce. I'd love a chance to get to know you better and there's something I'd like to talk to you about. I think it might be just the ticket for you...and for me too."

"Well, that certainly sounds mysterious." Marci's eyes lost a little of their sadness. "I'll definitely be back, and thanks again for the discount." She picked up her bag and left smiling.

Savannah turned to greet another customer who had entered the store. "Good afternoon Mrs. Dodge," she said to the lady and waved goodbye to Marci. "How may I help you today?"

Dave Wright came into the showroom and went over to his David Yurman section. He returned the less expensive pair of earrings to the display shelf and chuckled. There was more to Wright's generosity today. Marci would not realize that Savannah had also switched the pairs and given her the more expensive earrings until she opened the jewelry pouch later. He wished he could be there to see the shocked expression on her face. His daughter had taken an immediate liking to Marci, as she always did with those in trouble or to rescue dogs or birds with broken wings. Savannah was a born nurturer...and sometimes it got her and occasionally him into trouble.

CHAPTER 2

Marci drove back to her rented townhouse, after stopping at Publix for a few groceries and at Total Wine for some California Chardonnay. She put her key in the door lock and simultaneously picked up a small pile of mail that had been left on her doorsill. The communal mailroom and main public space for the townhouse complex was closed for renovation, so the mail carrier left the resident's mail on their doorsills.

Marcy put her groceries and the bag from *Wrights* on the kitchen table and thumbed through the bills and advertisements, relieved that there was only an electric bill and one for her cell phone. She had put herself on a strict budget in an attempt to stretch her alimony payments to the fullest while she was getting herself resettled and her new life going. She had even stopped her cable television service and given up her Starbuck lattes. She was not used to making budget decisions like this but nothing about her situation now was like anything she'd prepared for.

Stan, her ex, was a wealthy man and Marci, who considered herself the injured party in the divorce, had expected a much more generous settlement from him. Regrettably, her lawyer had not been able to convince the court to do more. The judge ruled that Marci was still young and should be able to support herself. She had no ongoing medical problems that would keep her from working or children to raise. He ordered what he thought was fair settlement after fifteen years of marriage, but he expected her to return to school or find a job and become self-sufficient.

Life was ironic. Marci had gone from being a supremely comfortable woman to one who suddenly needed to earn a living. Her husband had handed her a wakeup call on his way out the door. She took the funds from her portion of the sale of their house in DC and gave them to a stockbroker to invest. She swore she would not touch the principal under any circumstances. She might need it when her alimony stopped and for her old age.

She looked in dismay around the one-bedroom place, sparsely furnished with just a few favorite pieces from her old life. She wondered if her hasty decision to move to Florida to get as far away from Stan and their social circle, the one that appeared to be closing ranks around him, was the right one. But Florida, with its allure of sunshine and pristine beaches, fit her mood. And she should fit in because much of the population were transplants.

She glanced ruefully at the two metal clothing racks she'd bought at Target and were standing side-by-side along the living room wall. Her bedroom closet was jammed with resort attire, haute couture dresses and hangars full of silk blouses and linen slacks…clothing she doubted she would have an occasion or a place to wear now. On the bottom of the crammed closet and the clothing racks were at least thirty pair of designer stilettos, athletic shoes and flats. Her wardrobe had once been intrinsic to her identity. But who would she be now?

In her previous life, as the wife of a prominent attorney, Marci had lived in a large house in Northwest Washington, DC. Her walk-in closets alone were more spacious than her whole bedroom in Ft. Lauderdale. While she was married, she had successfully run her home with the help of a housekeeper and a gardener. Her everyday life consisted of ladies' lunches, weekly massages, workouts with a personal trainer and extravagant vacations.

Her former friends had been frivolous, but Marci had also always spent part of her week doing meaningful volunteer work. She diligently pursued ways to help children. While she was grateful for her affluent lifestyle, and often discomforted by its excesses, she never took it for granted. She was a giving and generous person.

Suddenly, on his fiftieth birthday, Marci was blind-sided when Stan calmly announced over an Italian dinner that he wanted a divorce. Stiffly, he explained that he had probably lived more than half of his life, and that there was someone else, someone who could give him the family she could not. His harsh words brought tears to her eyes. In spite of surgery for painful endometriosis, she had been unable to conceive. He had refused to consider adoption or hiring a surrogate to carry their child. It was as though he preferred to be childless over being happy. And, he could blame his misery on Marci. He never stopped to consider that their fertility issues could have been his fault. Several doctors intimated that, but he had refused to be tested.

Marci's eyes welled as she replayed a mental reel of arguments upon argument followed by long stretches of silence. She had begged him to try counseling, but Stan wasn't interested in that either. Why hadn't she seen this coming? She cringed as he described his new love - the young woman who worked in his office. She could not compete with youth or a fertile uterus. He announced that he was done with her and with their marriage. In fact, he moved out that night.

Marci had reeled from her husband's betrayal and initially sought solace in yoga and chardonnay. But eventually, she realized that she needed to get over her ex, once-and-for-all, and build a new life for herself.

Moving to Florida had been a first step. Meeting Savannah had been a blessing. Maybe they could become friends.

As she brought out the vacuum cleaner and began tidying up, she wondered why Savanah wanted to see her. But no matter the reason, she was looking forward to socializing with somebody new. She glanced at her watch. It was almost five o'clock. Time to change into something appropriate for Happy Hour. It was exciting to finally have a reason to dress up.

She thought it would be a nice gesture to wear her new earrings and went to open the bag from *Wright*. She was stunned when she found the more expensive pair of Yurman earrings nestled in the jewelry pouch. Happy tears formed in her eyes. She instantly understood what Savannah and her father had done for her and she was amazed at their generosity. It had been her lucky day when she'd ventured into *Wrights*. She finished dressing and put on the new earrings, wearing a grin, she locked the door behind her. Happy Hour awaited.

CHAPTER 3

Marci casually strolled into the bar. Several heads turned to admire her as she entered the room. She stood almost six feet tall, wearing a stunning red and white Pucci dress with matching Louboutin red high heels. Oblivious to the appreciative glances her arrival was causing, she casually scanned the room until she spotted Savannah sitting at the far end of the massive oak bar. She was perched on a metal stool; her legs provocatively crossed to reveal just enough tanned thighs to attract attention from the males nearby. She was chatting amicably with another bar patron and enjoying her drink. When she saw Marci, she signaled for her to come over and held up a glass. Happy hour was in full swing and every stool and booth was occupied. Cages was a popular bar and restaurant and attracted many of the young professionals who lived in downtown Fort Lauderdale. The drinks were strong. The music and chatter were loud and the hamburgers were delicious and affordable.

"I should have suggested someplace quieter where we could talk," Savannah apologized. "I'd forgotten how loud this place can get. I come here a lot after work to unwind and never paid attention to the noise level before. There's a patio area out back. We can take our drinks and move out there, so we don't have to shout and can talk more privately.

"That's not necessary. I don't mind the noise, if you don't. And by the way, thank you so much for the earring switch. I was flabbergasted when I opened the box earlier." Marci looked around the room, noting the attractive people indulging in their cocktails and flirtations. "It's been so long since I've been out anywhere. I love the energy here. I didn't know Fort Lauderdale could be this lively. One normally only hears about South Beach and the clubs in Miami. I guess we'll just have to exercise our vocal cords to be heard."

"You're welcome regarding the earrings. And as to Cages, it attracts all ages," Savannah admitted. "Even my dad likes it here. But I wanted to talk to you about something serious. Maybe we should we go out back?" The disc jockey had turned up the volume of the music. Some of the crowd enthusiastically joined in, singing and fist pumping to Neil Diamond's *Sweet Caroline*.

"Tell me why you wanted to meet with me, please. But first, I'd like to finish this delicious Cosmo you ordered for me. Thanks for that, by the way." Marci grinned, taking a large gulp of the cocktail. Then she waited for Savannah to begin speaking. She still had no idea what her new acquaintance wanted to discuss, but she was intrigued.

Savannah's lips formed into a hint of a smile. She was sure that what she had to say couldn't compete with a great cocktail, so she took another sip of her own and began cautiously. "I hope you won't be offended. I don't want to presume too much." She tried to catch the bartender's eye to order another round.

Marci raised her eyebrows. "Just go for it," she laughed cheerfully. "I've been offended by better people than you."

"Okay. Here it is." Savannah turned to face Marci directly. "My dad's been running *Wrights* by himself since my mom died. I was nine at the time and now I'm almost forty. Don't misunderstand, he has loved every minute of managing the store, but Dad just turned sixty. I want him to be able to slow down and back away from the daily grind of managing our business. He's taken a day off here and there, but it's not enough. He's an avid golfer, a devoted fisherman and a football fanatic but doesn't have time to enjoy any of those things.

"I've thought about how we could ease him out successfully. I need to find someone who would 'get' our business, and who we would like and trust to help me out at the store. I've started interviewing people but for one reason or another, there's always something lacking in them. Until today! I'm not sure why, but the minute you walked in and started talking, I made an immediate connection with you. When you mentioned your budget and your need to watch your money, it gave me the idea. I discussed it with Dad. He has great people sense and thinks my idea might work."

"What do you have in mind? What's this have to do with me?" Marcy was curious.

"I'd, or rather we'd, like to offer you a full-time job working in our store. I know I'd personally enjoy having another woman my age around. I'll teach you everything I can, and work right alongside of you. When you feel comfortable with the inventory and ready to handle the sales floor by yourself, I'll move into my dad's office in the back and begin to take over that aspect of the business, relieving him of those responsibilities.

He has a keen interest in increasing our on-line presence and expanding to other locations. If you come onboard with us, it would free him up to pursue those interests. If all goes as well, I expect that in a year or so, I can ease Dad out so he can enjoy the golf course – and his other interests, and you and I will run *Wrights* together. What do you think? Does the job appeal to you?"

Marci was flabbergasted. She knew she needed to find a job, but she never expected one to literally drop in her lap. And not just any job – this was one she'd actually love. She didn't need any time to think it over. *Wrights* would be perfect for her. She was thrilled at the opportunity being offered her. This unexpected job was the chance she needed to make a new start. Stan was not going to get the best of her. *Thank you, God…and Savannah.*

"Yes! Yes!" Marci beamed with excitement. She wasn't going to waste a minute playing hard to get. She wanted the job, wanted it very much. "I'd love to work with you and your Dad. This is a dream come true. How can I ever thank you?"

"No need to thank me," Savannah grinned happily. "You'd be doing me a tremendous favor. I know we'll make a great team. Here's to a bright future for us and for *Wrights*." She clinked her glass with Marci's. "Let's go back to the shop and we'll iron out the details."

Marci smiled innocently. "Oh my gosh. I know I haven't asked about the salary, or how many hours you'll want me to work. This is so new to me, but as long as I can make a decent wage, I'm all in. I'll try my best not to let you down. But I do have one important question to ask. It's a possible deal breaker." She giggled and hovered over Savannah. "As part of my employment package, will I get a jewelry discount?"

CHAPTER 4

Marci began work at *Wrights* the next morning. She was a quick learner and absorbed everything Savannah taught her about the jewelry business and the daily routine of the shop. Dave Wright watched them and was delighted by how efficient and professional the two were. They made a good team. Marci displayed a knack for sizing up a customer and knowing what the client would like. She also had an appealing way with them, was warm yet professional, stylishly enough attired to make them trust her sense of taste, but was not intimidating or judgmental. After six months, Savannah had been happy to step back and take over the business side of *Wrights*, managing stock and new orders, while Marci handled the sales operations. It was a perfect arrangement.

Marci had become a real asset to Savannah and Dave, both personally and professionally. Being a member of *Wrights'* team gave Marci a sense of belonging, a feeling of being part of a family. She was proud of what she had learned and about her new-found skills as a salesman. The fact that she sold a record amount of jewelry during her first few months gave her a much-needed confidence boost…and a large bonus. Marci enjoyed every minute of her time at the shop, especially her blossoming friendship with Savannah.

The two women became inseparable despite their differences. Savannah was a take charge, type A personality with clear goals and aspirations. She was driven and had big plans wanting to make *Wrights* a national brand with satellite stores throughout Florida and eventually expand into other states. Her looks were deceiving. When people first met her, they tended to dismiss her because she was so beautiful and playful. But, as they got to know her, they were astounded to find that she was an astute and cunning business person. She was funny and creative and always smiling.

Where Savannah was blond and petite, Marci was model tall with dark luxurious hair and deep-set green eyes. She was shy and a little introverted, especially after her recent divorce, but always pleasant and engaging. She was still hesitant to do anything spontaneously or to take any emotional risks, and whenever Savannah offered to fix her up, Marci resolutely refused. She did, however, enjoy going out with Savannah and her friends. Marci was a follower, not a leader.

Wrights was having a banner quarter. The millennials living and working around Las Olas had discovered the shop and flocked there to make purchases. Many of the male customers flirted and asked her out. She steadfastly but always politely refused. Marci had no interest in complicating her life with new emotional entanglements. She was content with her job and doing girly things with Savannah. She didn't need or want a man in her life at the moment.

Marci was pleased that because of her job she had someplace to wear some of her lovely designer clothes. She was conscious of the image she wanted to project as the face of the store now that Savannah had slipped into the back office. The two women were congenial coworkers and best friends who spent their workday hours together, and much of their downtime too. They kidded each other that if things didn't change, they might end up one day as roommates like Rose and Blanche in *The Golden Girls.*

One afternoon, only minutes before the store was due to close, Marci was beginning to lock up the inventory when a very attractive man pushed the front door buzzer, impatiently waiting to be admitted. Bearing an impressively expensive crocodile briefcase and juggling several cell phones, he anxiously peered through the glass door hoping to be admitted. Marci responded by pushing a button on the side of a display case and let him in.

He rushed over to her. "Thank goodness you're still open." He dropped the briefcase and phones on the nearest stool. "I need a gift for my grandmother. Damn if I didn't forget that today's her 90th birthday. Believe me, I'd never hear the end of it if I showed up for dinner tonight without a present."

Marci looked at him sympathetically and grinned. He was very handsome with gorgeous aqua colored eyes and an impish grin. His triceps were amazingly developed and she noticed that he sported a unique rose tattoo on his forearm. His longish blond hair was windblown and disheveled. Small beads pf perspiration glistened on his forehead and cheeks. He must have sprinted for blocks down Las Olas to reach the store before it closed. The only words she could think of to describe him were "adorably disheveled."

"Don't worry. We'll stay open. Take as long as you need," Marci assured him and handed him a cold bottle of Evian. "What are you thinking of for your grandmother's gift? What might she like?"

"I really don't know," he answered earnestly. "She has so much jewelry as it is. But even at ninety, she still loves new pieces. Although she rarely goes out and has nowhere to wear it, it's her single best source of delight. Do you have any suggestions?"

While he looked around the shop, Marci noticed he took the time to appraise her, stealing glances at her as she moved around the glass cases selecting various pieces that she thought he might like. Evidently, he liked what he saw about her. She was very pretty, tall and slim. Her smile was warm and her voice was gentle. He was instantly interested in her.

Marci was surprised at herself. She felt a strong attraction to the man, but forced herself to keep her voice level and her eyes off his handsome face. After the hurtful way her marriage had ended, she was not about to engage in even a mild flirtation…and certainly not with a customer!

"Tell me," she asked, trying to focus on something besides his physical appearance and her unexpected discomfort, "is your grandmother a formal person or more casual?"

"Oh, very formal," he answered instantly, pushing a strand of damp hair off his face. "She's never without makeup and at least a strand of pearls. And now with her eyesight starting to fail, she seems to favor her bigger pieces. The bigger the better. Whatever I buy her, as long as it's egg-sized and gaudy, she'll love it."

"I see," Marci tried not to smile, but she couldn't help it. The man had painted a vivid picture of his grandmother in just a few simple words. "I don't think we carry anything I'd call gaudy, but we do have some rather over the top items. I'll show them to you, if you'd like. By the way, my name is Marci."

"Alan," he said grinning. "Alan Trent. I didn't mean to offend you, Marci, by requesting something gaudy. It's clear that this is a tasteful shop. It's just that my grandmother is suffering from the early stages of dementia, so I really want to make this gift special. Let me assure you, she's keenly aware that today is her birthday, and she's expecting me to make a big fuss."

"No offense taken." Marci's eyes twinkled. "Come with me over to the last counter on the left. I think I have something that she'll like, just as long as cost is not an issue. You didn't mention how much you're prepared to spend."

"Money's not an issue at all," he stated matter-of-factly and followed behind Marci. Again, she got the sense that he was using the moment to evaluate her and especially her long legs as they crossed the room.

"Here's it is." Marci unlocked the case and brought out a huge coral and diamond brooch which she placed delicately on a black velvet board. "What do you think, Alan? Is this something your grandmother would wear?"

"Well, it's certainly flashy. Not my taste at all, but probably right up her alley." He picked up the unique piece shaped like a pumpkin and turned it over in his hand. "It's very heavy. I suppose that's good. What's the price?"

Marci knew the price of every item in the store, but pretended to look at the discreet little tag attached to the piece. "It's $55,000 and it's a one-of-a-kind brooch that contains 5 carats of VS clarity, brilliant cut diamonds which surround the large piece of authentic red Mediterranean coral. It's a real conversation piece. I've never seen anything quite like it."

Marci tried not to show her distaste. In her opinion, the piece was absurdly ugly…and to use Alan's words, gaudy. She wondered why *Wrights* had it in their inventory in the first place. It wasn't the kind of jewelry Savannah and her dad normally selected for the store. It seemed very out of place and Marci assumed there must be a story. She had to remember to ask Savannah about it later.

"I'll take it." Alan quickly announced. "It's just tacky enough that Grandmother will adore it."

He reached in his pocket for his wallet and fumbled around saying he was looking for his black Amex card. Then he had a change of heart and went over to the stool where he'd left his alligator briefcase. Marci's jaw dropped as he pulled out stacks of hundred-dollar bills and began to count them, one at a time, and stack them in piles of thousands. "I assume for a cash transaction of this size; your store will absorb the Florida state tax to seal the deal?"

"I really don't know," Marci stuttered. "That's above my pay grade." This was a first. Even with all of her former wealthy friends, she had never seen any of them carry around so much cash. "I'll have to go ask the owner. Excuse me please. I'll be right back." She walked to the office to confer with Savannah.

Moments later Savannah came out to the showroom with Marci and introduced herself. "Mr. Trent, I'm Savannah Wright. My father and I own this store. Quite frankly we've never had a cash transaction of this size, but given that we won't have to pay a substantial credit card fee, *Wrights* will be happy to pay the local state sales tax on your behalf. I will note that on your receipt, and we sincerely thank you for your business."

"You are quite welcome."

"And you should know that this beautiful saleslady," he indicated

Marci. "She's very good at her job and the sole reason I'm making this large purchase." He turned his attention back to Marci. "Will you please put the brooch in a gift box and wrap it?" He looked at his watch nervously. "I have to get home for Grandmother's dinner."

"Yes, of course." Marci took the coral pumpkin and soon brought it back, with a receipt and wrapped with Wrights' signature green foil gift paper.

"Thank you for your business," she smiled warmly at Alan, still stunned by the sizeable cash transaction. *Who carries that much money around the streets in a briefcase?*

"I'm sure this will be the first of many transactions between us," he said flirtatiously as he tucked the box in his now nearly empty briefcase and strolled nonchalantly to the door. "Nice to meet you Savannah. And Marci, I'll be seeing you again very soon. You can count on it."

After he left and Savannah had locked the stacks of cash in the office safe, she turned to Marci. "Nice work, my friend. After that sale, let me buy you a drink."

Marci smiled and nodded her agreement.

"That man just bought the ugliest piece in the store's collection. We've been trying to get rid of it for years. Dad made a huge mistake when he purchased it. He thought some eccentric person would want it for - oh, I don't know – as a Halloween gift, maybe? Boy was he wrong. We've been stuck with it for years. You're quite a saleswoman, Marci. Thank you."

Savannah turned off the shop's lights and locked the front door, carefully setting the alarm.

"Let's get that drink and we'll call Dad and tell him the good news. He'll be ecstatic that you sold the pumpkin. As a matter of fact, he'll probably treat us to dinner in celebration."

CHAPTER 5

After the evening out with Marci, Savannah had trouble sleeping. She tossed and turned and finally got out of bed to get a glass of water. In her mind, she kept running through the strange transaction with Alan Trent. Why would anyone carry around that much cash in a briefcase? She hoped he wasn't into something illegal. Drugs? Prostitution? Sex trafficking? Paying cash for a large purchase was not in itself illegal. But it was certainly more than a little suspicious.

As a young girl, Savannah had loved the Nancy Drew mystery series by Carolyn Keene and fantasized that someday she would have the same sleuthing abilities as the heroine. By the time she was in the eighth grade, she had read every volume of the series, her favorite title being *The Secret of the Old Clock*. She still had the collection stored in boxes in the attic, hoping one day to pass them on to her own daughter. Savannah's dad still teased her about her passion for detective work and lovingly nicknamed her "Nancy".

Over the years, Savannah had put to use what she learned in those

books. As a young teenager she'd spotted their housekeeper helping herself to Dave's liquor supply, substituting water for his vodka. Once when
she became suspicious, she followed a former employee to a Jupiter pawn
shop and caught her trying to sell merchandise that had gone missing
from *Wrights* weeks earlier. Savannah was not suspicious by nature, but
had a keen internal warning system when she thought something was
not on the level. Her instincts were very good, and she had always been
correct, so far.

Wrights was doing well financially and especially since the addition of
Marci. However, the business was entering into the time of year when
their expenses were the greatest. Estimated quarterly IRS taxes were
due and the shop's air conditioning compressor needed replacing. The
strong national economy was inexplicably beginning to stall. The stock
market see-sawed, and with concern about an uncertain financial future
ahead, many of *Wrights*' loyal customers worried about their portfolio
balances and were reluctant to spend money on expensive jewelry. In
addition, Savannah and Dave had taken on Marci with a generous salary
and health benefits – all of this just when the store needed extra cash to
replenish its inventory ahead of the holiday season and for the following
year. The unexpected cash windfall from the sale to Alan Trent would
help the bottom line.

Savannah was due to purchase a major portion of next year's inventory at the upcoming annual international jewelry show in Las Vegas. It
was the one time of the year when the shop spent a great deal of money
on replenishing and updating inventory, and it was always hoped the
pieces she and her dad selected would appeal to their clientele and sell
considerably above cost. The markup on jewelry was often 100% - 200%.

Carrying outdated stock that didn't move was the financial kiss of death in the business. Customers were always looking for new pieces that were the new trend or classic recognizable brands. They counted on *Wrights* to have beautiful and unique pieces.

The annual JCK International Jewelry Show was the leading jewelry event in North America and traditionally drew over thirty thousand of the most influential jewelry professionals in the world as exhibitors and/or purchasers. It's the venue where new trends and innovations are first introduced and displayed by international designers. Vendors from around the world present their wares and compete for purchase orders. Antique time pieces, the newest, lightest metals, fine jewelry and gemstones…diamonds, emeralds and rubies, are available for purchase for any taste or any price-point.

Savannah and her Dad had shopped the June show together for over a decade. They loved the networking and reconnecting with the numerous venders who attended annually. The show was serious business for everyone involved, but also a fun time for the participants. This year, Savannah planned to surprise Marci by taking her in Dave's place. Her father had agreed to leave the golf course to cover the store in their absence and thought the show would be a great educational experience for Marci.

Savannah purchased airplane tickets and made hotel reservations at Caesar's Palace. She was excited to share the jewelry show experience with her new friend and planned to surprise her with news of the trip in the morning. They would leave in two weeks. She knew Marci had never been to Vegas and Savannah was looking forward to showing off the famous strip. While they had serious buying to do for the store, she also wanted them to have a good time.

Savannah finished her water and returned to bed. She was still agitated and couldn't stay still. Tossing and turning, she finally fell into a fitful sleep in the early hours of the morning, dreaming about Alan Trent standing in front of her, counting piles and piles of money.

CHAPTER 6

Savannah poured a cup of coffee from the Keurig machine in the office and cautiously approached Marci who was rearranging the shelves in the pearl case. "Hi," she said wearily, exhausted from her restless night. She was definitely an eight-hours-of-sleep-a-night type of gal.

"Hi yourself." Marci looked up from her task. "What's up?"

"I have some news that I hope you'll like. It involves taking a trip with me."

"A trip?" Marci was excited at the prospect of going somewhere with Savannah but curious. She was aware that the stalling economy had thinned the store's revenues so this certainly didn't seem to be the optimum time to take a vacation.

"It's to Vegas," Savannah announced with a grin. "I'm taking you to the biggest jewelry show in North America. Dad and I attend every year and as a reward for your hard work, he's agreed to let you go in his place this year. It'll be good for you to learn something about the buying side of the business. He'll man the store for us until we return."

"Wow! Thank you! With all the traveling I've done; I've never been to Vegas. My ex just never had any desire to go there. When do we leave? What should I pack? I gather it can be very hot there."

"Whoa, Girl. I'm glad you're so enthusiastic," Savannah joked. "One question at a time. The show begins in two weeks, and we'll stay for five days. It's a lot of work, moving around from vendor to vendor, but our nights are free and we'll have fun. The show's held in the Vegas convention center and it's always freezing in there. Bring jeans and a sweater and comfortable shoes. We'll do a lot of walking. Our nights will be our own, so we can gamble a little, or take in some shows. The restaurants in Vegas are unbelievable. We'll have a great time – although because we're really there to work, we'll just have to tuck into bed at a decent hour. It used to be that everyone dressed to the nines there, but no longer. The jeans you wear in the daytime can take you right into night, just change into a pretty blouse and nice shoes. With your wardrobe, you'll be the belle of the ball. Did I answer all your questions?" she laughed, pleased that Marci was so excited.

"Yes. I can't believe this Savannah. Thank you so much. You have been like a fairy godmother to me since the first day we met. Look how my pathetic, lonely life has turned around since you and your dad took me under your wings. I've been able to save some significant money, and now a trip to Vegas. Life is good!"

Marci had developed a wonderful rapport with Dave Wright. She found him to be very sophisticated and yet totally down to earth. She had always been comfortable around older men. She'd even married one. Stan had been fourteen years her senior. She enjoyed Dave's company whenever he was in the shop and had learned so much about the jewelry business from him. They often chatted about sports, Broadway shows and occasionally politics. He was charming and knowledgeable and she missed those talks now that he was in the shop less often. In her way, she realized she had developed a little bit of a crush on him. Well, maybe that was the wrong word, though she couldn't quite put a name on their evolving friendship. She was grateful that he was sending her to Vegas and hoped to learn a lot to better repay him for everything he'd done for her.

Savannah wanted to say more about their trip, but a customer was ringing the bell for entrance. "We'll talk later. Duty calls." She nodded towards the shop's front door and was shocked, and not pleasantly, to see Alan Trent standing outside.

"Oh God," Savannah thought uneasily. "I hope he doesn't want to return the pumpkin brooch. Dad was so happy to be rid of it."

Marci buzzed him in, curious also as to why he was back so soon. His grandmother must not have liked her gift. She hated that she'd have to refund his money. She knew Savannah and the store needed it.

"Good morning, Alan," Marci said pleasantly, trying not to betray her anxiety. "What brings you back so soon?"

"Hi Marci," he answered jauntily. "I came to report that my grandmother loved the coral piece and asked me to thank you personally."

Marci sighed with relief. The fifty-five thousand was safe. "I'm so glad the gift was a hit." She was curious about the elder Mrs. Trent. "If it's not too personal, does your grandmother normally do her own jewelry shopping?"

"Not anymore." He frowned slightly. "I may not have mentioned it, but she's confined to a wheelchair now. I do all of her errands, all the shopping. I buy her clothes, groceries, medicines… you name it. But it's my pleasure. She's been great to me so it's the least I can do. My two sisters live out of state and do nothing to help out. I think they're simply waiting for her to die so they can carve up her estate. Neither has called her in months."

"That's shameful and a big burden on you," Marci offered sympathetically. She was impressed by his unselfish devotion. Not too many men were as attentive to their grandmothers as he appeared to be.

"Yes, it's hard sometimes, I must admit. She has some dementia and fading eyesight as I mentioned before. She doesn't have the energy she once did, so she saves it for outings with Consuela, her full-time caregiver, and for her doctors' appointments…of which she has many." He added ruefully. "Older people sure spend a lot of time with their physicians and Grandmother's a world-class hypochondriac."

Marci hardly heard him. She was so relieved that he didn't want his $55,000 back. She turned towards Savannah who was standing behind her and gave her a discreet thumbs up sign that Alan could not see. She knew her friend must have worried about having to return the money, too.

"Is your grandfather living?" Marci asked, "if you don't mind me asking."

"No, he passed a few years ago and that's when my grandmother started her decline. It seemed to happen almost overnight. I'm glad that I've been here and able to help her. I'm a tax accountant and I work at home, so it's not been a hardship to supervise her care. She has a devoted staff, but nothing replaces family. I'm not married, so I can give a lot of time to her well-being. In return she lets me live in her guest house rent free. It's a pretty good deal."

Marci looked at him with new respect. Unlike her ex, here was a man who was steadfast and loyal, with a deep appreciation of family. She could never imagine him cutting and running like Stan had. He was obviously a loving and considerate grandson. And also, for some reason, hearing that he wasn't married, made her happy.

Alan reached out and took her hand. "Thank you, again Marci. I'm so happy we met. I know this might seem very sudden, but would you have dinner with me, tonight or tomorrow? I think there could be something special between us."

She gently withdrew her hand. She did not want to hurt his feelings, but she was not in a place yet where she would consider dating, even though she found Alan to be exceedingly handsome and likable.

"I'm sorry Alan. It's nothing against you personally, but I'm not dating. Lady scorned and still healing." She tried to make light of her situation. "It's an old story. But thanks for the nice invitation."

Alan took a step back and searched her face. *How could such a pretty lady not have a man in her life?* He was not easily put off, but he'd give her a little time to reconsider. "I'll accept your "no" for now," he said softly, "but I hope you'll reconsider. I promise, I don't bite."

"I'm sure you don't," Marci said uneasily. His persistence was making her uncomfortable. "But I'm afraid I won't change my mind."

"We'll see," he said evenly. "In the meantime, since my grandmother loved the coral piece so much, I'd like to get her the matching ring that I saw in the display case yesterday. She's a size seven. Do you still have it?"

"Yes, we do, but I believe that ring is a size eight. We can resize it for her in a few hours if you'd like to come back this afternoon." She went to the case, withdrew the ring and handed it to him. "It's priced at $23,000."

He studied the ring for a moment, held it up to the light and nodded his agreement. "I'll be back around four. Also, I'll need appraisals for the brooch and the ring. I'll be paying with cash again."

"No problem, of course," Marcy answered. "I was going to mail you the appraisal from yesterday in fact, but possibly because of the late hour, we didn't take your address. My apologies."

"I live on my grandmother's estate. It's located in Coastal Beach." He wrote down the address and added his cell phone number. "It's practically around the corner from here. You should come by sometime."

Marci knew Coastal Beach. It was one of Fort Lauderdale's most exclusive and expensive neighborhoods. She'd discovered it soon after moving and often drove around it admiring the enormous homes. No wonder Alan could afford to buy expensive jewelry.

"I'll have everything ready at four o'clock," she assured him. "Thanks again for buying from *Wrights*." She was trying hard to act professionally, but she was still shaken by his attention and his dinner invitation.

"Okay then. See you later. And please think about my offer." He turned and left.

"What was all that about?" Savannah asked, as soon as she saw Alan leave the building.

Marci rolled her eyes and suppressed a smile. "He'll be back later today for the ring. Do you believe it? He just spent another $23,000 without batting an eye. His two purchases – cash purchases - should put *Wrights* in good shape for the Vegas trip.

"Well, it won't cover a smidge of what I plan to spend, but every little bit helps." She cautioned Marci, "I think there's something's a little off about that man. I have a funny feeling he's not as he appears. I'm going to the bank right now to deposit the cash he gave us yesterday, and I'll do the same thing first thing tomorrow. I want to be sure the bills aren't counterfeit. If he should come back with more cash before I get back, stall him. I don't want any more jewelry leaving here with him until I know his money's good."

"All right, but I think you're over-reacting. He seems so nice. I can't believe that he's anything other than exactly as he appears, a nice man, completely devoted to his ailing, and apparently very rich grandmother."

"You've been duped by men before, Marci." Savannah reminded her gently. "I'm just being cautious. I may be wrong about Alan. Let's see what the bank says."

"Okay," Marci said reluctantly. She didn't know why she was upset by Savannah's suspicions, but she hoped her friend was wrong. She wanted very much to believe Alan was who he said he was.

CHAPTER 7

Savannah returned from the bank. "The money's good," she announced with relief. "I don't know where Alan gets it, or why he carries it around with him, but the bills are definitely not counterfeit. I still think it's weird, but who am I to judge?" She looked around the empty shop. "As long as Alan's not come back yet, why don't you Google him while I write up his appraisals. Maybe we can find out more about him."

Marci was surprisingly relieved about the money. Although she had no interest in dating Alan, she did find him interesting. And, yes, good looking too. She liked his devotion to his grandmother and wondered why he showed any interest in her. Someone so eligible should have a girlfriend or a wife. Why was he still single? Marci didn't know how old Alan was, but she thought he must be about forty, and living with his grandmother, no matter how convenient, seemed odd at that age. She went to the office computer and began to type Alan Trent into the Google search bar when the bell on the front door rang. *Damn*, she thought and reluctantly abandoned the search to wait on the customer.

The hours went by quickly. A few customers came by and made their selections. However, their purchases were nothing compared to Alan's. The day's sales were for small items, earrings and bracelets totaling in the hundreds, not the thousands. But every little bit helped the store's bottom line. And with the jewelry industry's retail mark-up, in Alan Trent's case, the brooch he purchased yesterday for $55,000, added $43,000 to the store's profit. The ring would add $18,500 to that windfall. While Savannah had been a Godsend to Marci, Alan was rapidly becoming a Godsend to Savannah and her father.

Savannah prepared the two appraisals and placed them in an envelope for Alan when he returned. She announced that she had an appointment and would be taking off the rest of the day. She asked Marci to close and lock up.

"Let's meet for a burger around 7:00," Marci suggested. "I feel the need for dinner, somewhere by the water. Are you up for that?"

"Absolutely." Savannah pulled out her car keys. "Is Shooters okay? I can meet you there."

Marci kept busy cleaning the jewelry display cases and rearranging the antique watches in between waiting on the odd customer. She impatiently kept checking her watch. The hour hand was not moving fast enough. Four o'clock seemed so far away. Why was she so eagerly anticipating Alan's return? She had turned him down for a dinner tonight and meant what she said about a woman scorned. Then why was she so anxious to see him again? What was wrong with her?

At precisely four o'clock, Alan drove up to the front of the store, double-parked and left the engine of a red Porsche running. He tapped lightly on the door and smiled through the glass. "I'm sorry but I'm in a hurry and have left the car running. I have to be back at the house to meet with my grandmother's estate attorney. Otherwise, I'd love to chat more with you." He smiled mischievously. "Have you reconsidered my dinner invitation?"

"I'm afraid the answer is still no," she said softly. "I'm not ready to date anyone, but I'm flattered by your attention." She turned away as her face was beginning to turn red. Reaching into a drawer, she pulled out the appraisal envelope and a small gift-wrapped box. "The ring is now a size 7. I hope your grandmother enjoys wearing it."

"I'm sure she will." He sounded slight annoyed. "I am not giving up on you, Marci. Sooner or later, I'll break you down and you <u>will</u> go out with me.

"Don't count on it," she countered, but didn't sound too convincing, even to herself. However, she had to ask herself why he was being so persistent.?

"Well, unfortunately I don't have the time to argue with you now, but I'll be back." He handed her a manilla envelope and told her it contained the $23,000. "Do you want to count it before I leave?"

"No. I trust you," she said. "I know you're in a hurry to get to your meeting. I have your address now, so if anything's missing, I'll know where to find you." She realized what she'd just said sounded stupid and childish. She was crazy not to count the money on the spot. What was happening to her common sense? She prayed he had not shortchanged her, and that she didn't have to confess her error to Savannah and her father. They would surely fire her, and rightly so.

Alan turned around with the appraisals and the gift box in hand. "I'll be back. You can't escape from my charms so easily."

She watched him climb into his expensive car and drive away before she counted every dollar. Marci was enormously relieved that he had brought the right amount. She placed the cash in the safe, locked the front door and went through the checklist of what had to be done before she turned off the lights and exited by the rear. As she was about to leave, she turned around and walked back into Savannah's office to check the client rolodex, jotting down Alan Trent's address.

CHAPTER 8

Marci was late getting to Shooters. She arrived flustered and visibly excited. Savannah was waiting for her at a table on the dock with a glass of Chardonnay, and she was halfway through it.

"Sorry I'm late," Marci apologized. "I did a very shocking thing for me, and I can't wait to tell you about it." She signaled the waitress and ordered a glass of Malbec.

"I can't imagine you, "'miss goody-goody-two-shoes'" doing anything scandalous," Savannah chuckled. "Did you run a yellow light or jaywalk?"

"No really," Marci insisted. "I'm serious. Just listen to me. When Alan came by the shop this afternoon with another twenty-three thousand in cash, I started wondering about him too. You made me a little suspicious and planted a seed of doubt when you wondered whether his money might be illegitimate."

"So?" Savannah sat up straighter and looked curiously at her friend. "What have you done?"

"Since Alan's address was in the office file, I put it in my car's GPS. Then, I drove by his house on the way over here." She looked smug and very pleased with herself.

"No, you didn't?" Savannah was surprised. "That's not like you at all."

"Yes, I did," she boasted proudly. "And I must tell you, it's a pretty impressive place. The red Porsche he drove to the shop today was parked out front of a huge stucco mansion with a four-car attached garage. The main house sits on a large point lot with an enormous yacht docked in the back on one side. I also was able to see the guest house where Alan lives, but that "'so called'" guest house is as big as most normal homes. Savannah, from what I could see, Alan Trent's the real deal and his grandmother is loaded."

"Well, aren't you a regular little spy these days," Savannah toasted her friend. "I'm impressed. Usually, I'm the one poking around where I don't belong. I didn't know you had it in you."

"Neither did I, but that's not all," Marci grinned. "I drove over to the next street to see if I could peek into his back yard. The homes in that neighborhood are so humongous that they take up most of the lots, but I could see between them from several different spots. The main house has a tennis court off to one side and an infinity swimming pool on the other. The yard is gorgeous with beautifully mature and manicured landscaping and green, green grass. I'm no expert but the yacht that's docked there has got to be at least 175 feet long. The name on its side said *Pampered.* I counted at least five decks and there was what looked like a hot tub on the very top deck."

The waitress came over to take their orders. As soon as she left, Marci looked at Savannah and whispered. "Alan can certainly afford the jewelry he bought from us, though I don't understand why he pays with cash. A man with his means must have dozens of credit cards."

"Maybe he has a weird quirk. Wealthy people are sometimes reputed to be eccentric. Remember the strange stories about Howard Hughes?"

"Yes, I suppose you're right." But Marci was still concerned. "Other than the money thing, he seems so normal. I'd really like to find out more about him. He intrigues me."

"Didn't you Google him?"

"Yes, but there are a lot of Alan Trents around the country. I couldn't find any in Ft. Lauderdale or anywhere in Florida that sounded like him for that matter. It's as though he doesn't exist but of course he does, and we know where he lives. It's strange."

"Maybe not so much," Savannah observed. "Many people of great wealth who want to protect their privacy, go to great lengths to keep a low internet profile. Not everyone is a Palm Beach attention-seeking socialite or business tycoon."

Marci was silent. She stared at her red wine glass lost in thought.

"Well, there's one way to find out more about him," Savannah continued. "You could accept his dinner invitation. Just don't end up falling for the guy."

Marci looked up at her friend and shrugged.

Savannah was wary. She knew Marci was naive and suspected from all appearances that Alan was out of her league. Marci had married money, and was comfortable with the way of life it allowed. But whatever she had enjoyed in DC, it was nothing to equal the Trent lifestyle she had just described. And, with Alan's sophistication and wealth, why was he so interested in a jewelry store sales-clerk anyway? He probably could have his pick of any number of the glamorous young women in town. Why was he so enamored with Marci? *Maybe I'm being too critical,* Savannah thought. *Maybe Alan simply has a taste for beautiful women and Marci is certainly that.*

"No, I'm not falling for him or any man," Marci answered a little too emphatically. "But I can't help it if I find him fascinating. And I want to understand why he carries around so much cash. Although Fort Lauderdale is a pretty safe town, there are still criminals and hoodlums here too. He's an easy target for a robbery and should be more careful."

"I'm sure he's perfectly safe. No one would suspect he had that much cash on him. Most rich people deal with credit cards. Anyway, let's leave the topic of the mysterious Alan Trent alone for a while." Savannah wanted to change the subject because she could see that Marci was becoming defensive. "Let's talk about our Vegas trip instead. Are there any particular entertainers or shows you'd like to see? Cirque du Soleil? Or maybe Celine or Lady Gaga?"

As they began to plan their trip, Marci relaxed now that she did not have to further explain her fascination with Alan. Why had talking about him made her uptight? Her palms had begun to sweat.

The server returned with the women's plates. Marci picked up her burger and gazed appreciatively around the beautiful waterfront restaurant with its large blue umbrellas shielding the diners from the sun or the rain. She wanted to enjoy her meal and the rest of the evening with Savannah.

"What was the name of the yacht you saw?" Savannah asked suddenly. Even she couldn't get Alan out of her mind. She knew a lot of boat owners in the area and had spent many happy hours on the water over the years. Maybe they knew Alan and his yacht. At 175 feet it would be hard to miss.

"*Pampered.* And I repeat. It is gorgeous. Why?"

"Because as long as we're googling Alan, we might as well check out the boat. If it's that big, I'm sure there'll be a picture of it on the internet… maybe even a deck plan. I'd love to see it. Dad likes to cite the famous quote about the best two days of a boat owner's life being the day you buy a boat and the day you sell it." Savannah laughed.

"I know boats are supposed to be a hole in the water that you throw money into, but Alan's is really awesome." Marci smiled and without thinking, pulled out her cell phone. "I took pictures of everything, the Porsche, the house and even the yacht, but frankly I was embarrassed to tell you. I didn't want you to think I'm some crazy lady stalking Alan."

"Come on, don't keep me in suspense. Show me the pictures. We'll stalk him together."

Marci handed her phone to Savannah and the two friends spent the next half hour commenting and dissecting the photos.

"I think you *should* spend some time with Alan if he asks you out again," Savannah suggested cautiously. "Call it research. I want you to keep your head and not get involved with him. Maybe if he thinks you're interested in him, he'll open up and tell you more about himself."

"Maybe." Marci suddenly felt tense, like she was standing on the edge of a precipice and afraid of taking a serious misstep. "My brain says maybe I should, but my heart says probably I shouldn't."

"Whatever," Savannah laughed. "We're over-thinking this. How about we ask for the check and we'll head home?" She glanced at her watch. It was only ten past eight. If she ditched Marci soon, there would be enough time for her to drive by and take her own look at Alan's property and yacht herself before it got too dark. Thank God for Florida's long sunny days and for daylight savings time.

CHAPTER 9

Savannah and Marci continued to work side by side at *Wrights* every day. They were counting down the days until their Las Vegas trip and had purchased tickets to see the Cirque du Soleil at the Luxor on the second night and Lady Gaga on the fourth night. The jewelry show would begin the day after their arrival. They had made lists of the vendors they wanted to visit and also what other hotels and tourist attractions they hoped to see in their free time. Marci wanted to check out the Eiffel Tower in *Paris*, and Savannah wanted to show her the *Wynn* and especially the famous dancing fountains at the Bellagio.

Savannah had thoroughly briefed her father on all the recent transactions that had happened in the shop as well as inventory and revenue. Dave for his part, since taking a step back from the business, had been busy working with a web designer on an enhanced site to increase the shop's on-line business. He had also looked seriously at commercial properties in Palm Beach and in Miami that he thought might be good locations for other *Wrights*. He was working on the costs for such expansions. He and Savannah conferred regularly about his progress.

She'd been thrilled to turn over some of the work to him while she became more comfortable managing the tasks associated with his former end of the business.

Savannah showed him the ledger and the taxes she'd paid on the shop's behalf. She even reminded him about the two unusual purchases made in cash by Alan Trent and mentioned her previous concern that the money could have been counterfeit.

Dave didn't seem alarmed and assured her that he had seen stranger things during the many years he'd been running the store. He could handle any situation that might come up while she was away. He was proud of what his daughter had done with the business and thrilled that Marci had come onboard and made herself so useful. She continued to impress him with her kindness, style, and quick-study enthusiasm to learn the business.

As their trip approached, Marci couldn't help but feel a little disappointment that Alan had not come back to the shop. Ten days had passed without a word from him. Each time the bell rang announcing another customer's arrival, she glanced up at the front door eagerly, hoping to see his face. She was angry at herself for being such a schoolgirl, and yet she could not help herself. He had promised her that he'd return, but maybe that was simply a pick-up line. All men lied. He obviously was not as attracted to her as he had led her to believe. She had twice turned him down for dinner. Maybe in his mind she wasn't worth risking a third rejection. *Had she been too rash? Too protective of her heart?*

Savannah had sheepishly admitted that she'd driven by Alan's estate after their Shooters dinner and confirmed Marci's impression of the property. Together they agreed the land and the two homes were worth at least twenty-five million dollars, probably more. Savannah took her own photos of *Pampered* and checked out the mega yacht on the internet.

She confirmed that it was a 180-foot yacht worth close to 60 million. The boat boasted twelve staterooms, a panoramic glassed- in gym on the top deck, a salon with a 22-foot onyx bar, a driving tee on the aft deck and every imaginable luxury, including a gold-plated sink in the master bathroom. It was built by a famous German ship maker, in 2010 and was registered to a corporation in the Bahamas. That was not unusual, as most owners of expensive super yachts took title out of the United States to avoid paying huge luxury surcharge taxes, which for a boat this size could run easily into significant seven figures. A full-time crew of twenty was needed to maintain and service the boat and its guests. The on-line write-up noted that the yacht could be leased for a mere $500,000 a week without provisions or gratuities. The friends joked that when they won the lottery, they would charter it for a month and sail around the Mediterranean together.

Since there were no customers in the store at the moment, Savannah called Marci into the office and handed her a plane ticket and her badge for the jewelry show. "They are very strict at the doors," she explained seriously. "No one gets in without a badge. So, don't lose it. Getting a replacement is almost impossible."

"I promise. I'll guard it with my life." Marci smiled and crossed her hands over her heart. "I feel like a kid the night before Christmas. I…"

Their conversation was interrupted by the insistent sound of the doorbell being pushed repeatedly. "Back to work," Marci sighed, tucking the ticket and badge into her handbag. She went back onto the show-room floor and pushed the entrance bell before looking up. *All right. All right, hold your horses,* she thought to herself. Someone continued to stab ferociously at the bell. She looked up and put on a pleasant smile, trying not to show her annoyance at the customer's rudeness. Then Alan nonchalantly sauntered in.

"It took you long enough." He sounded annoyed, but then backed down quickly looking hurt. "Didn't you want to let me in?"

"Don't be silly. I had no idea it was you. I was in the office with Savannah and it took me a few seconds to get out here to release the door. What's your hurry anyway?" She was as irritated as he was, and had not expected his sudden appearance, although she had been hoping for it. She was not prepared for how handsome he looked in pressed chinos and a black silk shirt unbuttoned just enough to show a sliver of chest hair.

He looked into her emerald green eyes and his expression softened. "Sorry, I was just impatient to see you again. I've been out of town visiting a client. I haven't even been home yet. I wanted to see you first."

She looked outside, but didn't see his red Porsche. He saw her eyes searching the street. "I Ubered from the airport," he explained casually. "That's what I get for thinking you'd miss me. Did you even notice that I wasn't around?" He sounded peeved. "I was hoping you'd be pleased to see me again."

Marci smiled to herself but kept her lips from betraying her feelings. "Sorry Alan. I hadn't noticed," she fibbed. "We've been busy doing inventory and preparing for our trip to Vegas. I haven't had a second to think about much else." She took a deep breath, silently congratulating herself on maintaining her composure and telling the lie with a straight face.

Alan seemed puzzled. "What trip? You never mentioned going to Vegas."

"I didn't know I had to run my schedule by you, Mr. Trent," she countered sharply. "And besides, you said you'd been away. How would I have told you about my trip, even if I wanted to?"

"Good point there," he admitted sheepishly. "Suppose we start over again?" He walked over to the front door, turned around and then approached her again with an ingratiating smile. "Good afternoon, Marci. You are looking exceptionally pretty today. I thought I'd swing by and say a quick hello."

Marci laughed in spite of herself. "Good afternoon Alan. It's nice to see you again."

They continued to banter back and forth or was it flirting? Another customer arrived and Marci left him to help her. Alan wandered around the store and stuck his head in the back office. "Hi Savannah," he said cheerfully. "I hear you're going to Vegas."

Savannah looked up from her paperwork, annoyed at the interruption. Her office was off- limits to customers. "Oh, hello, Mr. Trent," she said stiffly. "Yes, we're leaving tomorrow for the international jewelry show."

"Well, have a good time and watch out for my girl. She doesn't seem the Vegas type."

Savannah gave him a weak smile and returned to her paperwork. *My girl?* She thought sourly. *Since when did he become so possessive of Marci?*

"Oh, there you are." Marci came up behind him. "I turned around and you'd disappeared."

"I went to say hello to Savannah but she didn't seem too friendly."

"She's probably distracted. There's a lot to do before we leave. I'm sure she didn't mean to be rude."

"I'm disappointed that you're leaving town. I was going to invite you to The Broward Center Saturday night to see *Hamilton*. I have the house seats." He smiled enticingly.

"That would have been nice," Marci said wistfully. She had been dying to see the famous musical. Then she caught herself. "I mean, I've wanted to see the show, but I told you Alan, I am not dating…you or anyone."

"That's too bad. Then I guess I'll take my grandmother. It won't be quite the same." He wrinkled his nose. "Being with you would have been much more fun."

"I'm sure you know lots of girls to invite. Fort Lauderdale's full of single women."

"I don't want lots of girls. I only want you." His blue eyes bore into hers intensely. She felt her knees buckle slightly. *Why do I react to him this way? We barely know each other*, she thought.

Something about his adoration made her uncomfortable, yet also strangely simultaneously happy. She felt like an awkward teenager with a crush, not sure how she felt or how to act.

"I'm flattered by your interest in me Alan, really. But I just got through a nasty divorce and, really, I have no desire to get into a relationship with any man now and probably never again."

"Don't say that," he chided her. "I'll wear you down eventually, just give me time. How about if we don't date? Instead, we enjoy spending a little time together. Do you play tennis?"

"Yes, I play and I used to be pretty good," she laughed. "Let me think about it, and we'll talk about it when I get back from Vegas." Marci was flustered by his persistence and wanted to change the subject. *Would an occasional game of tennis be so bad? That wouldn't be a real date.*

"Where are you and Savannah staying?"

"Caesars. It'll be my first time in Vegas and I'm really excited."

"Well, I hope you have a wonderful time. Vegas is an interesting place. I'll miss you." He turned around, blew her a kiss. "Have fun."

She stood still and stared after him, not knowing what to make of the entire encounter. On one hand, she was pleased that such an attractive man showed a continued interest in her, but his pushiness also unnerved her. Thankfully, she was going away and would have the five days to think more clearly about him and possibly reconsider his invitation to play tennis.

Savannah came out of the office in a huff. "That man is insufferable. Who does he think he is? I've changed my mind about you getting to know him better. He's a rich, self-indulgent playboy and you could be badly hurt...again."

"Wow. What set you off?" Marci asked. "Never mind, please let's forget about Alan." *But could she?*

CHAPTER 10

Marci's eyes grew wide as the jet flew low over the Las Vegas strip. Gazing in wonder out the window, she could see the enormous number of spectacular hotels fanning out below.... the Luxor, New York-New York, Paris, the Mandalay Bay, Caesar's Palace, the Venetian, the Bellagio, the Wynn and many more. The dazzling, blinking florescent lights from 5,000 feet were mesmerizing. Marci thought she knew what to expect from photos she'd seen, but the reality was so much more fantastic. Savannah looked at her with amusement and completely understood. That man-made desert playground was hypnotic, cheap, sensual, and beautiful, all at the same time—and never ceased to stir her.

"It's quite something, isn't it?" Savannah remarked.

After picking up their luggage, they took a taxi to their hotel. Driving through the streets, Marci had the same sense of awe that she'd felt on the plane. The iconic hotels were as spectacular up close as they had been from the sky. They passed by the Hard Rock and the Flamingo before pulling into the huge portico of Caesar's Palace. Marci noticed that there were glistening water fountains everywhere, and many of the hotel staff were dressed in togas or Grecian wear.

As soon as the two women entered the hotel to register, they were enveloped by the clanging sound of the slots. Everywhere they looked, people were seated in front of the colorful machines, pulling levers or pushing buttons. "Let's quickly drop our bags off in the room," Savannah suggested. "Then I'll take you on a tour of the hotel. We'll need to put on our comfortable shoes. We can walk several miles inside this building and never set foot outside."

"I can believe that," Marci answered as she gazed around the massive lobby and the thriving, crowded casino off to the right.

After signing in at the registration desk, they dragged their rolling suitcases down several long halls and into one of the many passenger elevators. When they finally reached their floor, Savannah pulled out her key and held it up to the pad. "For fun, I got us a special theme room," she grinned. "It's complete with two heart-shaped beds, mirrors on the ceiling and a champagne glass shaped bathtub in the middle of the room. I thought you'd get a kick out of it."

"No?" Marci laughed. "You didn't?" She'd seen pictures of those rooms in brochures and magazines, but never expected to be staying in one of them. "Stan and I traveled a lot during our years together but I've never seen anything quite like this place."

As soon as they walked in, Savannah and Marci froze, almost tripping over each other. "What the…" Savannah looked around the room in disbelief.

"I've never seen so many roses," Marci exclaimed. "We must be in the wrong room." There were dozens of long-stem red roses placed in vases on every available table or flat surface. The scent was overwhelming. It was so intense Marci gagged. "It smells like a funeral parlor in here."

Savannah looked at the key again to be sure they were in the right room. Then she ripped a card off one of the huge arrangements. Even before she showed it to Marci, she knew who had sent them.

Marci took the card from Savannah. "Lovely roses for a lovely lady. Love, Alan."

"Oh, my goodness." Marci dropped the card in dismay. "Why on earth would he do this? A dozen roses would have been a lovely gesture, but this is …garish and way over the top. I feel like I can't breathe in here. Can we get rid of them, please?"

"I'll take care of it," Savannah picked up the phone to call housekeeping.

CHAPTER 11

The housekeeping staff arrived promptly with several luggage carts and removed all the offending flowers from the room. Savannah suggested they take them home for themselves or give them to other hotel guests. She and Marci didn't care. They wanted them gone. The overwhelming smell in the room was nauseating. Marci flung open the balcony doors to let the fresh air in.

Although she normally adored fresh flowers, she was appalled by the ridiculous extravagance and questioned Alan's intentions. Was he trying to impress her, or was he sending her some kind of bizarre message? Did he think he could buy her affections with such a grandiose gesture? If so, he had badly miscalculated. Marci's taste tended toward understated and classic, not gaudy and attention-grabbing. She was not like his grandmother.

She had hoped her time in Vegas would be part a learning opportunity and part a fun time with Savannah. Instead, the trip was starting out to be all about Alan and his ridiculous obsession with her. She was torn between thinking he was a nice if eccentric man, in the way the super wealthy can be, and suspecting something more sinister - that he could be emotionally unbalanced. Whatever the reason for the roses, this was a trip for two, not three. She didn't want Alan elbowing his way into her time away with Savannah.

"Let's not let this ruin our trip," Savannah soothed as she watched Marci's dismay. "Now that the damn flowers are gone, let's change and take a walk around the hotel. We're having an adventure and Alan Trent be damned."

"You're right." Marci unzipped her suitcase and pulled out a pair of comfortable shoes. "I'll deal with Alan when we get home, but from now on, his name is *verboten*, agreed?"

"Agreed." Suzannah said solemnly. "Pinky swears. But she wasn't so sure that would last. His outrageous gesture had already tainted the trip.

The two left their room and began slowly roaming around the large casino taking in the sights and sounds of the hundreds of gamblers intent on winning jackpots. They walked past the baccarat and craps tables, by roulette wheels, and poker tables and into the blackjack area.

They wandered into the Forum shops - the upscale shopping mall attached to the hotel. And Marci was mesmerized by the larger-than-life moving statues, twisting and turning in theatrical presentations while thunder roared from speakers and streaks of lightening lit up the ceiling. It was like a Disney presentation.

The Forum shops, measured by the sales per square foot, was the highest grossing mall in the United States. Most purchases were made for thousands of dollars at stores and boutiques like Cartier, Louis Vuitton, Dior, Christian Louboutin, Chanel, Burberry and the like. Marci had been used to shopping in expensive stores during her marriage, but she had never seen anything to equal this display of extravagant merchandise.

Even Paris and Rome didn't have as many shops in such close proximity. In addition to the shops, there were world famous restaurants everywhere. Savannah and Marci checked out the menus at Rao's and Mr. Chows before deciding to grab dinner at Gordon Ramsey's Hell's Kitchen. There they spent a wonderful hour and a half at the trendy eatery and enjoyed delicious food and wine. As per their agreement, neither brought up Alan's name, but he was ever present in their minds…like a hovering, dark cloud.

CHAPTER 12

The convention doors opened at eight a.m. Marci and Savannah were one of the first registrants in line. They picked up maps of the convention floor and marked the location of the many vendors they wanted to visit. Savannah had a long list of items she needed to order for the shop - the meat and potatoes of any good jewelry shop. Nailing down those selections was her first priority. She wanted to show Marci what went into her decision making...why one line of necklaces or one designer's bracelets would probably outsell another. These were decisions not made from data, but rather ones made from her gut after a decade of experience. She wanted to see Marci's reactions and get her opinions. Fresh eyes were always good and she respected Marci's good taste.

"What do you think of these?" Savannah asked Marci holding up some gold earrings. "I think these will appeal to a lot of our customers, especially if we order bracelets from the same collection." She made a notion on her laptop. "These, bought in sets, will make wonderful

Christmas, birthday or Mother's Day gifts and the price point is afford-able. I'd say these are a definite yes."

Marci nodded in agreement and moved slowly around the display case studying other pieces. She didn't want to miss anything that might be a "winner" for *Wrights*. This particular stop was the fourteenth vendor they had visited since the morning, and there were dozens more still left to see tomorrow and the next day.

Marci had spent hours trailing after Savannah from booth to booth, meeting the vendors and analyzing their goods, talking trends, prices and the pros and cons of various collections. Marci felt she had learned so much already and now had a good idea about what merchandise appealed to *Wright's* customers. She was thoroughly enjoying the experience and tried to ignore the fact that she was bone tired, that her feet were sore and her lower back ached from standing so long on the concrete floor of the convention center. She needed to find a place to sit down, for just a minute.

"How many more booths today?" She asked trying to hide her fatigue.

"Two more in this section." Savannah answered compassionately. "I can see you're exhausted, and you've been a real trooper today, soldier-ing on like this on your first day. Why not go the room and take a nap? I'll be up in another hour or so. Remember, we have the Cirque du Solei tickets for tonight."

"Are you sure you don't mind? I can last another hour," she smiled weakly. "I don't want to abandon you."

"No, go on ahead. I won't be long. Can you find your way out of this maze?"

"Sure. I'll be fine." Marci rubbed her lower back and started walking slowly down the aisles towards the nearest exit doors. The show was so interesting that even though she wanted to lie down and rest, she couldn't keep herself from glancing at the exquisite merchandise in the booths that she passed. She was almost to the exit door when she spotted a large hand-painted sign hanging above one of the booths. In bold red print it said, "Previously Owned". That surprised her. Everything she'd seen so far had been new and original items. She strolled over to the booth and began to engage the man behind the counter in conversation.

"I didn't realize the show featured jewelry that's been previously owned," she remarked casually.

"Normally it doesn't. He answered. "I'm the only booth permitted to carry used jewelry --, more politely referred to as previously owned. This booth was grandfathered into the convention years ago. It would never be allowed today. I sell the pieces outright or on consignment. My supplies usually come from estate sales or pawn shops in wealthy zip codes like Palm Beach, Miami, Manhattan's Upper East Side and Beverly Hills. The workmanship and quality of the stones are usually quite remarkable. Thanks to the hits the rich took from Bernie Madoff, my inventory really spiked. This is only a small sample. Please feel free to browse. Do you have anything special in mind?"

"No, nothing special. I was just leaving the show for the day but your sign intrigued me." Marci started looking at ruby and emerald necklaces that looked exactly like what the grand dames of Palm Beach society wore to their charity and social events. Most of what she saw was much too heavy and ornate for her taste or for the regular clients of *Wrights*, however, the pieces were undeniably significant. The shelves contained dangling, sumptuous, diamond earrings, bracelets and brooches of every description. *The owner's insurance must be off the wall,* Marci thought. *This stuff is worth a fortune.*

"Thank you," she said as she started to walk away. "I'm glad I found your booth. You have some extraordinary pieces."

He started to wave when she glanced at the brooch nestled on the black velvet lined case. She froze. "May I see that piece please?" she asked in a startled voice.

"Sure, you've got a discerning eye, Miss. This is a real show stopper, genuine Mediterranean red coral. I received it just this morning. Here, please take a look."

Marci held out her hand. The jeweler dropped the pumpkin shaped lady's brooch into her open palm. "Oh my God. Where did you get this?" she demanded. "I just sold a piece exactly like it to a customer in Fort Lauderdale."

"It came by Fed Ex," he replied, taken aback by the accusatory tone of her voice. "I haven't had time yet to log it into my inventory."

"But where did it come from?" Marci persisted. "Who sent this piece to you? And how much do they want for it? Please, I have to know."

The jeweler looked at her oddly and pulled a recently discarded purple and orange Fed Ex box from the trash can. He glanced at the return address. "The return address is an apartment building - The Connaught - on Collins Avenue in Miami Florida. I get a lot of merchandise from that address. Some of it I buy outright, but I'm taking this piece on consignment. As I said, I just got this and I haven't had the time to appraise and price it yet. If you're interested, I'll hold it for you until I can give you a definite price." He reached his hand out to reclaim the brooch.

"Oh no. I'm so sorry. I don't want to buy it. I'm just curious if it's the same piece I sold to a gentleman as a gift for his grandmother. If it is the same piece, I can't imagine why he would try to sell it through you.

Why wouldn't he have simply brought it back to my store and asked for a refund?"

"I don't know, Miss. Maybe he needed the money and was too embarrassed to go back to your store and ask for it."

"I doubt that. My buyer is from a very wealthy family." Alan certainly didn't need the money. "May I take a picture of it?"

"Suit yourself. But they're can't be too many red coral pumpkins of that size around. If you change your mind and want to buy it back, I'll give you a sweet deal."

"Let me think about it," Marci replied. "I'll be back in the morning."

"Okay, but I warn you, pieces like this don't last long. It's one of a kind."

Marci had not heard his last remark. She was running back down the aisle, desperate to find Savannah.

CHAPTER 13

Marci ran up and down the aisles, frantically dodging other registrants until she tracked Savannah down. When she found her, without taking the time to explain, Marci took her by the arm and dragged her to the "previously owned" booth. Unfortunately, it was now covered with a heavy black tarp and padlocked closed. The man behind the counter had left.

"Damn!" Marci swore. "He was here ten minutes ago."

"Who? What's going on, Marci? I know this booth," Savannah sighed. "Everyone does. There's nothing here I'd be interested in. The guy is grandfathered into the show because his stuff is pretty dated and super expensive. I think all the wealthy old ladies around the country dump their unwanted jewelry on him to sell. I guess it's been more trouble for the convention committee to close him down than to let him keep his booth. Why did you bring me here, anyway?" Savannah was tired and wanted to go back to their room.

"I'll explain when we get back to the hotel." She pulled Savannah forcefully towards the exit and could not help but think that no matter what she did or where she went, Alan Trent was with her, in spirit, if not in person. It was creepy.

As soon as they walked into their room at Caesar's, Marci went to the mini bar and poured herself a bourbon. Offering Savannah one, she blurted out. "I was just leaving the convention center to rest when I saw that booth. I don't know why, but I was curious and walked over to take a look. There was a lot of fancy jewelry there, but as you said, nothing that would be for us. As I was about to leave, I noticed a piece in his case. It's exactly like the pumpkin brooch I sold to Alan." She nervously took a large swig of her bourbon and continued.

"I held it in my hand and looked it over closely. I swear it's the same brooch, or an exact duplicate. I took a picture." She reached for her cell and handed it to Savannah.

"It certainly looks like the same ugly piece. But why would Alan have sent it here? Why not bring it back to us?"

"That's what I want to know. Alan assured me that his grandmother loved it, and he even bought the matching ring for her, as you know. It doesn't make any sense."

"Did you ask where the salesman got the piece?"

"Yes. Of course. He said it came from an address in Miami, and that he frequently receives pieces from that address. He didn't seem overly concerned, and had agreed to take it on consignment."

Savannah looked at her watch and was surprised by how late it was. "Whatever happened with that pumpkin, we can't do anything about it now, so let's change and grab dinner. The Cirque du Soleil show starts at 8:00."

Marci went into the bathroom to apply more make up. She was still unsettled by what she'd discovered, and as hard as she tried to forget about it, she felt uneasy. Her intuition told her that something was not right. As soon as she got back to Fort Lauderdale, she would check in with Alan and be sure his grandmother still had the brooch. *But would he tell her the truth?* She was also going to address the elephant in the room and ask why he carried so much cash around. The more she thought about it, she couldn't come up with a reasonable explanation for any of this.

Savannah had waited for Marci to leave the room and once the bathroom door closed, she grabbed Marci's cell phone and quietly slipped out onto the balcony. From there she made a hasty, whispered call to her father and forwarded him the picture of the brooch.

CHAPTER 14

The rest of the convention week passed quickly. Savannah and Marci spent long days on the jewelry show's floor placing orders and scouting out new designers. They took time off to enjoy massages and foot rubs at the Caesar's Palace spa, and in the late afternoons they sat by the glistening hotel pool, people watching and sipping frozen daiquiris. Their evenings were spent at the excellent restaurants they'd booked and one night they attended the spectacular Lady Gaga show. The two women stuck to their resolve not to talk about Alan although both were dying to confirm that Mrs. Trent still had her brooch.

On the last day of the convention, Marci left Savannah for a few minutes and went back to the "Previously Owned" booth. A different salesman stood behind the counter.

"I was here a few days ago," Marci explained. "I was shown a very unusual pumpkin shaped red coral brooch. May I see it again, please?"

The man searched the case and then consulted a black notebook on the counter. "I'm sorry," he said. "That piece has been sold."

"Oh, what a shame. May I ask what it sold for? I had hoped to purchase it." Marci lied.

"Unfortunately, I'm not allowed to share that," the salesman said. "All of our transactions are confidential. There are a few other brooches here. Can I tempt you with one of them?"

Marci feigned interest in the others, but soon backed away. "Sorry, but that was such a one-of-a kind piece. I don't see anything else here that I like as much. Maybe next year." She nodded politely and walked away. It was hard to imagine that with all the pieces of jewelry in the convention center, that one brooch had sold so quickly.

The next day, after they checked out of the hotel, Savannah and Marci made their way towards the taxi line. Savannah impulsively stopped and reached into her purse. She pulled out a single dollar bill and fed it gently into the nearest slot machine. She and Marci had been good and had refrained from gambling the entire trip. Placing one bet on the way out of town would not break the bank. The buying trip had been successful in every way. She was pleased with her orders and the new designers the shop would be introducing. The two friends made quite an effective team.

Savannah turned to pull her suitcase towards the taxi line, when suddenly the slot machine she'd fed began making a loud clanking noise and lights blinked on and off. Soon a casino attendant appeared and handed her a printed receipt for her winnings. She had hit the jackpot.

Stunned by the sizable amount of her winnings, she approached the banking cage to turn in the receipt. Smiling broadly, she hugged Marci. "You have been my lucky charm this whole trip and a great partner, so half of this windfall is yours."

She peeled off $1500 in one hundred-dollar bills and handed them to her friend. "Thank you. Thank you, Savannah. Are you sure? I don't deserve this. It was your dollar."

"Absolutely you earned it. We're a team. One for all and all for one." She put her arm around Marci's waist and the two very happy friends left for the airport. *I'm not the only one who can hand out cash*, Savannah thought ironically, momentarily forgetting about her pact not to think about Alan Trent.

CHAPTER 15

Savannah and Marci took the weekend to settle back in their separate homes. No one, except Savannah's father, knew they were in town again. After catching up on the bills, finishing the novel she'd begun in Vegas and doing her laundry, Marci was more than ready to return to work Monday morning.

Savannah had gone in early to log in the orders she'd made and show her father pictures she'd taken of her selections. Returning from the annual jewelry show always made her feel like it was the beginning of a new year. The pieces she'd bought would arrive in a few weeks and then she and Marci would have fun rearranging the display cases to highlight them. It was like spring cleaning and she looked forward to it.

Dave Wright was still there when Marci arrived. He bowed graciously to her and gave her a quick hug. "I'm sorry but I can't stay around with you girls but I have an appointment this morning."

"That's too bad," Marci said. "I was hoping you'd have time to chat. I've missed our talks."

Her remark made him smile and he was sorry that he had to leave. They had started talking together one on one when he visited the store and Savannah was busy or out. Each enjoyed getting to know the other better and developing their own friendship. But Dave now was meeting his realtor to look at a Palm Beach property again. It was time to make a decision about it or someone else would snap it up. It was an ideal location for the next *Wrights* and if Dave didn't put in an offer soon, someone else would.

"Before I go, I need to speak to Savannah for a second." He took Savannah's hand and led her into the office, closing the door behind them. That was unusual. Normally Marci was privy to whatever went on in the store, but apparently this morning Dave wanted some privacy.

Marci began dusting and wiping down the glass countertops. Dave was a wonderful person and an excellent jeweler, but he was not particularly tidy. His housekeeping skills were sorely lacking. There were fingerprints and smudges everywhere. His wife probably did the cleaning when she was alive and then the chore had fallen to Savannah. Marci sighed and went first to the pearl display case, with Windex in hand, and busied herself there.

The store's doorbell rang. She looked up eagerly, anticipating the first customer of the day and was upset when Alan marched in. She suspected he would come to see her on her first day back, but she had hoped he'd wait till later in the afternoon. Instead, he strutted right up to her, standing only inches from her face. "Did you get my roses?" he launched right in. "I thought you might have called to say thanks. Or do all your boyfriends send you twelve dozen roses?"

She was taken aback by his abrasive manner. He had always been so polite. She continued wiping down the countertop so she would not have to look directly at him.

"I did get them," she answered cautiously. "And, while I love fresh flowers, you sent too many. I had to give them away. The hotel room was so overrun with them that there wasn't enough space for Savannah and me to move about, much less unpack. And the smell was suffocating."

"Well, honestly, what did you really think of them?" His demeanor softened and he grinned. "I wanted to make a grand statement. To show you how much you mean to me. I guess I overdid it a tad."

"A tad?"

"Well, it's just that when I want something, I go after it 100%, and Marci, I'm sure you know by now that I want you."

"Yes, I'm beginning to get the message." She backed away from him. "What I don't understand is *why* you want me? We barely know each other. How could you possibly think I'm the woman for you? It's way too soon."

"No, it isn't. Not from my perspective. From the moment I saw you I knew you were the woman I've waited to be with all my life. I have absolutely no doubt. I can clearly see us married with a houseful of beautiful children running around." He tried to take her hand, but she stepped back, out of his reach.

"That's ridiculous Alan. I told you it's too soon for me. I'm barely out of my marriage. If there's ever to be anything between us, and I'm not saying there can be, we need to move very slowly. You are pushing way too hard and scaring me to death. I hardly know you. You hardly know me. And FYI, I'm not sure at age thirty-six that I want to start a family with any man."

Her words stung him, but he persisted. "Okay, Marci, I'll back off, but the only way you can get to know me is to spend some time with me…

away from this place. I can't keep buying jewelry as an excuse to see you." He grinned and winked at her. "Seriously, can we begin with a simple game of tennis? That sounds harmless. That doesn't scare you, does it?"

She studied his face carefully. He looked so handsome and eager. Little beads of perspiration dotted his upper lip. He was trying so hard to convince her. She nodded reluctantly. "Yes, I guess a game of tennis sounds all right." As much as she was afraid of getting involved, she knew that she should give him a chance. Besides she had so many questions she wanted to ask him, especially about the pumpkin brooch. Playing tennis together would be a good start. "Okay," she answered softly. "When and where?"

"Tell me where you live. I'll pick you up this afternoon at 6:00 o'clock. It stays light till almost nine o'clock, so we can get in a set or two before it gets too dark."

She jotted her address down on the back of a *Wright's* business card and handed it to him. "By the way," she couldn't help herself. "Is your grandmother still loving her brooch?"

"Absolutely. She wears it every day." He looked puzzled. "Why do you ask?"

"Because I'm not sure if I told you that *Wrights* will take back any piece of jewelry within 30 days of purchase, if the buyer changes his mind for any reason. That's always been the store's policy."

"No need for that. I swear, I couldn't tear it away from her." He started towards the door, "Marci, thank you for agreeing to tennis later. I promise it will be the first night of our future together. And," he laughed and his eyes twinkled, "You don't have to commit to having my children yet."

"*Oh Lord,*" she thought uneasily. "*What have I gotten myself into?*"

CHAPTER 16

Alan arrived promptly at 6:00 as promised. He led her to his Porsche, opened the door and helped her adjust her seatbelt. He was behaving like a perfect gentleman.

"Thanks for agreeing to this," he smiled hopefully. "I'm sure we'll have a nice evening."

She nodded and pretended to be interested in the scenery. As they drove along the beach, they chatted amiably. Sitting so close to him, she could not help noticing that his tennis whites were immaculately pressed, showing off his toned and tanned thighs. He was a beautiful specimen of the male physique wearing his Tom Ford sunglasses and a tennis sweater tied loosely across his shoulders. He could have been on the cover of GQ magazine. She had previously thought that he was movie-star handsome, but now, seeing him in this casual new light, she was awestruck and surprised by her intense physical reaction to him. Self-consciously tugging her own short, pink and white tennis dress down closer to her knees, she wondered if he was as taken with her appearance as she was with his.

She did not have to wait long for her answer. He gently reached over and placed his right hand protectively on her thigh. His warm, masculine hand on her soft skin made her entire body tingle. It had been a long time since a man had touched her admiringly and, it felt wonderful.

"You take my breath away, Pretty Lady," Alan said in a husky voice, taking his eyes off the road momentarily to gaze at her. "You're so damn gorgeous." She was not used to such extravagant praise. He made no attempt to remove his hand from her thigh. It felt good there and she was in no hurry for him to remove it.

"Here we are," he said proudly when he brought the car to a halt in front of a huge stucco mansion.

Marci did not reveal that she'd been there before on her furtive photo taking excursion. Instead, she looked at the house and pretended surprise. "What a lovely home. Your grandmother must be very proud of it."

"Yes, she is. Before she became ill, she threw magnificent parties here all the time. She thrived on entertaining and showing off this house and its grounds. Now, she still appreciates the beauty of the property, but it's mostly widows, who come over to play cards with her or for an occasional cocktail. Grandmother still loves her daily Old Fashions. Most of the time she can't remember the names of her old friends or what card game she's supposed to be playing.

"And with her failing eyesight, it must be hard for her to read the cards."

Alan stared at her for a beat and then gave her a wide smile. "You're an excellent listener besides all your other wonderful attributes. But, yes, the staff and I help her out with that. She so enjoys having people around. It's worth the effort it takes from us.

"I encourage her to keep being social because being with people cheers her up. That's why I buy her jewelry too. She has no place to wear it now-a-days, but it makes her happy. I love her smiles when I give her a new piece. Grandmother employs an excellent house staff, including a full-time companion, a butler, a chef and several housemaids. They also keep her company. We all look out for her as best we can. But, believe me, it's a full-time job."

"There must be a gardener or two here," Marci mused. "The grounds are so beautifully planted and maintained." On their way to the tennis pavilion, they had walked down a winding stone pathway, past a shimmering swimming pool. The guest house was set off to one side and was surrounded by a tall hedge of red Hibiscus.

"Yes. Grandmother has always had a twice-weekly landscaping service here, but truthfully, Pedro, her trusted butler, supervises everything. He really runs the place. He's the power behind the throne, so to speak. Believe me, you don't ever want to cross him. He can be quite fierce when provoked. He's extremely protective of Grandmother. He and Consuela, her companion, take excellent care of her."

"That must be a great comfort to you. Will I meet your grandmother, tonight?" Marci asked hopefully. "I'd really like to."

"Not tonight," Alan answered hastily. "She's gone out for a rare dinner with Consuela. She's let the rest of staff go for a well-deserved night off. I'm afraid it's just you and me here."

"Oh, I'm truly disappointed. After what you've told me about her, I'm eager to meet her. And I wanted to see her enjoying the brooch and the ring. That would give *Wrights* and me such satisfaction."

"You'll meet her in time, I promise," he assured Marci. "But we came for tennis, so let's get started." He grabbed his racket and a fresh can of balls.

"This place is truly paradise," Marci remarked enthusiastically. "If I lived here, I'd never want to leave." She kept seeing more and more to admire and appreciated every detail of the pristine property. It looked like a movie set.

"If I have my way, that's exactly what will happen," he grinned. "You'll never want to leave...not the property and not me. Now come on, Pretty Lady. Your serve or mine?

CHAPTER 17

Savannah was out for the evening, having dinner at Seasons 52 with friends. However, she was having a hard time concentrating on the lively conversation. Normally she was the life of the party but tonight she was distracted by thoughts of Marci being with Alan. She hoped Marci would get the chance to meet Mrs. Trent and see or ask about the pumpkin brooch for herself. If Mrs. Trent didn't have it - or couldn't produce it – it would mean that the brooch that Marci had seen in Vegas was the one Alan bought.

Savannah had called her dad from Vegas to tell him about the strange pumpkin jewelry coincidence but after that one conversation, he had not brought up the subject again. She felt sure that if Dave suspected something was wrong, he would have told her and warned Marci against Alan. Lately he seemed very protective of Marci, and not quite – Savannah sensed - in a fatherly way. She wasn't sure how she felt about that.

Savannah wondered if her dad was secretly attracted to Marci. A few times she'd come back to the shop to find them engaged in conversation.

She assumed it was playful banter or professional mentoring, but now she wasn't so sure. He was a handsome, well-educated, single man with a love of life and a tremendous sense of humor. Most women found him appealing and considered him to be quite a catch. He had broken a few hearts over the years, but not intentionally. He didn't want to remarry, and unfortunately most of the women he dated were husband hunting. He was looking for companionship, not a wife.

Now that her dad and Marci were on her mind, she wasn't sure how she'd feel if they began to date. There was a huge age difference between the two. Her father dating her best friend would take some major getting used to. Just the thought of it felt weird. At least for now, she didn't have to worry about it because as far as she knew, he hadn't asked Marci out and Marci, she knew, had no interest in starting a romantic relationship with anyone. Anyway, why borrow trouble? *I'll decide how I feel about it if and when Dad actually askes Marci out, and not before.*

"Savannah, Savannah," one of her friends tapped her gently on the shoulder. "Where are you tonight? You've been miles away. Are we boring you?"

"No, no, not at all," she blushed. "Sorry, I do have something on my mind but there's nothing to be done about it right now. How about we order. I'm famished."

For the rest of the evening Savannah focused on her friends. She put Marci and her father out of her mind. After dinner, someone suggested going to the Blue Martini for a nightcap.

"I think I'll pass," she covered a yawn. "I'm pretty tired and I have an early day tomorrow. You all go and have a good time."

She handed the parking attendant her ticket and had every intention of heading straight home and going to bed. But somehow, she found herself driving slowly into the Coastal Beach neighborhood and past the Trent estate. She wanted to see for herself that Marci was okay.

Savannah brought her car to a halt at the tip of the Trent's driveway. Without thinking her plan through, she spontaneously jumped out and started moving casually towards the mansion hoping to get a glimpse of Alan and Marci somewhere. Alan's red Porsche was parked in the driveway, but the main house was completely dark. Even the gas lanterns on either side of the front door were turned off. It appeared no one was at home there.

Savannah started walking cautiously towards a pathway she spotted on the left, searching for the tennis court. The sun had set earlier and there was not enough light left to play, so she guessed Marci must be with Alan in the guest house. She suddenly stopped short and reprimanded herself. Just what did she think she was doing, coming onto the grounds like this? *What had she been thinking with her Nancy Drew antics?* Disgusted with herself for not having a better plan, she turned around to backtrack to her car.

When she reached the driveway again, lights on the second floor of the mansion came on. She glanced up at the brightly lit window and thought she saw a woman looking out. On second glance, there was no one there. Had she inadvertently tripped a motion sensor or a silent alarm? Had someone in the dark main house seen her creeping around the property and panicked?

Bright outdoor spotlights, mounted several feet apart all around the roofline, came on simultaneously, casting an eerie white light across the lawn and the massive gardens. Had someone spotted her as an intruder and called the police? She did not want to be arrested as a trespasser.

Savannah ran to her car and sped away, shaking with fear and embarrassment for being so stupid. She was thankful that she passed no police cruisers as she left the Trent estate and pointed her car toward her own place. Apparently, no one had called the authorities. She was safe, for the moment.

CHAPTER 18

Alan was a very strong tennis player, and Marci had to fight hard to give him a competitive game. His serve was too fast for her to return successfully and he was a wiz at the net. After two sets, which he easily won 6-2 and 6-1, they moved to lounge chairs by the infinity pool to watch the sun finally drop below the horizon, and sipped lemonade that Pedro had left for them to enjoy.

"You have a terrific back hand," he observed, "for a girl."

"Thanks," she smiled, not sure if she liked his phrasing but appreciating the compliment. "My game's not up to yours, but I used to play on the county club team when I was married back in DC. It seems like so long ago. I really enjoyed playing again with you. Thanks for suggesting it. I never get any exercise anymore. *Wrights* keeps me too busy, or maybe I've just become lazy. I'm sure I'm going to be very sore in the morning. My muscles got quite a workout."

"We'll play again soon, if you'd like." Sipping his lemonade, he seemed relaxed and happy. Not at all the obsessed, aggressive man she had originally thought him to be. Conversation was easy and she found herself relaxing too. It was impossible not to savor the surroundings. *What had she been so afraid of?* She was thoroughly enjoying herself and was sorry she had wasted so much time putting him off. Maybe there was room in her life for another man, though she was still scared of being hurt again. Nevertheless, she found herself really enjoying Alan and didn't want the evening to end. How would she ever explain her change of heart to Savannah?

"Would you like to see where I live?" he asked lightly. "I'd love to show you the guest house. And then, I asked the chef to prepare a cold supper. It's in the fridge. We can bring it out here by the pool or take it onto the dock and watch the yachts going up and down the intracoastal waterway as we eat."

"That sounds nice," Marci said happily. "I'd love to see the guest house."

He led her away from the pool area into a miniature version of the main house. They entered into an open concept great room and kitchen area. There were no interior walls in that space, just two enormous white leather sofas facing each other, two red leather comfortable looking armchairs on each side and colorful throw rugs and pillows. An enormous flat screen television hung on one wall and six floor-to-ceiling windows were covered with white plantation shutters for privacy. The ultra-modern kitchen had no dining table, but there was a wide granite island with four brightly colored red leather stools. The appliances were glistening stainless steel and there was a Wolf six burner gas range and a huge wine refrigerator. It was a cook's dream kitchen, immaculate and spacious.

"Alan, this place is impressive. "Did you decorate this?"

"Along with Grandmother's interior designer. The furniture is completely my choice though. I love sitting on cool leather in our hot Florida climate."

"And with this spectacular kitchen, do you cook a lot?"

"Yes, as often as I can convince my friends to join me for a meal. Grandmother always takes her meals inside the main house in the formal dining room. I join her frequently, but, whenever she has other plans, or doesn't feel up to my company, I cook for myself here. It's relaxing and therapeutic. After I graduated from Yale, I spent one summer abroad at the Cordon Bleu School in Paris learning basic techniques and have loved cooking ever since. It's my favorite pastime."

"My goodness." Marci was flabbergasted. "You are a man of many talents." There was so much more to this man than she ever suspected. She chastised herself for judging him so quickly. Clearly, he was an educated man who knew want he liked. She had originally been put off by his brashness, but no longer. She found everything about him to be fascinating and hoped he'd invite her for dinner soon. She thought men who cooked were very sexy.

He took her hand and guided her toward the back of the guest house. "Over here is my bedroom." He opened the door to a huge room and urged her to step inside. There was a king size bed, covered by a bold red and white print duvet, another white leather sofa facing another flat screen television and an area he obviously used as his home office. A clear Lucite desk held a printer and two computer screens. There were several thick glass shelves along the wall, holding dozens of books. She walked over to glance at the titles. Alan's reading tastes were eclectic. There were several mystery and spy novels, presidential biographies and dozens of cook books. She noticed there were no tax or accounting books, which she found strange. She thought he'd have them around as references for his work.

"Over there," he broke into her thoughts, "is the master bath with a hot rock sauna and a steam shower. Further down the hall are two more bedrooms, each with its own bathroom. The house is just the right size for me, but it would be perfect for a small family too." He interjected slyly. "Just saying," and he grinned when she blanched. "Just saying."

"It *is* a perfect house," Marci agreed, but she was becoming a little uncomfortable lingering in his bedroom. "Can we check out the fridge for that supper you mentioned? I'm starving."

"Certainly, of course. I'm not being a very good host." He took her hand and led her back to the kitchen. "Everything's in a picnic basket on the top shelf. If you can grab it, I'll bring the wine? Red or white?"

"White. Chardonnay if you have it."

"Right here," he said as he opened the wine cooler and brought out two chilled bottles of Napa's Far Niente. "Let's head to the dock to watch the boats. It's a beautiful night."

The temperature had cooled off and the stars were beginning to appear. They ate a delicious supper of cold roasted chicken, potato salad and crusty French bread at a table on the dock. Alan, playing the ever-attentive host, kept refilling their wine glasses as many luxurious boats paraded past them. He pointed out the ones he knew and told her stories about their owners. He had a wealth of nautical knowledge and was eager to share it with her. He explained that his grandmother's yacht, *Pampered* was docked on the other side of the property. Of course, Marci knew that from her previous visit to the property. Alan promised to show it to her another time and maybe take her away for a weekend cruise to the Bahamas, if she'd agree. The mega yacht was a costly extravagance his grandmother no longer used and she had recently decided to put it up for sale. To maintain it, she continued to pay the salaries of many crew members and a full-time captain.

Marci thought she would most certainly agree to the trip on *Pampered* after what she'd seen of Alan tonight, but she held her tongue, not wanting to appear too eager. Then she noticed lights going on all around the main house. "Your grandmother must be back from dinner."

"So, I see." He acknowledged the lights. "She dislikes the dark. When she's home, she lights up the place like a carnival. Maybe she's afraid of a ghost," he joked. "I suppose I'd better be getting you home. I'm sure you have to be at the shop early in the morning."

"Yes, I do," she said reluctantly. She had completely forgotten about having to go to work the next morning. She had been having such a wonderful evening.

"Leave everything here. Pedro will clean it all up in the morning." He took her by the hand and led her around the side of the house. The moon was bright and the sky was lit up with thousands of stars, but they were hard to make out against the brightness of the spot lights.

Alan glanced up at the windows and gave a slight wave. "In case Grandmother's watching."

Marci hoped Alan would lean in and kiss her. She surprised herself but she actually hungered for the taste of his lips on hers. Instead, he simply opened the car door and helped her settle inside. She tried to hide her disappointment. His deferential gallantry was her fault. She had warned him to take things very slowly. But did he have to take her suggestion so literally?

They drove to her townhouse in comfortable silence. When they arrived, she was torn about whether or not to invite him in for a nightcap. She didn't want the evening to end. They walked up to her front door but before she could suggest coming in for a drink, he kissed her chastely on her cheek. "Thanks, Pretty Lady, for a wonderful night."

He got into his car again and drove off with a casual wave.

Well, that was an interesting ending to the evening. She was annoyed at herself and at Alan. *Why had she foolishly insisted that she needed more time?*

As she was dropping off to sleep, she relived the details of being with Alan and the perfect evening they'd shared. She'd been so mesmerized by him that she'd forgotten to ask him about why he'd bought the pumpkin brooch with cash instead of using a credit card. Pulling the covers up to her chin, she smiled. She couldn't wait for the morning and to get to work. There was so much to tell Savannah.

CHAPTER 19

How was last night? Did you find out anything about Mrs. Trent's pumpkin piece?" Savannah was too embarrassed to admit to spying on Marci, so she kept quiet about her ill-advised visit to the Trent estate.

"I had planned to, but it was never the right time. The evening turned out to be amazing. Alan is nothing like he appeared when I first met him. You know, with those obnoxious roses…I think he was trying too hard to impress me then. Honestly Savannah, last night he was charming and considerate. We had a wonderful time and I learned so much about him. He's a man of many talents."

"Like what?" Savannah was skeptical and thought Marci was naive and too easily impressed. Had she forgotten about him running around town with a briefcase full of hundred-dollar bills?

"Well, for one thing, he's funny and a natural-born storyteller. We ate dinner on his dock and watched the private yachts traveling up and down the intracoastal waterway. He pointed out some interesting details and told me stories about almost each boat that passed. He knows what he's talking about. He grew up traveling on his parent's and grandparent's yachts and loves everything nautical. And, he's an excellent tennis player. Oh, and another thing," she knew she was babbling but she wanted so much for Savannah to see Alan as *she* did. "He studied cooking at the Cordon Bleu school in Paris after Yale. How's that for something you would not have expected?"

Savannah was surprised, but she still had reservations. There was something about Alan she just didn't trust. "That's all fine, Marci, and I'm glad you had a good time. But more important, did you meet his grandmother and see her pumpkin brooch?"

"No, she was out for dinner with her caregiver, but Alan wants me to come back and I'm sure I'll get a chance to see her soon. Also, he was quite emphatic that his grandmother loves the brooch and wears it all the time. That means the one I saw in Vegas had to be a copy."

Savannah knew there was no copy. Her dad had told her much more about the piece, which she had not shared with Marci yet. "So, you're willing to take Alan at his word?

"Yes, and no. I mean yes, I have no reason not to believe him. And, as I told you, Mrs. Trent was out for the evening so there was no way for me to actually see it. Why are you so hung up on this?"

"Because I don't believe there is a copy," Savannah answered. "Dad says it's not possible. Did you at least get to see inside the main house?"

"No, but Alan gave me a tour of the guest house. It's beautifully decorated and comfortable. Not at all crazy over the top like those god-awful roses he sent me." She made a face at the disturbing memory. "It's a real home, not some contrived bachelor pad. I was very impressed. And, he's quite a reader. In his bedroom, he has shelves and shelves of interesting books on all sorts of various topics." She would have gone on raving about Alan and his home, but she could see from Savannah's dubious expression that she wasn't buying into Marci's euphoria.

Realizing that she was not going to convince Savannah to change her mind about Alan, Marci switched topics. "Anything special on the schedule for today?"

"Yes, as a matter of fact. A few board members from one of our largest local charities, *Abandoned Kids*, are coming over to buy items to auction off at their annual gala this fall. They do this every year and I normally show them our lower end items and then they mark them up considerably and raise quite a bit of money at the event. It's always a very successful auction. Also, *Wrights* usually donates a few items from our inventory that haven't sold. It's a way for us to get rid of stale merchandise and take a charitable deduction from the IRS at the same time. You know, Marci, for the last two years I've offered them that atrocious pumpkin piece. Even they had the good taste and common sense to turn it down."

Savannah sighed but decided she'd said enough and that they had to move on. "I started making a pile of those items for donation this morning. They're in a wicker basket on my desk. Do you want to handle the society ladies today? It will be good for you to get to know them. Privately, they're good customers. They refer a lot of customers and send their husbands in to buy them birthday and anniversary jewelry."

"Sure," Marci said eagerly. She was always willing to pitch in and do whatever Savannah or her Dad wanted. She loved her job and was working hard to make herself indispensable. "I'll be happy to meet with the ladies." Marci was relieved that Savannah had dropped the subject of Alan Trent.

The morning dragged on with a few customers straggling in, mostly "lookers" as Marci and Savannah called them. These were people who came in, wandered around the showroom looking at all the most expensive pieces, maybe trying on an item or two and left the shop without making a purchase… but always with a promise that they'd "think about it" and be back. Marci made one small sale and then the three ladies from *Abandoned Kids* arrived. She introduced herself to them and began to show them lower price point jewelry. After an hour or so, the women were happy with their choices and wrote a check for fifty-two thousand dollars. They explained they expected to make three times that when the items were auctioned.

As Marci was writing up the sales receipts, the three women leaned against a nearby counter and chatted amongst themselves. "This may be our most successful event ever." one of the ladies said. "It's just too sad about Margie. She brought us a long way and would have been so proud to know this."

"Yes, but the poor dear won't even know," another of the ladies stated, slowly shaking her head. "Margie's long since forgotten that she used to chair our Board. She hardly knows who she is anymore or where she is. Damn Alzheimer. It's such a horrible disease. I feel very sorry for her. She's all by herself in that enormous house and must be terribly lonely. I dropped by last week to visit, but Pedro informed me she's no longer receiving visitors. She's being cared for by her staff and her companion/ nurse. It's very sad. Getting old is not for sissies, as someone wisely said."

"She has some lucid moments," the third lady spoke up in her friend's defense. "And I know she'll be so pleased if we set a new record this year. Every penny we take in goes directly to the children. She's always loved this organization. Don't be so quick to discount her. Maybe," she said thoughtfully, "we shouldn't listen to the butler. We could all try again to visit her. It might really cheer her up."

Marci finished writing out the receipts and was now putting the various jewelry pieces in gift boxes. She had overheard the women's conversation and wondered if Margie could possibly be Alan's grandmother? The circumstances certainly fit.

She remembered that Alan had mentioned that she had early-stage dementia but not that she was so ill that she couldn't see her friends. And hadn't she been out to dinner last night when she and Alan were playing tennis? Marci was tempted to ask the ladies if it was Mrs. Trent they were discussing, and did she have a grandson named Alan, but they might not appreciate her eavesdropping. *I'll ask Alan more about his grandmother's health the next time I see him,* she vowed as she finished wrapping the last of the gifts and handed them to the women in several shopping bags.

"I hope your gala is a huge success and thank you for letting *Wrights* be a part of it again this year," she said politely watching the three women gather their packages and leave. Then she started toward the back office to fill Savannah in on the sales and to ask if Alan's grandmother could be the same person to whom the ladies referred. As Savannah had only dealt with the auction committee, and not the non-profit's executive board, she might not know. But she didn't get the chance. The doorbell rang. She buzzed a delivery man inside.

"Is Marci Morgan here?" he asked, looking around at the impressive display of jewelry.

"Yes, I'm Marci Morgan. How may I help you?"

He pulled one single, long stem red rose from behind his back. "This is for you then. I'll be seeing you every morning. I have instructions to bring you one of these every day. There's no card. The gentleman who placed this order said you'd know who it was from."

Marci smiled in spite of herself. Alan had definitely heard her "less is more" message. He had listened and was trying not to scare her away with extravagant gestures or by coming on too strongly. She clutched the beautiful flower to her chest. It was turning out to be a great day. She forgot all about asking Savannah about Mrs. Trent and the charity auction.

CHAPTER 20

Savannah was frustrated that she could not talk freely to Marci about her misgivings concerning Alan. Marci refused to listen to anything derogatory about him. She was acting like a love-struck teenager, and after only one date. Every time Savannah tried to mention the pumpkin brooch mysteriously showing up at the JCK International Jewelry show, Marci insisted there had to be a reasonable explanation and that the original designer must have made more than one. Savannah tried again to tell her why that was not true. She believed Alan.

Savannah had been worried when she saw the picture Marci had taken of the brooch. She knew for sure that it was the same piece her father had purchased years ago. When Marci left the hotel room, she'd called her dad. He also was concerned. Initially, the large, all-cash payment had been the first sign that something might be off. In all their years in business, they had never seen anything like it. Then, they both wondered why Alan had lied about his grandmother loving it, and what prompted him to send the brooch to the secondhand jewelry vendor to sell. Why not bring it back to *Wrights* with its generous return policy? And why continue the farce by buying the matching ring?

Father and daughter were beginning to have some ideas.

The next morning Savannah made an excuse about having a dentist appointment and left the shop around noon. She walked four blocks in the bright Florida sunshine to a downtown address and took an elevator to the seventeenth floor, to the offices of *Blake, Turner and Blake, Attorneys at Law*. The receptionist recognized her from past visits and told her that Mr. Wright was waiting for her in Mr. Blake Senior's office, and she should go in.

"Hi Dad. Hi Sheldon." Savannah greeted her father and their family attorney. "I hope I didn't keep you waiting. It's such a beautiful day that I took my time walking here."

Sheldon smiled warmly. He had known Savannah since she was a young girl and he respected her immensely. His firm represented the Wright family in personal matters, and in regards to their jewelry business. "Your Dad was just filing me in about your suspicions…that you suspect someone may be using your business to sell stolen jewelry, and possibly launder money. Does that about sum it up?"

"Well, that sounds a little harsh, but generally that's what we suspect." She looked the attorney in the eye and nodded her head. "We have very little to go on except our gut feelings. Did Dad explain about the coral pumpkin brooch?"

"Just that your sales associate sold it to a local man, Alan Trent, who paid a great deal of cash for it and supposedly gave it to his grandmother, Marjorie Trent as a gift. I don't know the grandson, but I have certainly heard of the Trent family." Then he looked at his notes and continued.

"When you were recently in Vegas at the jewelry show, that same sales associate, Marci Morgan, found an identical brooch at a booth selling pieces that were "previously owned. Is that correct?"

"Yes, that's right. But the thing is," Savannah looked at her father for reassurance. She did not like trashing someone's reputation, even if she didn't like him. "Dad purchased the piece as a lark, misguidedly thinking some attention-getting nouveau Hedge Fund person looking to make a splash in local society might purchase it. We featured it in several expensive ads at Halloween that year and again at Thanksgiving, but we had no takers. It's actually quite ugly and I though Dad had lost his mind when he bought it. Of course, it never sold, and we often referred to it as the albatross in our collection. Then out of nowhere, Alan appeared and snapped it up."

The attorney looked at his old friend. "Where did you get the piece?"

"From a designer I know in Italy. He has a small shop in Capri and makes all his own jewelry there. He has a wide following among summer visitors to the Amalfi coast. He NEVER makes the same piece twice. The coral pumpkin Marci saw in Vegas had to be the original, the one Marci sold to Alan Trent."

Mr. Wright pulled a black velvet pouch out of his pocket and handed it to the lawyer. "When Savannah called me from Vegas and told me what Marci found, I immediately became worried. I had a friend in L.A., Lois Catcher, call Mr. Jangles and made him an offer for the piece. They negotiated and agreed on a price of $110,000. She wired him the money that same day and he sent the piece here by overnight mail, and here it is." He handed the pouch to the lawyer. "I want you to have it for safe-keeping. If Savannah and I are right and something illegal is going on, it will be evidence. However, if everything turns out to be on the up and up, then I was dumb and spent $110,000 to find that out."

"Oh my God, dad! I didn't realize you were the one who bought it. You know you can't afford it. That's twice what we sold it for! What were you thinking?" She was stunned. It was not like him to be so impulsive.

"I was thinking that Alan is probably a clever con man and I don't want you and Marci, or the store implicated in his shady dealings. You can't put a price on reputation." He gave Savannah a rueful smile. "Besides maybe another knucklehead will come along and buy it again."

Savannah didn't know what to say. Her father rarely surprised her, but he had this time. Confused, she looked at him and back to Sheldon Blake. "I guess you made the right decision," she said in an unsure voice. "You'll keep it safe, won't you Sheldon?"

"Of course," the lawyer assured Savannah. He was curious and opened the pouch. "*Oy vey*," he snickered. "It really *is* ugly."

"Isn't it?" Savannah laughed… her sense of humor restored. "Sheldon, we also need your help us find out who sold it to the Vegas jeweler in the first place. Was it Alan? and if so, for how much? Marci tried to find out but got nowhere. Buying used jewelry is the crux of that vendor's business. I suppose if he's operating on the shady side of the law, his livelihood would suffer if he revealed his contacts. All she could determine was that the seller was from Miami and uses a Collins Avenue address."

"I can't make any promises," the lawyer stated soberly. "But I'll do my best. I'll have a private detective agency our firm works with look into it all. They are pretty creative about discovering things we need to know, as long as we don't ask too many questions about their methods or question their bills."

"I was sure you'd know what to do." Dave looked relieved. "I don't care what it costs. Our business reputation is priceless and we must protect it. It's Savannah's legacy. In the meantime, what do we tell Marci, and what should we do if Alan wants to buy more jewelry from us with cash?"

"Since we don't have actual proof of his doing anything wrong, I suggest we keep this strictly between the three of us for now. There's no reason to worry Marci and she might inadvertently mention something to Alan. Just act like everything is normal until I get back to you."

"But Sheldon, Marci's my best friend," Savannah protested. "And she's getting emotionally involved with Alan. I don't want her hurt or worse yet, mixed up in something illegal. I think we have to warn her."

"I agree," Dave said earnestly. "We should protect Marci. I'm very fond of her too."

"I understand, but you need to trust me on this. The last thing you want to do is warn Alan that you're on to him. If Marci is romantically involved with him, she might make an innocent comment that would alert him and give him time to cover his tracks. You can't afford to take that chance. As long as she is in the dark and not knowingly participating in anything illegal, she won't be liable for any legal consequences."

"That's right, Honey. We have to be smart about this." Dave relented. "Don't question Marci anymore about Alan. Let's see how this plays out. As Deep Throat famously warned, 'follow the money.' If we do that in this case, what do you think we'll find?"

"That's the point," Sheldon said. "Why would a supposedly wealthy man put himself at risk to sell his own grandmother's jewelry? Wouldn't he inherit it in the end anyway? Something's fishy. Unfortunately, we can't follow the money trail any further until we have more information."

Sheldon wrote a few more notes before standing up to shake hands with Savannah and her father. "Just lay low, act normal and wait to hear from me. And, call me if Mr. Trent buys any more jewelry."

Savannah and her father left the law offices together. He kissed his daughter goodbye. She walked slowly back to the store. She was upset and confused and had so much on her mind. Savannah was determined to act normal. She was not an actress and not a deceptive person by nature. It would be hard to keep the truth from Marci, but she knew she had to.

Over and over in her mind, she kept wondering, why Alan would buy the pumpkin piece for cash in the first place and then sell it so soon. He'd bought it from *Wrights* for $55,000 and then sold it a few weeks later. Why? He certainly didn't need the money, unless things were not as they seemed. She wanted answers and promised herself that she would find them.

Savannah's imagination went wild. She put on her Nancy Drew hat. What if the mansion and the yacht were mortgaged to the hilt? Or if Mrs. Trent had somehow lost her money in a bad investment, or if she was a secret gambler and had lost her fortune at the track before she got sick. There were so many possibilities, but no proof of anything. Nothing about the situation made any sense to her. *What in the world was going on? What was Alan really up to? And what did he want with Marci?*

CHAPTER 21

Marci was alone in the shop when Alan next appeared. Savannah was not back from her dental appointment.

"Hi." She felt a little awkward. She didn't know whether to go up and kiss him on his cheek or stay put, so she smiled and remained in place. He was so damn attractive. She felt herself yearning to touch him. He seemed more handsome today than ever.

"You left your racquet by the pool." He grinned from ear to ear and handed it to her. Then he took a seat on one of the stools in front of the diamond display counter. "I had a really nice time last night."

"Me too," she beamed. "Your place is fabulous. Thank you for inviting me."

"You're most welcome, Marci." He reached inside his jean pocket and pulled out an envelope, the kind banks use to return cash to their customers. "At my meeting with my grandmother's attorney he instructed me to begin to divest her estate of as much jewelry and fine art as possible before her death. It will reduce the estate taxes and make probate go faster. I hate to think of her dying, but I have to be realistic. She is ninety. I'm uncomfortable doing it, but her lawyer was insistent that as her personal executive, it would be financially irresponsible of me not to take his advice. It's ironic. Here I am, buying her new jewelry to make her happy, and at the same time, I'm being told to sell as much of her jewelry as I can. Does *Wrights* buy estate jewelry?" He looked into her eyes, waiting for the answer.

"Yes, technically we do." She saw instant relief spread across his concerned face. "But we don't keep the items here. Estate pieces don't interest our younger clientele. This is Mr. Wright's domain, really. He takes the pieces on consignment as a favor to his regular clients and sends them to his associates who own jewelry shops in Palm Springs and Beverly Hills. Those stores then sell the pieces and pay us a small fee which they deduct from the proceeds. It works out pretty well for everyone. Let me see what you have."

Alan opened the envelope and emptied out several large diamond cocktail rings, a set of peacock earrings with the plumes encrusted in rubies and emeralds and two Piaget ladies' watches.

"I can't quote you a price, but I can speculate that they're worth a great deal of money." Marci picked up one of the diamond cocktails rings and examined it closely. The center stone appeared to have excellent clarity and she could see no flaws with her naked eye. It was at least 8 karats in size. "Mr. Wright will take over from here. I'll give you a receipt and see that he gets these right out to his people in California. Is that okay? Unless you'd like to take them somewhere else. Maybe a shop in Miami or Palm Beach? They might handle the sales in-house and you'd get the funds sooner."

"No, I trust you and I'm in no hurry for the money. I just want a fair deal for my grandmother. I have more pieces to bring you but didn't want to overwhelm your shop all at once."

"Maybe you should hire an auction company to come in and take all the pieces off your hands at once," she suggested helpfully. "It would certainly save you time and be more efficient."

"I thought of that, but Grandmother would be upset at the idea of a lot of strangers bidding on her things. I think by taking a few pieces at a time, and bringing them to you, will be the best and least troubling way for her. Sometimes she doesn't understand what her attorney or I tell her. With any luck, I can keep buying inexpensive new pieces to replace them and she won't miss her old ones."

"So, Alan, your grandmother doesn't know what your lawyer asked you to do?"

"No, I don't think she fully understands. Whenever I bring up the subject of selling a piece of jewelry or a painting, she becomes agitated, so I've learned to just stay quiet about it. It's the kind thing to do. Her jewelry and art are reminders of the wonderful life she had with my grandfather. I can't take that away from her all at once."

"I understand," Marci said in sympathy. She was impressed by his love for his grandmother. "Watching her mentally decline must be so difficult for you. I know you're doing your best to keep up her spirits by your visits every day and having her caregiver take her out from time to time." Marci felt empathy for Alan. Taking care of Mrs. Trent's needs was obviously consuming his time and his emotions. "I wish I could be of more help."

"Just do your best, please, with the pieces. It's the best way to respect her life, and her legacy to us." He looked momentarily lost in thought, but soon a broad grin spread across his face. "Are you up for a rematch and a home cooked meal? Bring a bathing suit and we'll take a swim if there's time. Maybe I can convince my grandmother to join us for dinner in the guest house. Consuela can bring her down in her wheelchair. How's tomorrow night? I'll pick you up at 6:00 again."

"Sounds wonderful. It's a date. And I do hope your grandmother will come." She wanted to ask him more about his grandmother's health and whether she had ever been involved with the *Abandoned Kids*. She would see Mrs. Trent tomorrow night and ask her herself.

Instead of questioning him, she heard herself saying the words, it's a date…words that she thought would never cross her lips again. She surprised herself at how quickly her attitude had changed. She no longer felt like a woman whose husband had cruelly rejected her, but a woman admired and desired, one on the brink of an amorous, exciting adventure. And she was eager for it to begin.

Alan picked up the receipt for the jewelry and blew Marci a kiss. "See you tomorrow evening, Pretty Lady. I can't wait." He was gone before Savannah returned.

CHAPTER 22

Savannah returned from her clandestine appointment with her dad and Sheldon Blake. She was nervous about having to face Marci, and pretending everything was all right. It was not in her nature to be devious, but the family lawyer had given her no choice. The bottom line was that neither she nor Dave trusted Alan and they had committed to protecting Marci from him.

"Look Ma, no cavities," Savannah faked a cheerful smile.

"A clean bill of health?" Marci joked, "If you'll excuse the pun."

"Yep, everything's fine. Anything going on around here?"

Marci was hesitant to bring up Alan and his grandmother's jewelry, but she had promised to help expedite the sale as quickly as possible. "Alan came in while you were out."

"Oh?" Savannah tried to keep her voice level. "Asking you out on another date or wanting to buy more jewelry?"

"Yes, he asked me out, but that wasn't his only reason for coming in." She showed Savannah the envelope of Mrs. Trent's jewelry. "His grandmother's attorney wants him to sell as much of her jewelry and fine art pieces as possible before her death to reduce the taxable value of the estate."

"Oh, my goodness. Is Mrs. Trent dying?" Savannah asked with concern.

"No, no. Not right now anyway. It's just that she's ninety and will die sooner rather than later. The lawyer has advised Alan it's best to get her affairs in order before then. This isn't easy for Alan. He's so concerned for her well-being. It's lovely to see."

"I suppose so," Savannah said, but she really didn't understand. It seemed ghoulish. "So, what are we supposed to do with these?" She pointed to the watches and the rest of the jewelry.

"I told him how your Dad handles antique jewelry," Marci answered. "How *Wrights* only takes estate pieces on consignment as a favor to existing customers and that we send them to your dad's jeweler friends out of state to sell." Alan was okay with the procedure.

Savannah turned away from Marci and headed for her office. "I'll show the pieces to Dad and let him handle them. I'll be working on the bills, if anything comes up." She left abruptly clenching her teeth. Alan wasn't wasting anytime pulling Marci into whatever he was doing. *What was he really up to?*

Marci could tell that Savannah wasn't pleased about being stuck with Alan's jewelry. She had said many times how getting rid of estate jewelry was an inconvenience and a bookkeeping nightmare and how she wished her dad would stop agreeing to take in the pieces. Marci felt torn between helping the man she was falling for and annoying her best friend and Dave.

She busied herself the rest of the afternoon with cleaning and rearranging the cases and helping customers. Savannah did not come out of her office and Marci knew enough to stay away. Sometimes silence between friends was important and Marci sensed this was one of those times. It made her sad that Savannah was so unwilling to give Alan a chance, but hoped that maybe she would come around in time. She thought she would suggest to Alan that they invite Savannah to join them for dinner one night soon. Maybe that would break the ice and ease the tension.

CHAPTER 23

Marci was looking forward to her evening with Alan. She was eager to sample his gourmet cooking. Le Cordon Bleu, where he'd studied, was probably the most famous culinary school in the world and graduated many five-star chefs -- like Mario Bateli, Giada de Laurentiis and Julia Child.

As he had before, Alan picked her up promptly. He wore tight black jeans and a Tommy Bahama aqua colored silk shirt. His hair was still damp from his shower. Marci thought he looked as sexy as any man she'd ever seen. She'd decided to dress up for their dinner in honor of meeting Mrs. Trent. She wore a bright orange Armani midi dress with a gold metal belt secured around her tiny waist and matching gold strappy heels. Alan whistled appreciatively when he saw her. "Grandmother will love you," he said with affection. "And Armani is one of her favorite designers."

"How would you know this dress is an Armani?" Marci was flabbergasted and curious. Most men would not know the difference between the Gap or Dior.

"Remember, I've done all the shopping for my grandmother for a long time, so I know her tastes and I'm pretty good at guessing designers."

Marci chuckled. "Did I tell you that my dream had once been to go into clothing design? I majored in it at college."

"What made you give it up?"

"A man, a marriage and a bad decision."

"Well, you're single now. You could go ahead and take whatever courses you need. Certainly, that would be a better career choice than selling jewelry for *Wrights.*"

"Yes, that's exactly my plan. I want to take courses at night and complete my degree. Thanks for your encouragement."

"I didn't mean at night." He said sharply, as though he was suddenly sorry that he'd raised the issue. "That would eat into our time together. I was thinking you should cut your hours at the store, maybe only work two days a week there and go to school on the other days. I want it understood that your nights are mine now." A definite scowl had crossed his face and Marci was alarmed at how quickly his playful attitude had soured.

She said nothing. She didn't like his possessive attitude. Maybe getting romantically involved with him wasn't a good idea.

But when they arrived at the estate, his attitude changed again and he was back to being his good-natured self. It was as if he was an entirely different person from the man who had been so dictatorial only minutes before. He took her hand and they walked to the guest house.

"Something smells heavenly," she said. "What are you cooking?"

"Leg of lamb. It's Grandmother's favorite, so I'm making it for her. I hope you like it."

"Yes, I love lamb, but whenever I've cooked it, it never smelled that good."

Alan preened. "The secret is in the marinade, and then there's my special mint sauce. The meat has to cook for a while longer, so let's have a drink by the pool. Afterwards I'll go up to the main house and ask Consuela to bring Grandmother down to join us. She's very eager to meet you and thank you for pointing me to the pumpkin brooch and ring. I swear she sleeps with them on. But please don't mention the sale of her jewelry. As I told you, it will upset her. Of course, she doesn't know the full extent of what I'm doing. She thinks I'm selling the occasional piece she never wears anymore. So, if she asks please don't say anything different."

Marci was a little taken aback. She did not want to start her relationship with Alan's grandmother by lying to her. Hopefully the subject would not come up or Marci would be able to give vague answers. The situation made her uncomfortable and she did not like Alan putting her in that uncomfortable position. This was a matter between Mrs. Trent, her grandson and their attorney. Marci didn't want to be involved.

Before she could say anything, Alan grabbed an envelope off the counter and handed it to her. "Here are a few more pieces for Mr. Wright to handle. Why don't you put them safely away in your purse and I'll make the drinks? Are you up for a martini?"

They sat by the pool with their cocktails and savored a delicious crab and artichoke appetizer that Alan had prepared in advance. They were having such a nice time that Marci did not want to risk starting an argument. She would try to decline taking the jewelry later. She knew Savannah didn't want her to accept any more estate pieces.

"If you don't mind taking off that luscious dress, we can skip tennis and have time for a quick dip. You brought your suit, didn't you?" He winked seductively. "Or we could skinny dip."

"Yes, I brought it." She ignored him and hurried inside the guest house to change while Alan went into his bedroom to find his swim suit. When they were ready, they walked poolside together, holding hands.

"This is heavenly," Marci said after she dove under the water and swam the length of the pool. Alan swam up behind her and gently ran his fingers down her back.

"You're just as beautiful from behind as from the front." He grinned as he turned her around to face him. Before she knew what was happening, he took her face in his hands, and began kissing her ardently. Their wet bodies melded together, as their passions swept them away. Alan moved his hands expertly down her body under the water, cupping her breasts gently and then moved his hands slowly down her thighs and then back up to her erect nipples. Masterfully, he undid her bathing suit top with one hand and it floated away to the pool's floor.

Marci moaned with pleasure. It had been a long time since she had felt this excited by a man's touch. Her hunger for a passionate connection was suddenly released and she gave into her emotions. They stood in the shallow end of the pool, touching each other everywhere and kissing deeply. She clung to Alan like he was her lifeline.

Finally, Alan forced himself to break away. "My God, Marci, I have no restraint when I'm near you." He was breathing heavily and his eyes were hooded with desire. "But if I don't go inside right this minute, the roast will burn and my reputation as a chef will be forever ruined. The guest house might go up in flames. Grandmother would not be pleased."

"We can't have that," she giggled, grateful for an excuse to regain her composure. "I need to put on a little make-up and fix my hair before I meet her."

He stroked down the pool a few yards and retrieved her swimsuit top. Marci grabbed it, suddenly embarrassed by her nudity. They tossed towels around themselves without taking time to fully dry off and hurried inside. Alan went right to the oven to check the roast. "The lamb's okay," he reported happily. "I'll take it out and let it rest. Let's get dressed quickly and we'll go get Grandmother together. I'd like to show you some of the main house and some of the paintings that are still there. She owns quite an impressive collection. My grandfather spent many years acquiring the pieces he wanted."

Minutes later they reunited in the living room. Alan was tenting the roast when his phone rang. "That's Grandmother," he said matter-of-factly, shaking his head. "Her personal signal on my phone is a barking dog."

"That's really a coincidence, Marci's eyes misted. "Before my parents died in a horrific car accident several years ago, my father's signal was a barking dog and my mother's was a chirping bird."

Alan gave her hand a gentle squeeze and walked away speaking softly into the phone.

"Regrettably, Grandmother's not feeling well enough to come down. She's tired and is going to have some soup and get into bed," he explained sadly. "She apologies. I can tell she feels badly to have disappointed you. And now we'll have all this left-over food." He pointed to the huge lamb roast.

"Oh, that's too bad. I was looking forward to meeting her. Do you want to go up to the main house and check on her?"

"No. Consuela is with her. Mother does tire easily these days, and I told you she's a bit of a hypochondriac. A good night's sleep always restores her. I'll check on her before I go to bed tonight."

Alan pulled a pitcher of vichyssoise soup out of the refrigerator and poured it into cut crystal glass bowls that he'd placed in larger bowls of shaved ice. "This is my favorite soup, but it has to be served icy cold." He indicated where Marci should sit at the counter and pulled out the stool for her. "I hope you like it. It's truly my best recipe."

Marci had never tasted anything so delicious. Only her desire not to look like a pig kept her from asking for a second bowl. She loved the way he served it over shaved ice and admired the beautiful table settings Alan had created. He had used clear Lucite eating utensils and red contemporary square china dinner plates with matching Lucite water and wine glasses. The effect was stunning. The island countertop looked like something out of *Florida Today* or a *Martha Stewart* magazine.

The leg of lamb was cooked to delicious perfection. Alan served it with baby new potatoes and fresh snap peas. He filled their wine glasses with a bold Pinot Noir. Dessert was a cold chocolate mousse and then a magnificent cheese course completed the feast.

"That was amazing." Marci sat back satiated. She could not swallow another bite of anything. "Honestly Alan, you should open your own restaurant. That meal was as good as any I've had anywhere."

"Thank you." He bowed graciously. "You are too kind. I do love compliments. Would you like more wine or a brandy, perhaps?"

"Oh no. Nothing else, thank you. I've reached my alcohol limit. I am not much of a drinker although I do love a good wine." She glanced at the clock over the stove top. "I hate to mention it because it's been such a wonderful evening, but it's late and time for me to go home. I'm a working girl, remember?"

He looked at her hopefully. "I thought maybe you'd stay the night here with me?"

"No, not yet, Alan," she said. "I can't. Please be patient. I'm not ready to take that step. It's too soon."

"Okay, but you can't blame a guy for trying. One more thing." He looked at her earnestly and grabbed her hand. "I think we have gotten far enough along in our relationship that you can leave your tennis racquet and bathing suit here so you don't have to schlepp them back and forth every time you come over. Is that pushing the envelope too far?"

"No, it's all right," she smiled sweetly. "I guess that would be okay."

"And I have an interesting thought. Maybe the next time we go for a dip, you won't wear a bathing suit at all. That will give me something to look forward to."

Marci blushed and changed the subject. "We'll see about that. For now, let me help you with the dishes."

"No need," he answered. "Pedro will be here in the morning and he'll clean everything up then. God knows Grandmother pays him enough. It's the least he can do."

"Should we take the leftovers up to the main house. Maybe your Grandmother is still awake and hungry?" Marci was dying to see the inside of the mansion and maybe catch a glimpse of the elusive Mrs. Trent.

"No, I don't think so. Pedro and Consuela would have put her to bed by now and set the alarm. And to be honest my grandmother has never been one to eat leftovers. She can be a bit of a snob that way, God bless her."

"Okay." Marci was disappointed, but what he'd said made sense. Although, surely Alan knew the code and could disarm the alarm. He'd said he'd check on his mother before he went to bed. She started to ask him about that but he silenced her with more fervent kisses.

They stayed in the kitchen making out like teenagers for a few minutes until Marci reluctantly broke away. "Seriously, Alan. I need to go home now."

"All right," he sulked like a petulant boy. "But you don't know what you're missing."

Alan drove her home with his arm draped protectively around her shoulders while they listened to soft jazz. He kissed her deeply at her front door, which she returned in kind. They finally tore themselves apart. "I'll call you in the morning," he promised and drove off.

Marci was too keyed up to sleep. She made a cup of chamomile tea and sat at the kitchen table reliving the magic evening. It was not until she was finally relaxed and was lying in bed that she realized the beautifully appointed bar where they had eaten their fabulous meal had only been set with two placemats. It was as if Alan knew in advance that his grandmother would not be coming to dinner.

CHAPTER 24

Savannah and her father were enjoying a rack of baby back barbeque ribs at Bobby Rubino's restaurant in Pompano Beach. "These are the best ribs in the world," Dave enthused. "The meat literally falls off the bone."

Savannah laughed. "You say that every time we eat here, Dad, but I agree." She picked up the last rib on her plate and sucked the remaining sauce off the bone. "The trouble is, there's no way to eat these in a ladylike manner." The restaurant's secret sauce was all over her fingers and face.

"Here's a *Towelette*." He handed one to his daughter and used another two for himself. "It is a very messy meal, but worth every bite!"

"Remind me never to bring a date here. Seeing me devour these ribs like a cannibal would scare any sane man away." She giggled and wiped her face.

"Not if he's a rib connoisseur. And you better not date anyone who isn't," he joked. "What man wouldn't love this meal? And by the way, speaking of men, you haven't mentioned anyone special lately." He gave her an appealing smile.

Dave was worried about her still being single. She was such a warm and giving person. He hoped she would find a husband and have a wonderful marriage, like his had been with her mother. Savannah had been impulsive and married too young. She needed to let go of the past and move forward. He was always telling her that, but so far, his fatherly advice had fallen on deaf ears. What child ever listened to their parents once they passed age thirteen? And as he had predicted, she raised her hand in a protective gesture of "stop". He would have to move on too. The topic was closed.

"Not to change the subject, but on a serious note." Savannah took a bite of coleslaw and looked intently at her father. "I want to talk to you about Alan and Marci. I'm really worried that she's getting into something way over her head. She's getting more and more involved with him and I just know he's using her to unload more and more of his grandmother's jewelry through us. You and Sheldon told me not to warn her about him, but I'm really uncomfortable with that. She's being played like a fiddle and we're standing by silently and letting it happen."

"Honey, I appreciate your concern, I really do. We haven't heard back from Sheldon, though, so we don't have any hard evidence that Alan is scamming her. All we really know is that, for whatever reason, he sold the pumpkin piece right after buying it from us and no doubt, made a pretty profit in the process. He hasn't come clean Marci, but that's not a crime."

"I know, but I smell something fishy. You know my instincts are usually correct. And why wouldn't Alan's attorney handle the sale of Mrs. Trent's jewelry himself, or insist they use an auction house like Sotheby's or Christie's? They could do a much better job and get them higher prices than your jeweler friends. And it seems strange that Alan brings the pieces to us in dribs and drabs. It's almost like he doesn't want to raise any red flags. Do we know that his grandmother has actually authorized these transactions? Do we have anything in writing from her?"

Dave Wright admired his preceptive daughter. "Here you go again, honey, playing Nancy (Drew). But you may be onto something. No, we don't have any written permission or instructions authorizing us to sell the jewelry…all we have is Alan's word for it. What do you suggest we do at this point?"

"For one thing, get Mrs. Trent's signature on a permission slip authorizing *Wrights* to act on her behalf. We have that as a standard form in the office. I'm appalled that we let that important detail slip. We always have our clients sign it. That document protects us and them.

"Also," Savannah continued earnestly, "if Alan is not on the up and up, it will hurt Marci to learn the truth, but better she finds out now before she gets in any deeper. He's already in full-blown courting mode. She's spending all her free time with him. If he's innocent, great…but if not, we need to spare her a lot of grief down the road."

"Okay, I can see that." Of course, he didn't want Marci to get hurt. He had grown very fond of her too.

"There are a couple of things we can do," Savannah said. "Depending on what Blake hears from his private detective we can turn the matter over to the police."

"The police? Savannah, you're scaring me a little. I know you love mystery novels and NCIS and all, but this is real life. If Alan is really doing something illegal, he won't appreciate you snooping around. In fact, if he thinks that you suspect him of something, you might be in real danger."

"I know, Dad." She reached across the table and put her hand on his wrist. "But I truly believe he's not only roping Marci into his scheme, but *Wright*s too. We can't let that happen." Her blue eye blazed with resolve. "Listen to what I have in mind, and if you agree with me, then we can start doing something, tomorrow morning in fact."

Dave Wright looked somber and nodded his agreement. He signaled the waitress and ordered another beer for himself and another glass of wine for Savannah. "I'm all ears, honey."

CHAPTER 25

Marci and Alan had been spending every evening together. She now drove herself directly to his house after work and could hardly wait to be with him. There was nothing in her life now as important as Alan. She rarely saw Savannah outside of *Wrights* anymore. Her world revolved solely around her boyfriend now. She had forgotten all about her comfortable talks with Dave and her little crush on him, and about taking night classes too.

The two played a lot of tennis and kissed constantly in the pool. Alan cooked them one delicious dinner after another, something he was able to do working from home. He told her Pedro did the shopping for him each day, and then he got dinner started in between his work calls. On weekends the couple spent hours sitting on the dock or by the pool, sipping wine, playing cards or Backgammon. Marci joked that they were as boring as an old married couple but without the legal entanglements. She loved every minute of her time spent with him. They were in a world by themselves and she was totally content.

She loved Alan's stories about growing up in the big house with his grandparents… about the glamorous parties they had given and all the important people he'd met. He had loved traveling with his grandparents and seeing the world. But his happiest memories were around *Pampered*. Everything changed for him when they bought the yacht. He loved the boating lifestyle and he learned everything he could about navigation from the ship's captain. As a child, he had yearned to become a captain himself. He told her that it saddened him that *Pampered* was now for sale, but that was the right thing to do at this stage of his grandmother's life.

In turn, Marci told him about her upbringing in DC. She explained that her parents were not wealthy people but were well-connected and respected in their professional fields. Her mother had been a pediatric nurse and her father, a political commentator for the *Washington Post* newspaper. Congressmen and senators often dropped by her family home to discuss politics and seek her father's advice. They hadn't been happy when she married so young, putting her fashion dreams aside. She felt sad that she had disappointed them. That she and Alan had both lost their parents at relatively young ages drew them even closer. They had a shared tragedy and it drew them together.

Alan's parents had died when he was five. He barely remembered them. It was his grandparents who raised and loved him, and he was so grateful for the life they'd given him that he felt obligated to take care of his grandmother now. He owed her that much.

One night, when they had plans for dinner in South Beach – their first time venturing out of the guest house bubble – Alan apologized at the last minute and asked if she would mind if they cancelled. He was afraid to stray very far from the house. His grandmother's health was deteriorating rapidly. Even though Consuela was with her all the time, Alan said he felt obligated to be stay nearby.

Marci wasn't especially disappointed not to go out on the town; she didn't need fancy restaurants or clubs to feel content. But she was sad because the turn in Mrs. Trent's health suggested that now she might never have the opportunity to meet her. Every time Alan had planned anything, she had a "spell" or had begged off because she'd been too tired. Now it looked like the clock was running out and she was destined to never meet the family matriarch.

Marci had long since given up the hope of ever spending any time in the main house while Mrs. Trent was alive because she no longer permitted visitors, not even her closest friends. Alan swore that Pedro fiercely guarded the door and was sometimes hesitant to even let him in. As many times as Marci was on the estate, she had never seen the mysterious butler either, although she admired how well he took care of the grounds and the guest house. There was never anything out of place. Everything was almost too perfect.

Alan told her one night that within the last few weeks his grandmother had deteriorated so badly that she'd lost all interest in her physical appearance. She no longer wanted to color her hair or have the manicurist visit the house. She stayed in her bed most of the day and saw no one except Pedro, Consuela and himself. He went up to the main house every day and made her lunch, sitting by her bedside as she picked at the food on a tray. Alan had let the chef go because his mother became finicky and would only eat Alan's food.

It was a waste of money to pay a large staff when no one but himself and Marci ever used the property or enjoyed the grounds. As soon as his grandmother passed, he was going to put the estate on the market. Alan explained that he didn't want to stay there without his grandmother. He said he'd find another place nearby, one hopefully where Marci would move in with him.

She could see the emotional toil the situation was taking on Alan. Sometimes he appeared depressed and angry, and she noticed he was drinking more than usual. She was usually able to cheer him up, but not always. Sometimes he seemed to settle in a dark place and she couldn't reach him. When that happened, she drove home and usually worried about him all night. The next day he would call her and act as if nothing had happened. It was as if he was two different people inhabiting one body. She was concerned about him, but there was nothing she could do, except be there for him.

Marci remembered wanting to invite Savannah to join them for dinner and had suggested it a few times. Alan always found an excuse to put her off. He finally confessed that their relationship was so special, and he cherished every moment with her and didn't want anyone intruding on it. He half-heartedly promised he'd invite Savannah one day soon. But he didn't mean it. Sometimes Marci wondered if the real reason she had not met Mrs. Trent was that Alan didn't want it to happen. He was so possessive of her. Could he possibly be threatened by his own grandmother spending time with her? She wondered about it, but never brought it up. Confrontation and arguments upset Marci. She wanted to placate, not stir up.

"Soon she will be gone and I can get my life back again," he told her morosely one night when he was having a particularly dark time. "I can't imagine living here without her." Now he was consumed with having to wait for his grandmother's unlikely recovery or more probably, her death. It was a stressful way to live and Marci did everything she could to comfort him. He had begged her to move into the guest house but she continued to resist that. She did not feel it was proper to openly flaunt their happiness in his grandmother's backyard, especially when she was so near death.

"That's being damn stupid, Marci," he ranted one night in agitation. "What's the difference? You're here every night anyway. She knows what's going on. She's old and dying but not dumb."

"I know," she answered softly. "But I just feel it would be disrespectful. If I had met your grandmother, and she approved of me and our relationship, I would have different feelings about it. Don't make a problem between us, please. Things are great and in time..." She didn't say after his grandmother died – "I'll probably move in. You know how much I love and want to be with you."

"So, you say," he pouted like a spoiled child. "Sometimes I wish the old bag would just roll over and croak. It's time she went to the pearly gates."

Marci looked at him, aghast. "You don't mean that? You're just frustrated."

"Maybe," he relented. "I know, I know. I love her very much. It's just that she's ruining my life when hers is all but over. It's not fair to either of us."

"I've certainly learned that life's not fair, but you can't give in to depression. You have so much to be grateful for, Alan. Look at what you have, not at what you don't." She hoped she didn't sound like Pollyanna, but it was true. He had everything a person could ever want but he never seemed satisfied. Once his grandmother died, would he really be any happier?

Marci had seen this petulant side of Alan before and learned the best way to get him out of his funk was in the bedroom. Smiling seductively, she slowly slid off her shirt and shorts and stood before him in her black string bikini panties and lace bra. Every time he saw her in her lingerie, his lust smothered his bad mood. Under her sweetness and naivete there raged an ardent, sensual woman. He became instantly aroused and almost dragged her to his bed where they pleasured each other for hours until she insisted, she had to leave.

Not wanting to argue after such passionate love making, he abruptly turned over in bed and mumbled something to her about driving home safely. Marci quickly dressed and as she was about to leave the bedroom, he rolled back over. "There's another envelope of jewelry for Mr. Wright on my desk."

Reluctantly, Marci picked up the envelope that was like all the others and shoved it into her purse. She tiptoed quietly out of the bedroom and out of the guest house. He was already fast asleep.

As she walked up the path to the main house where she had parked the car, she was surprised to see lights going on and off on the second floor, as if someone was moving from room to room. She looked up but could see no one at the windows. Was it possible that Pedro was doing a final walkthrough before setting the alarm? Marci glanced at her watch. It was well past midnight. The household should have been sleeping by then…unless either Pedro or Consuela had suddenly become a night owl. Surely Mrs. Trent was sound asleep.

Feeling guilty for having been with Alan when his grandmother was so ill, she slid quickly into her car and drove off. She couldn't put a label on it, but she felt uneasy, afraid something bad was going to happen.

CHAPTER 26

When Marci came into the shop the next morning Savannah asked to speak with her. Savannah's tone of voice and facial expression were serious, which was unusual for her.

"What's up?" Marci asked nervously. "You're not firing me, are you?"

"No, of course not. But we do have to address the elephant in the room."

"I suppose you mean Alan?"

"Yes, exactly. And believe me, I wish I didn't have the suspicions that I have, but I do and they're not going away."

Marci sighed heavily and sat down. "Okay, what's the problem now?"

Savannah had to be careful what she said because she didn't want Marci to get mad and run to Alan with her accusations. Right now, he was her white knight and it would be hard for Savannah to convince her otherwise.

"Dad and I both think it's a little unusual that Alan is selling off so much of his grandmother's beautiful jewelry through us. In most cases, collections of this size are sent to an auction house, appropriately photographed and catalogued and then sold in lots, all on the same day. It's faster, tidier and the bookkeeping is much simpler than doing it in dribs and drabs like Alan has chosen to do."

"Oh, I can explain that," Marci said, visibly relieved. She was afraid it was something more serious. "Alan told me that his grandmother associates her beautiful possessions, jewelry, artwork and the like, with a time in her life when she was happily married, active and in good health. So, out of consideration for her feelings, he only takes a few pieces at a time and replaces them with inexpensive jewelry. That way he does what the estate attorney has requested and she isn't upset. I think the way he's going about this is loving and considerate. There's nothing suspicious."

Savannah had to consciously force her eyes not to roll upward. She wanted to shake some sense into her all-too-trusting friend. *Could Marci really be that blind?*

Trying to control her frustration, Savannah gritted her teeth. "That may all be true but Alan's decision to handle the sales this way puts *Wrights* and all of us at risk. We don't have any legal paperwork, any written authorization from either the attorney or from Mrs. Trent that gives us permission to sell her pieces. Usually that's the first thing we ask for, but as you recall, Dad and I weren't here when Alan brought in the first batch, and he's only given you the additional pieces when you've been alone with him. Am I right? Legally, we need Mrs. Trent's written permission."

"I'm sure that won't be a problem," Marci smiled. "Give me whatever you need her to sign and I'll have Alan take care of it tonight." She stood up; happy the subject was closed. "Anything else?"

"No that covers our concerns. Thank you. It'll be a big relief to have that authorization on file. I don't want anything to taint *Wright*'s good reputation."

"Nor do I." She gave Savannah a quick hug and returned to the showroom to start her day.

The next person into the shop was the florist delivery man with his daily red rose for Marci.

CHAPTER 27

n mid-July, Dave received a call from his friend in Palm Springs, California. "Dave, I've managed to sell thirteen of the twenty-six pieces of the estate jewelry you sent me in the first consignment and I got pretty respectable prices. The other batches have not moved nearly as well. I'm afraid Harry, in the Beverly Hills store, only managed to sell three pieces. I don't know why, but it seems the market for previously owned jewelry has dried up. We were flooded with items after the Bernie Madoff scandal, but now no one wants to touch the stuff. I'm returning all the unsold pieces you sent us, as is our policy after 60 days. I'll be sending you a check for $779,000 for your client. That represents the total sales, less your and my combined commissions of $62,000. It's all spelled out for you on the receipts as always. I'd advise your client to try to sell the remaining pieces at auction. It will be simpler for him and faster. If he doesn't want to use the national houses, his best bet is a big auction in Phoenix, Arizona in two weeks. I suggest you tell him about it."

"I'll pass that information on. Oddly, our customer doesn't appear to need the money. He says he's trying to reduce the inheritance taxes on the estate for when his grandmother passes. But I don't understand why. He'll have to report the money he receives from the sales anyway."

"I've known people to do that, but I think it's pretty cold-hearted."

"I agree, but that's apparently what his lawyer suggested. Of course, he'll have to pay taxes on this $779,000, but at a lower rate."

"And how's that pretty daughter of yours doing? Married yet?"

"No. At the moment, Savannah is married to our shop, and I'm frankly not happy about it. I'd love for her to find a nice young man and settle down."

"Give it time. She's too lovely to remain single for long. Give her my best and stay safe during this upcoming hurricane season."

Dave hung up the phone and called his daughter. He explained what had happened and that his California friend was returning the unsold pieces. "I know Alan will be disappointed about that but we got good prices for Mrs. Trent's first batch of jewelry. You can tell him he'll be receiving a check for $779,00.00 in a few days."

"I'll let Marci know. She sees him every night, much to my distress. I still think there's something weird about the guy. I did have the talk with her a few days ago like you and I discussed and she's promised to get us Mrs. Trent's authorization in writing. I think we should be smart and keep the money until we get it."

"Agreed. Let's see what happens. Tell Marci we can't disperse the money until we have the signed form. I'm sure she'll pass the message on."

"Okay, Dad. By the way, have you heard anything from Sheldon and his private detective? He should have some info on Alan by now."

"Not yet, but I'll give him a call after we hang up. Are you free to have dinner with your old man tonight? Morton's Steak house perhaps?"

"Sure, I can't turn that invitation down. What time should I meet you?"

CHAPTER 28

Alan paced around the room, alternately taking big swigs from a bottle of McCallum fifteen-year-old scotch and fighting the urge to scream with frustration. After months of plotting and planning, and tediously courting the simpleton, Marci Morgan, he was no closer to getting her to marry him than he'd been on the first day they'd met. He had counted on his charms to persuade her. Marriage was essential for his plan to work. But it hadn't happened. She continued to hold back.

If things had worked out the way they were supposed to, he would be sailing off to paradise by

now -- leaving her alone to face the authorities.

So far, he'd managed to accrue a lot of cash from selling the old bat's jewelry and art, but it would do him no good if he couldn't move the money out of the country to spend it.

He was exhausted from pretending to be the caring grandson and perfect boyfriend. He hadn't been sleeping well and often awoke from horrible nightmares, sweaty and dripping wet. His plan was taking too long to implement, and now timing was going to become a huge problem. He needed Marci to move into the guest house and marry him, but she was too damn noble and claimed it would be disrespectful to his grandmother. *What bull! The old lady was so out of it now-a-days that she'd never know. Why did Marci have to be so damn sanctimonious? If she wouldn't marry him voluntarily, then he'd have to force her.*

He slugged down more of the scotch that was quickly becoming his constant companion and went to his computer to once again Google the wealthy Brazilian plastic surgeon who'd come out of nowhere last week, screwing up his plan by wanting to buy *Pampered.* There was no question that he could afford the boat, even when Alan raised the price in an effort to deter him. Alan couldn't allow the sale to happen because he needed the mega yacht for his escape. If the doctor actually bought *Pampered,* he'd have to change all his elaborate plans. And he did not like change.

Alan stood up, dizzy from too much scotch, and staggered to bed. Time was running out. The Brazilian doctor's interest in the yacht had forced his hand. He couldn't wait any longer. He'd have to convince Marci to marry him, no matter what he had to do, and with no more delays.

CHAPTER 29

Savannah entered the dining room at Morton's Steakhouse and immediately spotted her father. He was seated at a table and chatting with the waitress. Savannah made her way towards him in the crowded restaurant, stopping to say hello to a few of the shop's clients on the way. *Wrights* was such a well-known entity in Fort Lauderdale that she was accustomed to running into its patrons around the city.

"Hi, Dad." She kissed him on his cheek and took a seat opposite him. "I see you've already ordered my favorite wine. Thanks." She picked up the glass and saluted him.

"My pleasure, Honey. I knew you'd be anxious to hear about my conversation with Sheldon, and this way the waitress won't interrupt us for a little while." He looked around the room nodding to a few people whom he recognized. He was a popular man, both at the shop and at his country club. Savannah was happy that because of hiring Marci, he was having an active life again, no longer quite so chained to the store.

"So, Sheldon heard back from his private detective?"

"Yes, coincidentally he spoke to him only an hour before I reached out to him today. He was about to call us with his findings."

"And?" She sat up straight and leaned in towards her Dad. "Did the detective find anything that might shed some light on Alan?"

Dave took a large gulp of his dirty martini and spoke in a low voice. "He learned that the pumpkin brooch was sent to Vegas from an address in Miami, the same one Marci had taken down but additionally he found an apartment number. After some pretty good sleuthing, the detective was able to discover that the apartment was completely empty. It contained no furniture at all and it appears that it's only used as a mailbox drop.

"Go on," Savannah fidgeted in her seat. "Dad, don't keep me in suspense."

"Hold your horses, Savannah. I'm just getting to the good part." He took another sip of his drink and continued. "The name listed on the lease was not that of an individual, but of a corporation...Pampered Partners, Inc."

"No?" She gasped, fully understanding the significance of that name. "*Pampered*, that's Mrs. Trent's yacht."

"Yes. Let me finish," he sighed. Savannah was always impatient and thinking two steps ahead of him. "The PI checked with the mailman on that route and the concierge at the front desk of the apartment building. The concierge said he'd never seen anyone come in or out of that apartment but both he and the mailman know someone empties the box quite often. I was thinking about it. Imagine if Alan is using other jewelers in addition to us. He could be raking in millions."

"If what he's doing is really on the up and up and on the advice of his attorney, why the cloak and dagger business of using a dummy corporation and keeping an empty apartment in Miami? Why wouldn't he use his grandmother's home address? Or the attorney's? The more we find out about Alan Trent, the stranger this all gets."

"That's why we need to figure this out quickly. And, let me caution you, Sheldon reminded me that it is not against the law for someone to form a corporation to house assets. And, having an apartment, but not living in it, is completely legal. We have to be cautious about defaming Alan's name and reputation until we have actual proof that he's done something wrong. We can't afford for him to sue us and drag *Wright's* name through the mud."

"What he's doing may be legal, but it certainly seems odd." Savannah was more worried than she let on. "Dad, are we in trouble for helping Alan sell the pieces?"

"No. Not according to Sheldon. Ours was a legitimate transaction. But we do need the authorization from Mrs. Trent. As long as we report everything to the IRS, we're fine. If Alan fails to disclose the money that he got from our California sources and from the Las Vegas vendor, then that's a different matter. He'll be in trouble, not us. In any case, we have to tell Alan that we can't handle any more of his mother's jewelry. Our sources don't want it. And what's more, I don't want *Wrights* involved in his shenanigans in any way going forward."

"Oh, my goodness. I've been thinking that my overly active Nancy Drew imagination was getting the best of me, but now I really believe that Alan is a bonified crook. Do you remember the plan I suggested to you when we had dinner at Bobby Rubino's? Tomorrow might be a good time to implement it."

He nodded somberly. "Let's order and we'll talk more about it. We need to decide who does what. I told Sheldon your plan. He had a few suggestions too." He signaled the waitress.

"Dad, if I go against Sheldon's advice and warn Marci, she won't take me seriously and it might ruin our friendship. Alan's got her completely fooled. They spend all their waking hours together when she's not at work. He makes sure she doesn't have time for anything or anyone but himself. She won't even have a quick drink with me at Cages after work anymore. He demands all of her attention and makes her feel guilty if she wants to do anything without him. Alan actually got mad at her last week when she went to get her hair cut after work instead of going right to his house. I think it's clear he's deliberately isolating and controlling her. But she doesn't see it that way. She says he loves her so much that he wants to be with her all the time when she's not working. He's brainwashing her and he's been trying to persuade her to move in with him. I'm afraid she may say yes."

"If he's a sociopath, which I think he probably is, that's the way the illness presents. A sociopath will lie and lie and hurt a lot of people in the process. They have no conscience. They isolate their victims until they have total control over them. Unfortunately, Marci has unwittingly put herself in the middle of a potentially dangerous situation. I agree with you, honey. We have to get her away from him for her own sake." He was worried sick about her himself and realized how devastated he would be if she moved in with Alan. Things for him had changed. He'd have to stop being afraid of rejection and tell Marci how he was feeling about their friendship…about her…before it was too late. Timing is everything.

The waitress brought their steak dinners to the table and refilled their drinks. Dave began to enjoy his meal, but Savannah had lost her appetite and was too upset to eat.

"Can we follow through on my plan tomorrow?" she begged her father. "Please."

"Yes. Either we're making a mountain out of a mole hill, or we're on to something criminal."

"Do you think the private eye can find out where Alan deposits the money he gets from the sale of the jewelry? It would be interesting to see if it goes into his grandmother's account or to the Pampered corporate account or to somewhere else entirely. . .like maybe his own pocket."

"I'll call Sheldon in the morning and ask him to get his PI to check it out. That's a good suggestion. You really are a Nancy Drew copycat, but much cuter." He winked at her and smiled.

Savannah was already lost in thought about how to put her plan into effect.

CHAPTER 29

brought some paperwork with me for your grandmother," Marci said casually while chopping tomatoes for the salad. Dave needs them for his files. It's purely routine." She dried her hands on a dishtowel and handed him an envelope from her purse.

Alan tossed the envelope onto the coffee table. "I'll take care of it tomorrow. If Grandmother's not lucid in the morning, I'll sign the paper for her. I have her power of attorney."

"That would be wonderful. I know Savannah's worried. She's super organized and likes to have everything in perfect order. You know she's a type A personality."

"Let's stop fretting about forms and Savannah. I want my girl all to myself tonight. Would you like to take some wine and sit on the aft deck of *Pampered?* It's a beautiful evening. I may not be able to take you on a cruise because it looks like it's about to be sold, but at least we can enjoy her at the dock ... and maybe christen the owner's stateroom?" He looked at her seductively. "I don't know why I haven't thought of that before. There's no crew on board anymore, so the place will be totally ours."

"That sounds delightful. I've wanted to go on board since the first time I saw her."

"Your wish is my command. Grab a bottle or two of wine and we'll head over there. Most of the provisions have been removed from the galley, but all the stemware and dishes and glasses are still there. They'll be sold with the boat."

Carrying two chilled bottles of Kistler Chardonnay they headed to the yacht and Alan helped Marci navigate the gangplank. "Be careful. It can be slippery."

"My God, this boat is gorgeous," Marci enthused as she stepped onto the deck. "Everything is spotless. The yacht actually glistens. I can't imagine what it must cost to maintain, and the manpower it must take to keep this boat looking so pristine."

"It's super expensive. In its prime, she used to carry a huge crew. Now Pedro is solely

in-charge but he does a great job. I don't know how he does it, but he washes down the decks and polishes the finishes every few days. We have to keep it spotless to show to potential buyers. And, I think we might actually have a live one. He's a plastic surgeon from Brazil who's been here three times already. Next, he wants to take her out for a spin, a type of sea trial actually. If that goes well, I think we'll have a sale."

"That sounds promising. Will you be sad when she sells?"

"Yes. Certainly. I've spent many happy hours onboard, but there's a time for everything and it's time for her to go to a new owner who will use and enjoy her. It's not good for the engines to sit idle in the water. Boats are meant to be used, not sit around like a floating hotel."

He poured Marci a glass of wine and they took seats on the aft deck chairs. The stars were out making bold patterns in the sky and a gentle night breeze blew across the intercoastal waterway caressing them. "Hmmm," Marci murmured contently. "How wonderful this is. I bet you'll miss your boat more than you think."

Not really, he thought smugly. *Because soon I'll have a mega yacht all my own that'll make this one look like a rowboat. And you, my pretty lady, are going to help me get it.* He reached for Marci's hand and gave it a squeeze. He had to keep up the pretense of being a loving grandson and devoted suitor for a little while longer. This was not the time to risk the fortune he'd been secretly accumulating. He'd have plenty of time to enjoy that in the future, but not until he convinced Marci to marry him.

"What do you say we go to the master suite and break in the bed?" He took her glass and set it down on a nearby table. "

Tipsy from the wine, she turned and threw her arms around his neck. "Oh yes, let's go fuck our brains out." Oh my God, she was mortified. She never used the F word. Where had that come from?

Shocked by her uncharacteristic speech, Alan grinned. "Yes indeed, my little potty mouth. I think I can oblige you. I see Kistler Chardonnay brings out an interesting side of you. Follow me."

They literally ran to the master suite and tossed all their clothes onto the floor before jumping onto the bed. "I know we're still at the dock, but I feel like we're rocking and rolling." She slurred her words.

"That's the wine," he laughed. "I think you've had enough. Maybe we should go back outside to the deck and get you some fresh air." He was afraid she might get sick and he'd have to clean up the mess.

Alan led her to the aft deck and tried again to persuade Marci to move in with him, and again she refused.

"All right then." He could barely hide his annoyance and he was getting angry about her stubbornness. "If you won't move in with me, will you marry me instead and then we can live together honestly? Surely you cannot think that marriage will offend my saintly grandmother?"

"Marry you?" She was stunned and ignored his snide reference to his grandmother. "We've never talked about marriage. How can you possibly think I'd be ready for that? We have a good time together and great sex, but I've told you from the beginning that I'm not ready for that and in fact I may never marry again after what I went through with my ex-husband. I haven't changed my mind. Please Alan, don't ruin what we have by pushing me too hard. I do love you…but that has to be enough for now. I can't promise you anything else."

"Of course, I won't push you," he said smoothly but was seething underneath his calm façade.

If you won't marry me willingly, then I'll have to find another way.

CHAPTER 30

D ave Wright unlocked the door to his shop, turned on the overhead lights and went back to the office. Shortly thereafter Marci let herself in and came in to say good morning.

"Sorry, but you're stuck with just me today," Savannah's dad said cheerfully. "My daughter had some personal things to take care of, so I gave her the day off. A little nepotism never hurts."

"Well, I guess not. That's one of the benefits of being the boss's daughter. It's really nice to see you again Dave." Marci smiled affectionately at him. "I've missed our little chats, but I suppose the golf course is more appealing. Is there anything special you need me to do today?"

"No, I don't think so. Business as usual but by the way, are you still dating that Trent fellow?"

"Yes. Why do you ask?" she blushed. She wasn't comfortable talking about her personal life with her boss. She knew he didn't think much of Alan.

"No particular reason. I just wondered. I wish Savannah could find a nice young man. She would never admit it, but I know she'd never expected to still be single and she's lonely. She'd hoped to have a house full of kids by now, and probably a dog and a big yard with a white picket fence. Do you think you could ask Alan if he might have a friend he could fix her up with? Maybe then the four of you could double date, or is that too old-fashioned? Do people still do that?"

"Yes, they do, and it would be fun," she confessed. "I haven't actually met any of Alan's friends. I'll be sure to mention it to him tonight though. I would love to introduce someone nice to Savannah. I don't get to talk to her much these days. And by the way, I don't think Florida homes have white picket fences. They have bougainvillea hedges."

"You're right," he grinned. "I'm hopelessly old-fashioned...I should wear a button-down Perry Como sweater and carry a pipe in my hand."

She smiled at him. His old-fashioned values were one of the appealing things about him. She then looked pensive, suddenly aware of how little social time she'd spent with her best friend since becoming so involved with Alan. She had neglected Savannah and been selfish. She needed to correct that, to make her friendship a priority. And now that Dave had mentioned friends, she wondered why it was that she had never met any of Alan's. It seemed strange. After all these months of dating, shouldn't one of them have dropped by his house or called him when she was there? When she met him, he had said he frequently invited his friends to dinner and that he enjoyed cooking for them. But he had never mentioned any of their names and they certainly had not been invited to the guest house since she'd been coming over nightly.

"It was just a thought," Dave said nonchalantly. Had he successfully planted a seed of doubt in Marci's mind? Truthfully, the very last thing he wanted was for his daughter to get mixed up with any of Alan's associates.

However, he needed Marci to believe everything about Alan was fine, until it was time to tell her otherwise. If he or Savannah made her suspicious, she would certainly run to him with their accusations. Before they said anything to her, they needed solid evidence.

The doorbell rang. A florist delivery man handed Marci a long stem red rose, smiled and departed. Over the last weeks, his arrival had become a morning ritual that Marci looked forward to. She placed the pristine rose in a Waterford crystal vase and added water but this morning, the flower did not make her smile. Dave's mention of Alan's friends and her realization that she didn't think he had any, disturbed her.

Dave wondered what would have happened between Marci and him if he'd given in to his impulse at the time and asked her out? He was not deterred by their age difference, though that might be hard for Savannah to accept. What would she think? What daughter wanted her father dating her best friend?

He had hesitated to ask her out because he had respected that she was entering into a relationship with another man and he was too much a gentleman to interfere…until now. Alan was a scoundrel at best and a con man and thief at the worst. Marci deserved better, much better, and he wanted a chance to prove that he was the right man for her. The two of them alone in the shop was the perfect opportunity for him to finally make a move to turn their friendship into something more. He prayed Savannah would not object too much, but for now, she had no need to know.

A few minutes later, fortified by a strong dose of caffeine, he casually walked onto the show room floor and approached her. "I hope you don't think this is too off the wall," Dave began hesitantly. "My country club has a terrific happy hour on Thursday nights. They serve great martinis, all kinds of appetizers and the most enormous cheese and charcuterie board you can imagine. There's a small band and it's always a fun evening. Would you care to join me there tonight? I would really love it if you would." He held his breath waiting for her answer.

Marci grinned. "Dave. That's a lovely invitation, but…"

"No buts, young lady. You've been an important part of the *Wrights* family for many, many months now and have become my daughter's best friend. I appreciate what you've done for us and yet, our talks aside, I hardly know anything about you. Please come with me this evening. You can go meet your boyfriend afterwards. Simply tell him you have to work late. Boss's orders. Happy hour can be our little secret, if you don't want to tell him. What do you say?" He was surprised by how much he wanted her to say yes.

Marci was taken aback. She had always thought Dave was a handsome man and young for his years. But she always thought of him as simply Savannah's attractive father. Now she was seeing him in a new light, as a possible date. She didn't know how to answer him. In fact, she didn't know much about him either beyond their conversations, which had never focused on personal topics. She was surprised that she was even considering going out with him and was already beginning to feel guilty about having to lie to Alan. But, why shouldn't she have a night out? Just because Alan had proposed, which she thought was ludicrous, it didn't mean that he owned her. Since working at *Wrights*, Marci had become an independent, self-supporting woman and as much as she loved Alan, she had every right to see another man if she chose to. And suddenly she knew that she did choose to.

Before she could change her mind, she smiled at Dave and whispered, "Yes, I'd love to have a drink with you tonight. But it has to be our little secret. I'm pretty sure Alan wouldn't like the idea."

"And I'm not at all sure how Savannah will feel, so absolutely, let it be our secret for the moment."

CHAPTER 31

Savannah adjusted her favorite Raquel Welch auburn wig so that the bangs almost hid her eyes. She hadn't worn this particular one in years but was grateful she still had it in her closet. Ten years ago, she had been forced to wear hair pieces for a few months after losing her own hair from chemotherapy treatments for her breast cancer. She had kept a closet full of wigs then, in all colors and styles. They helped her to feel pretty and light-hearted – a contrast to the worry and discomfort her disease and treatment caused. Keeping some of the wigs was just a reminder of her strength and how she came though such a difficult time. Now she felt confident that if Alan happened to be home and saw her, he would not recognize her. But running into the unlikable Mr. Trent was definitely not in her plans.

She drove past the faux gatehouse at the front of the private Coastal Beach community and to the front of the Trent property. Alan's red Porsche was not in the driveway. Savannah breathed a sigh of relief. Hopefully she had timed her arrival to coincide with when he would be out doing errands for his grandmother or maybe heading to Miami to retrieve his mail and checks. If that was the case, she'd have a few hours to snoop around, but if he only ran local errands, her safe timeframe would be much shorter. There was no way of knowing how long he'd be gone, so she had to work quickly.

Savannah moved her car around the block and parked it on the street in front of one of the neighbor's. Adjusting her wig one more time, she put on a pair of dark sunglasses and walked casually back in the direction of the Trent home. She was alone on the street. *So far, so good.*

Once she was in the front of the estate, she walked through the open gate and darted around the side of the main house, looking for the guest house. She needed to be positive that Alan wasn't inside. As she approached it, she noticed the tennis court and the swimming pool that Marci had described in great detail. Both were empty. She hugged the side of the winding path next to a row of flowering hedges, hoping none of the house staff would see her. When she got by the front door of the guest house, she peeked through a large window on the left. The plantation shutters were partially open so she could see that the kitchen-living space appeared deserted. She continued walking around the outside of the guest house. Marci had been right. It was the size of most normal homes and was every bit as attractive as she had said. Nothing appeared out of place. She recognized Marci's tennis racquet hanging from a hook and Alan's briefcase on the kitchen island.

When she had come full circle, and was convinced Alan was not at home, she moved slowly towards the dock. The mammoth yacht, *Pampered,* was tied up straight ahead. There did not appear to be any crew around, at least none she could see. From her vantage point, all the boat's decks appeared empty. The metal gangplank was in the down position, making entry easy. It was so tempting. Did she dare climb on board?

Scouting out the boat was not in her original plan, but the lure to take a quick peek was strong.

As she was deciding what to do, she heard whistling and saw the figure of a man wearing black shorts and a white tee shirt with the *Pampered* silhouette and name on the front. He wore a towel over his head to protect it from the sun and was walking directly toward her. He carried a large plastic container full of cleaning supplies. Savannah realized that she was trapped. There was no way off the dock without passing him unless she backtracked all the way to the guest house, but then he'd surely see her moving away. She had no choice but to throw herself headfirst into the nearest bushes and hope for the best. Oblivious to her presence, the man continued walking and passed within inches of her hiding place. He was seemingly in no hurry. At the bottom of the gangplank, he removed his shoes and started to climb onboard.

Thinking he'd heard an unfamiliar sound, he stopped and turned around, looking up and down the length of the dock. The bushes were a perfect shield. Savannah could see between the branches, but she was perfectly camouflaged. After a few seconds, the man shrugged and continued up the gangplank. He picked up a hose, uncoiled it and began washing down the deck and railings.

Suddenly she saw the salon door slide open and a tall attractive, woman dressed in street clothes, stepped out from inside the boat's salon and approached the deckhand. They talked for a moment. He dropped the hose and put his arm around her, and they kissed. Savannah could not make out the man's face from her position but she could not help but notice a large red rose tattoo on his right forearm. After they pulled apart, the woman disappeared back inside. The man picked up the hose and continued to wash down the deck.

Painfully Savannah twisted her body around so that she was facing the yacht head-on. Finally, when she could no longer see the deckhand, she sprinted out of the bushes and dashed around the corner to the guest house. From there, she abandoned her original plan and ran directly past the main house and to her car. She kept checking her rear-view mirror until she was confident no one was following her. If the deckhand had spotted her and stopped her to ask questions, what would she have said? Nancy Drew or not, she had to be more careful next time.

As she drove back to the store something began nagging at her. That rose tattoo…she'd seen it before. Hadn't she? But where?

CHAPTER 32

avannah called her father as soon as she got home from her harrowing visit to the Trent estate.

"Dad," she blurted out. "The place is beautiful and just as Marci described. I checked out the guest house to be sure Alan wasn't there. Then I was going to the main house, as we discussed, but I saw *Pampered*, the yacht, which has the same name as the corporation that the Miami apartment is registered to. I decided to detour and check it out. That was a mistake. I was almost caught snooping by a member of the crew and had to nosedive into the bushes to avoid detection. I have the scratches to prove it."

She gently rubbed her bruised shoulder and arm.

"Are you all right, honey?"

"Yes. I'm fine, but really bummed that I didn't get a chance to speak to Mrs. Trent. We need to think of a way to get Alan off the property long enough so that I can try."

"I'll devise some legitimate reason to get him to come into the shop. But we can't make Marci suspicious. In the meantime, take care of yourself and enjoy the rest of your day off. I'll see you in the morning. By the way, Marci never brought back the authorization. I guess I can use that as the excuse to get Alan to drop by the shop."

"Good idea." She began rubbing antibiotic cream on her bruised arm.

It was not like Dave to keep anything from his daughter. Normally he shared everything with her. But sensing Savannah would not be pleased, he didn't tell her about his upcoming date with Marci. If the evening didn't pan out, there would be no reason to tell her anything. But, if it was the beginning of something nice happening between him and Marci, then he'd tell Savannah when the time was right. He knew in the end, he could count on her support, but didn't want to jinx his date.

"One more thing." Savannah said cautiously. "I had a thought in the middle of the night. That's when I do my best detective work, you know. Do we have any proof that Alan is really who he says he is? Because if he's a full-fledged sociopath, as you and I and even Blake suspect, that could mean he's probably lying about everything else, including his name. Did you ever see his driver's license or any other personal identification when you took in his grandmother's jewelry for consignment sale?"

"I never asked for identification," Dave admitted, ashamed of his carelessness. "He was a friend of Marci's. I stupidly just didn't think."

"Don't worry about it, Dad. It'll be okay." She was trying to make him feel better, but they both knew that they had made a sloppy mistake. One or the other of them should have asked Alan to sign the form before they sent the jewelry out west. "How about his social security number. It's required by the IRS on the consignment forms? Do you have it?"

"I must admit, I didn't pay attention, but I'll check right away. Good thought, little Miss Nancy. You should definitely be a detective in your next life."

"I'll settle for just getting to the bottom of this one mystery," Savannah replied seriously. "See you in the morning. Don't worry. We'll figure this out."

She went into her kitchen and poured herself a glass of sweet tea. The rose tattoo was still bothering her.

CHAPTER 33

Marci and Dave were seated in at a corner table at the Coral Ridge Country Club overlooking the patio and the pristine golf course. They had helped themselves to full plates of shrimp cocktail, crab claws and oysters on the half shell. Marci was enjoying a Cosmo and Dave had his favorite drink in hand, a dirty vodka martini.

"I'm glad we're doing this," Dave smiled. "It's wonderful to have a gorgeous woman by my side. I haven't had time for much socializing lately. I've been working on some new ideas for the store."

"Well, I'm honored that you asked me out." Marci nibbled on a piece of shrimp and looked at the beautiful scenery. "Did you come here with Savannah's mom often?"

"No, we were too busy running the shop and being parents. I joined this club after my wife passed. It gave me a place to bring Savannah, where she could meet and play with other children. Being a single dad with a young daughter to raise was tough on both of us. She was only nine when her mother died, and I hadn't the first clue as to what to do with a young girl. I guess you could say we raised each other. She literally grew up at *Wrights*, building forts under the jewelry counters and after school doing her homework in my office while I took care of the customers. It didn't take long for her to become a favorite of our regulars."

He had a faraway expression as if recalling fond memories. "I bet she's never told you, but because of our membership here, she became quite an awesome swimmer. She excelled at the breaststroke and cap- tained the club's swim team. She could have gone to college on a swim- ming scholarship, had she wanted to."

"Wow," Marci answered. "Savannah said she used to swim compet- itively but I had no idea she was that good. She always talks so lovingly about you and her childhood. I congratulate you, Dave. You did a won- derful job raising her. Savannah is the best friend a girl could have and she's a direct product of your care and love."

"Whoa, don't give me all the credit. Her mother had a great deal to do with how she turned out. She laid the foundation. I just built upon it."

"Yes, I'm sure," Marci blushed. "I didn't mean to discount her. I just wanted you to know what an amazing job you did."

Dave looked embarrassed by her praise. "How about another drink? We can stay for dinner if you'd like. They serve a great veal parmesan and Caesar salad."

Marci looked at her watch. It was already 7:30. When she had called Alan with her working late excuse, she told him that she'd be at his house by 8. He had not been happy when she said she had to stay late. He accused her of loving her job more than him. It was a ridiculous state- ment for him to have made. She hung up the phone, not wanting to hear his nasty remarks or be pulled into an argument. Sometimes she couldn't believe how possessive and childish he was.

"Let me call Alan and tell him I'm still tied up and won't be coming over tonight." She hated to lie but she wanted her evening with Dave to continue. She stood up to make the call. "And I'd love to stay and have dinner with you. There's so much more I want to hear about you and Savannah."

She found the ladies' room and dialed Alan, knowing he would be upset. He'd become so obsessed with her lately, but she had not expected his reaction now to be so unpleasant. He was absolutely livid and warned her that she'd better not make a habit of working late or she'd have to find herself another job. He would not put up with it. He growled that he had no intention of sitting home alone at night waiting for her. Then he coldly announced that he'd be expecting her immediately after work the next day and she'd better not be late. His tone had been frigid and a little threatening. And he didn't bother to say good night.

Marci returned to the table, shaken by Alan's rudeness, but determined to enjoy the rest of her evening with Dave. She'd worry about her temperamental boyfriend tomorrow.

Dave procured a table for them on the patio and they enjoyed a wonderful meal with easy conversation. The sun set over the golf course, lighting up the sky in shades of pink and red. They kept talking and talking, without work interruptions getting in the way. With the leisure of a meal, and a nice bottle of wine, they talked for hours, finding that they had a lot in common...the same taste in books and a love of the outdoors. They were enjoying themselves so much that neither noticed they were the last patrons left on the patio or in the dining room. The country club waiters stood patiently off to one side watching them.

Dave finally looked up and got the message. "We should leave. I think the staff is waiting to clean up and go home."

"Oh, I hadn't realized," she laughed apologetically, looking around at the empty tables. "I believe you're right. But the evening's been so nice. Would up like to follow me home and come in for a night cap? There's still so much I want to know about you."

"You're on," Dave winked and they went to their respective cars and drove to her apartment.

Enjoying a glass of brandy, they sat on her sofa and talked for another hour. Dave was fascinated by Marci's stories of growing up around a journalist in Washington and she loved hearing about Savannah's youth – including Dave's honest opinion about his daughter's ill-advised marriage.

He was open and candid in confessing his own grief about the death of his wife, and how he had suffered from loneliness for so many years. Back then his time was so completely committed to caring for Savannah and keeping the business thriving that there was no time to think about dating, even had he wanted to. Finally, with Savannah becoming a healthy teenager preferring the company of her friends to his, he began to move forward again socially. Over the years he'd dated quite a lot of interesting women but hadn't found anyone special enough to marry. The more he talked, the more fascinated and intrigued Marci became. Dave was such a compassionate man, obviously a wonderful husband and a loving father. She marveled that he would have any interest in her. He made her feel safe.

After Stan's hurtful rejection and divorce, Marci's self-esteem had been at a low point. Alan's extravagant attention had helped raise it, but she was slowly realizing that what he described as love was really only his need to control her. Dave, on the other hand, was genuinely interested in her and saw her as a whole person, not an appendage. She could be her own person around him. She didn't have to fake anything.

Looking at her watch and yawning, Marci walked him to the door and waved goodbye as he drove off. It was after 2:00 a.m. She was about to close her door when she thought she saw a red Porsche idling further down the street. She started to step out to have a closer look but when she did, the car sped away. Maybe her imagination was playing tricks? Alan could not possibly be so insecure that he was spying on her, could he?

CHAPTER 34

Savannah and Marci were enjoying a rare private moment over a cup of coffee before the day's customers began to arrive. Marci had not said anything about her dinner with Dave or her suspicion that Alan may have been stalking her last night.

"I know we haven't seen much of each other outside of this shop lately," Marci admitted sadly. "It's totally my fault and I'm sorry. I've been so involved with Alan that I've neglected our friendship. That's going to change. I'm going to tell him tonight that I need a break, some time away from him. I need girl time with you (*and more time with your father*, she thought). We haven't had dinner or facials together in ages."

"And I've missed that. Although, won't Alan put up a fight? He wants to be with you every second. Don't you find that suffocating?" Savannah was edging on delicate territory, but Marci had opened the door to this conversation. She was not going to miss the opportunity to tell Marci what she honestly thought.

"I honestly don't care what he thinks. I'm thirty-six years old, for God's sake. I don't need a keeper. Sometimes, I don't know how I feel about him. When we're together, in the heat of passion, I feel like I'm madly in love with him. At other times, I'm not so sure. My feelings for Alan might be simply good old-fashioned rebound lust and the need for some male attention."

"Lust's a good thing," Savannah joked, trying to lighten the moment. "I love lust."

"Whatever this is, I know that I have to have a life apart from him. We can't be tied to each other's hips all the time. It's not healthy. And frankly, lately he's become so obsessed with me that it's a little frightening. He's gotten much too serious too soon. I think I'm ready to start seeing other people." She didn't have the nerve to tell Savannah about Alan's marriage proposal. She wanted her friend back and knew that would raise her hackles.

"Amen." Savannah nodded. "I'm so glad you've got the spunk to take a little break from him. Here's to us doing more things together again." She toasted her friend with her coffee. "How about I make us mani-pedi appointments for tomorrow and then we'll have dinner at Houston's afterwards. Just like the good old days."

"Great," Marci smiled. "I can't wait. I'll tell Alan tonight."

"What are you girls doing? Goofing off on my dime?" Dave joked when he walked into the office. "I'm not paying you two to over-caffein- ate yourselves and spend the morning chit chatting."

Marci jumped up and looked embarrassed, but Savannah only grinned. "Dad stop joking. You're scaring Marci."

"No, you're not scaring me," Marci laughed. She thought Dave looked especially handsome in his colorful shirt and khaki slacks. When Savannah looked away, he winked at Marci and she smiled back. They had had a wonderful evening together. There was something special happening between them and neither was willing to share the newness of it with anyone else yet. Marci had even promised Dave that she would continue to see him, no matter what Alan thought. They had already planned to have drinks again together next week at the club and take in a movie later in the week.

"Sorry," he apologized. "I didn't mean to barge in but I need to find some papers our accountant needs for last quarter's books and I'm in his doghouse." He handed Savannah a folded piece of paper. "Will you take care of this for me please?"

"And Marci," he continued. "I'd like you to contact your friend, Alan Trent and ask him to come into the shop as soon as possible to complete some paperwork. I know you gave him an authorization form before, but he never returned it. I need his social security number and his grandmother's signature on the consignment forms. Can you call him now, please?" He hated to deceive Marci but he didn't dare share his suspicions without some solid proof.

"Sure, Dave. I'll call him right now." Marci went to her purse and pulled out her cell. "I'll make sure he comes in today."

She was nervous about calling Alan since their heated argument the previous evening and her suspicions that he'd been outside her apartment spying on her. Normally he called her to say good morning every day before she left for work. She had not heard from him. He must still be angry. Unbelievable!

"She's calling him now?" Savannah gave her father a look after Marci left the room. "When did that start? Is there anything I should know?"

He ignored her remark. Savannah knew enough not push him and let the subject drop. "And I'll start pulling those papers together." She had noticed an exchange of knowing looks between Marci and her father. *What's going on?* She left them to their secrets and went to her desk.

Five minutes later Marci came back into the office. Dave could see that she was not happy. "I reached Alan. He says he'll be here around noon but I warn you, he's not in a good mood." He had been barely civil to her on the phone and abruptly hung up on her after agreeing to come in and sign the papers. He was acting like a spoiled little boy having a temper tantrum.

"Thanks," Dave said. "That'll be a big help." He felt badly for Marci. He didn't want to subject her to Alan's wrath, but he needed her help to get Alan to come into the shop. He must have been abusive again to Marci on the phone, just like last night. Dave promised himself to make it up to her. She didn't deserve to be treated so unkindly.

"And Dad," Savannah interrupted his thoughts. She picked up on what Marci had said about noon. "I can walk these papers over to the accountant. If you can cover for me, I'll go today during lunchtime. I have a few errands to run anyway."

"Sure, honey. I'd like to be here when Alan comes in anyway. I want to apologize to him for the inconvenience." He almost gagged on the words and made a show of collecting some random receipts from a file before he left the shop with a wave. "I'll be back before noon."

The shop's doorbell rang. Marci grinned when she saw the familiar florist delivery man. But today he was empty handed. He looked at her apologetically and explained that the standing order had been cancelled. He felt he should let Marci know. She was stunned. It wasn't the lack of receiving a rose that bothered her, but that Alan was so petty about her missing one night with him that he retaliated in such a childish way.

She realized things had gotten too complicated between them and it was time to break the relationship off. She was not going to let him dictate when and where she could go, or with whom.

Savannah slowly opened the folded piece of paper her dad had given her earlier. She read it quickly, grinning before tearing it into tiny pieces and tossing them into the trash.

"Nancy Drew, I've done my part…now it's up to you. The coast will be clear."

CHAPTER 35

t was noon. Dave sat expectantly in the office. Savannah winked at her dad and hurried out of the shop carrying the bogus papers she was supposedly taking to the accountant. Marci was occupied helping a customer select an engagement ring and nervously waiting for Alan. She dreaded facing him and hoped he wouldn't make a scene in front of Dave. He had been in a dark mood on the phone and that meant his behavior could be unpredictable. Lately he had begun to yell at her and to make some pretty cutting remarks about her failed first marriage. There were nice men in the world like Dave. She didn't have to put up with this abuse.

At twelve fifteen, Savannah parked her car around the block from the Trent's house as she'd done previously. She put on her auburn wig again and grabbed the clipboard she'd tossed on the back seat to use as a prop.

Cautiously, she gazed up and down the block. Seeing no one in sight, she started towards the Trent's estate on foot. As she neared the large Mediterranean-style house, she checked the driveway and the grounds beyond.

Alan's car was not in sight and there was no sign of anyone about. She took a deep breath and marched with determination to the front door. There was a freshly polished brass lion's head knocker mounted on one of massive double doors, and a sign to the side of it reading "No Solicitors."

Savannah was not intimidated. She used the knocker forcefully. After a minute, when no one answered, she knocked again even more loudly. There was still no reply. Not knowing what else to do, she shouted, "Mrs. Trent? Mrs. Trent are you home?"

She could hear someone moving about inside. Savannah had not counted on being ignored. Frustrated, she pounded on the door again and again.

"Mrs. Trent, I'm with the United States Bureau of Census and by law you must answer my questions. Please let me in. I can hear you inside. My survey is short, just a few questions, and I'll only take a couple of minutes of your time." She held her breath and hoped she had sounded official enough to warrant admission.

The bolt on the front door shifted slightly and a tall, beautiful woman in a white nurse's uniform partially opened the door. She glanced at Savannah cautiously. "My lady sick," the woman said in what appeared to be a Mexican accent. "She no answer questions." She started to close the door. Instinctively, Savannah stuck her foot on the threshold to prevent it.

"Then I'll speak to you," Savannah boldly pushed the door wide open and stepped inside the foyer. The nurse's eyes darted around the room in fear, but there was no one there to help her.

"Sorry. I don't mean to be rude." Savannah realized she'd been too forceful and apologized. "But this is my job and I have many more homes to visit today. I have to fill out this form on Mrs. Trent or the police will come here and do it for me. It's your choice. I'd advise you to cooperate." She was telling a bold-faced lie and prayed that her remarks would not be tested. There was no way the police would strongarm a citizen into cooperating with a census worker.

Savannah held up the clipboard and began to write. She had no idea where she got the nerve to be so bold. It was so unlike her. The nurse looked frightened but pointed to an upholstered bench positioned along one wall. "*Sientese usted.* Sit."

Savannah took a seat. This was not going as she had hoped. "My name is Patty Gross," she said, "and I'm with the Census bureau, and you are?"

"Consuela," the nurse responded stiffly. "Consuela Lopez. What you want?"

"I'm here because every ten years we conduct a national census to count the number of residents in the United States by each state and zip code. These numbers are then used to determine the number of elected representatives the states will get and how much money will go for things like transportation, education and health care." She rambled on recalling what the Census brochure had explained.

The nurse seemed to relax a bit but was still clearly nervous. Savannah had no idea whether Consuela had understood a word of what she'd said. Probably not.

"I assure you that our purpose is not to arrest or deport undocumented residents, or to get anyone in trouble. We simply need to know the number of people living at a specific address on a certain day, April first of this year, in particular. Do you understand? There's nothing for you to worry about."

The nurse nodded reluctantly. Undaunted, Savannah continued

talking and tried to reassure Consuela that there was no personal danger to her by answering the questions. "Let's begin." She wished she'd remembered more of her high school Spanish. She'd have to wing it.

Savannah continued making bogus notes and kept her eyes on the nurse. "As of the first of April, how many adults and how many children lived in this main house and how many lived in the adjacent guest house?"

The nurse appeared confused. Either she didn't understand the question or she was afraid to answer.

"*Quantas personas?* How many people? I'm not interested in any friends that may visit from time to time or in the staff that works here daily," Savannah explained patiently. "Only the number of people who actually sleep here every night." She folded her hands together below her jawline, making the sleep sign.

The nurse remained silent, but Savannah could see the nurse was shaking. What was she hiding?

"In this big house, how many people sleep here every night?" Savannah persisted, talking louder as if that would make her better understood. She held up her fingers to indicate the numbers one, two or three.

Finally, the nurse, whose face had remained impassive, responded by holding up three fingers. Savannah fidgeted and looked nervously at her watch. This census gambit was taking too long. Alan might return home at any minute and catch her in this ruse. She had to speed this up.

"Consuela, let me be clear. Are you saying that only three people sleep here normally?"

The nurse nodded, yes and clutched her hands together.

"And I suppose that would be you, Mrs. Trent and the butler?"

The nurse nodded in the affirmative. "*Si, si.*"

Savannah asked a few more questions that she remembered were usually on the census form to make herself seem more authentic… about the race of the occupants and their religions. The nurse continued to look frightened and never spoke again. She indicated her answers with a nod for yes or no.

"Okay, then. I believe we're done with the main house. Let's continue with the occupants of the guest house. I will ask you the same questions. We're almost done." She smiled weakly at the nurse. This was painful. Where was Mrs. Trent? Was she upstairs in bed? The idea had been to talk to her and ask specific questions about the pumpkin brooch and about Alan.

"How many people live in the guest house?" Savannah tried again.

Consuela held up her thumb and index finger, making the zero sign.

"No one? Zero?" Savannah was surprised. "Are you sure? I was told Mrs. Trent's grandson lives there."

The nurse became agitated and stood up, as if to dismiss the census taker. When Savannah did not move, Consuela blurted out in broken English. "I need get back to lady. She need medicine."

"I understand." Savannah wanted to scream in frustration, but she forced an awkward smile. "You've been very helpful, Consuela. However, I have to ask again about the guest house. I think the man who lives there is Mrs. Trent's grandson, Alan."

"I need get back to my lady," the nurse repeated again, her agitation mounting. To get rid of the census lady and without thinking, she screamed, "*La dama no tiene hijo.*"

Consuela glared savagely at Savannah and marched angrily to the front door. She had had enough questions and wanted the irritating woman to leave. Flinging it open, she shouted, "No more questions. Go away. No police. *Sin policia!*"

CHAPTER 36

Alan jabbed at the doorbell impatiently and burst into *Wrights* a few minutes past noon. He marched right up to Marci, who had been helping a customer, spun her around and possessively took her in his arms, kissing her fiercely on her lips. He bit down mercilessly on her lip and drew blood. "Don't think you can get away with cheating on me?" he hissed before releasing her. "I'm nobody's fool."

Marci was humiliated and deeply embarrassed. She pushed him further away. "Alan," she tried to keep her voice steady, but she was shaking with fury and her lip was bleeding. "I'm helping this gentleman pick out an engagement ring. Mr. Wright's expecting you in his office. Please go back there and don't keep him waiting."

She sent him a stony stare and turned back apologetically to her customer. How dare he act that way. He didn't own her. She would not allow herself to make a scene in the shop. She was irate at his reaction last night and now by this latest stunt, which was unforgiveable and the last straw. She was scared by his attitude and appalled by the vicious bite. She could only imagine his reaction when she told him she was going to stop seeing him. However, she didn't want to live in fear of Alan for another day.

"Well, hello Mr. Trent," Dave Wright said pleasantly when Alan appeared at his door. "Thank you for coming in. This will only take a minute." Alan's attention was elsewhere. He kept looking back at Marci, but her back was turned to him. He was upset about losing his temper and knew he had to behave better in order to keep her in line. Otherwise, she'd ruin all his plans. He could not allow her to slip away until he was through with her. He had to move forward quickly with his plan before she bolted for good.

Dave stole a look at his watch and worried about Savannah. Had she been able to talk to Mrs. Trent? Did she need more time? Should he keep Alan away from the house a little longer? He wished he knew the answers but thought it was better to err on the side of caution. "I'm sorry about this inconvenience," he said, trying to get Alan's attention. "Hopefully my inadvertent oversight will have a fringe benefit for you."

"What do you mean?" Alan fumed. He realized that overnight, Dave Wright had become his competition for Marci's affections and he wouldn't allow it. It was time to take action and wrap up this ridiculous situation.

"I'll give you a little extra time to spend with your girlfriend. Why don't you take her to a nice lunch? I don't mind at all. As a matter of fact, I insist. It's the least I can do for inconveniencing you...and lunch is on me."

Dave reached in his wallet and handed Alan a crisp hundred-dollar bill. "But don't keep her away too long. I'm by myself here today. I need her on the sales floor. I feel terrible about asking you to come all the way back here today, but my accountant insists this paperwork is absolutely necessary."

What the hell? Alan thought. *The dumb bastard has no idea that I know he was with Marci …my Marci, last night. She's mine until I say she isn't.* He was seething with anger at Mr. Wright and at Marci too. They were a bunch of lying losers and they weren't fooling him even a little bit.

Dave studied Alan's face. He could see that the man was very angry beneath his calm demeanor. His face had reddened and his fists were clenched. His eyes kept darting back to Marci and the customer in the other room. Surely, Dave thought, being asked to come back to sign a simple document had not generated such a reaction. It had to be something else. Could he possibly know about his date with Marci last night? Did he suspect anything?

"My accountant pointed out that I neglected to finish the paperwork the IRS requires regarding the jewelry pieces we took on consignment," Dave said seriously. "I just need your social security number and your signature." He thrust a sheet of paper at Alan and pointed to the signature line and where to put his social security number.

Alan could not concentrate on anything. His attention was directed solely on Marci. He kept looking back, hoping to catch her eye. Barely glancing at the paperwork, he automatically signed his name and added his social security number where Dave had indicated. He was completely distracted and trying to decide what to do, how to win Marci back for at least another day or two until he had everything worked out. He hated that he needed her cooperation, but he did. Everything was set in motion. He had overplayed his cards by hanging up on her last night and stopping the silly roses from being delivered. He had to make things right while there was still time.

As soon as the customer left the shop, Alan shook hands with Dave. "Sir, I'll take you up on your offer to take Marci to lunch. Thank you. We'll leave right now and I'll have her back soon." He couldn't wait to get out of that office and back to Marci.

He marched back into the showroom and over to Marci. "I'm sorry about our argument last night," he said in his sweetest voice. "I don't know what came over me, but I want to make it right between us. I'm going to take you to lunch. It was your boss's idea, so let's go, please. We need to repair this."

Marci didn't want to go anywhere with him. She had witnessed an unpleasant and frightening side of Alan that she never wanted to see gain. Savannah had been right. He was not the right man for her. She turned to Dave, a little baffled and silently begging him to veto the lunch, but he merely smiled at them both and mouthed the words, "Go, have fun." Why was he pushing her to leave with Alan? She knew that like his daughter, he didn't like or trust him. What was he doing?

Still uncomfortable but not knowing what else to do, Marci picked up her pocketbook. Alan possessively grabbed her wrist as though he was afraid she might try to run away. "I'm sorry about last night," he said again. "I was disappointed that you were ditching me for the evening. I'd planned a special surprise. Grandmother was in the guest house waiting to meet you, and have dinner with us. I didn't tell you earlier, because I was afraid that she'd back out again. Consuela brought her over a few minutes before you called to say you weren't coming." His voice was tight and controlled. "I was embarrassed that you'd stood me up in front of her. I'm sorry. Marci, will you forgive me?"

She relaxed a bit. "Alan please let go of my wrist. You're hurting me." She tried to read his eyes but they remained unexpressive. To avoid another argument, she gave him a stiff smile. "Yes, I accept your apology. I'm sorry that I disappointed you, and that I missed the chance to meet your grandmother. But we need to have a serious talk. I don't like the way you're behaving lately and furthermore, don't you dare ever bite or speak to me that way again."

"I promise." He crossed his heart and tried to sound contrite. "Let's go to lunch, Pretty Lady."

CHAPTER 37

Savannah rushed into the shop breathless. She looked around at the empty showroom. "Where's everybody?" she called out, frantic to talk to her dad. The front room was never supposed to be left unmanned during the store's operating hours...that was one of her father's hard and fast rules. Where was he?

"I'm right here," Dave stood up from behind one of the diamond cases. "Marci sold an engagement ring earlier today and I was rearranging the shelf. I urged her to go out to lunch with Alan after he signed the bogus paperwork because I wasn't sure how long you'd be tied up with Mrs. Trent. I was trying to buy you more time. So, it's just the two of us here now. How did it go? Did she confirm that Alan has the authority to sell her jewelry?" He looked at his daughter inquisitively. "Tell me everything Mrs. Trent said, word by word."

"Oh Dad, you won't believe it." Savannah's shoulders sagged. "I never got to speak with her. Her nurse claimed Mrs. Trent was too ill to answer questions and she seemed scared of something. I think she's probably in the country illegally and was afraid of getting caught. I tried to reassure her that no harm would come to her if she answered my questions. But there's a lot more."

Savannah sat down on one of the stools and took a deep breath. "How long do you think we have before Marci comes back?"

"I don't know." He looked at his watch. "They left about an hour ago, so it might be any minute. Why? What did you find out about Alan?"

"It's unbelievable. I still can't believe it."

"Honey." He put his arm around her and gave her a fatherly squeeze. "I can see you're upset. I'll make us some fresh coffee and you can tell me everything."

Thankfully there were no customers in the shop. Dave and his daughter sat on stools in the showroom sipping their drinks while Savannah recounted her meeting with Consuela.

"Dad, I asked the nurse how many people lived in the main house. After several attempts to get her to answer, she finally held up three fingers. Her English is very poor. And my Spanish is pretty weak, but I was able to confirm that three adults live in the main house, Mrs. Trent, her nurse and the butler. I think Marci said his name was Pedro."

"I'm surprised there aren't more live-in staff for a property of that size," Dave observed. "Maybe she doesn't like to have a lot of people underfoot."

"I don't know but that's not the point. I asked her about the guest house. How many people lived there? She seemed confused but finally held up her fingers to make the round, zero sign. Naturally I was surprised and asked her again. She kept making the zero sign so I told her that I thought Mrs. Trent's grandson lived there."

"That was dangerous Savannah. A legitimate Census taker would not know that."

"You're right. That was a mistake, and thankfully, she didn't catch it. She did, however, tell me something interesting just before she threw me out of the house. You'll never guess."

"For heaven's sake, Savannah. You're really dragging this out."

Savannah looked at him with a smug expression. "Mrs. Trent does *not have* a grandson. *La dama no tiene hijo!*"

"What? Are you sure?"

"Of course, I'm sure. Even though she said it in Spanish, I understood her. But, if Alan is not Mrs. Trent's grandson, then who the hell is he? And how can he get away with living in her guest house?"

CHAPTER 38

Marci studied Alan's face but couldn't read his expression. She used to think he was so handsome, but no longer. He seemed belligerent and angry. *Was he truly sorry for his behavior?* She didn't think so. When they arrived at the intersection that would have taken them to their lunch destination at the Capital Grille, he turned left instead of right.

"I think you made a wrong turn. The Capital Grille is the other way," she said softly, trying not to infuriate him further.

"But the airport's this way." Alan kept his eyes steadily on the road and refused to meet her questioning gaze.

"What do you mean... the airport?"

"I mean we're going to the Capital Grille, but not the one in Ft. Lauderdale. I'm taking you on a surprise trip to Chicago. There's a Capital Grille there. Grandmother chartered a plane for us, so we'll have lunch on board and be in town for dinner. You always complain that I don't take you anywhere, so now we're going."

Marci was shocked. She had never complained about not going any-where and she had been happy to stay at home with Alan. And how on earth would either he or Mrs. Trent know that Dave would give her time off for lunch with him today? "I can't just up and leave for Chicago," she protested. "What about my job? I can't desert Mr. Wright and Savannah. They expect me back this afternoon. And besides, I don't have any clothes. I suppose you mean well, but a trip right now is impossible."

"Why are you always so negative? Nothing is impossible," he said irritably. "I cleared this with Mr. Wright when I was in his office, and he not only approved of our little trip but gave me money towards it. He pulled out a hundred-dollar bill from his pocket and waved it in front of her. "You saw him. He said, "Go, have fun."

"Yes, but," she didn't know what to say. After last night, she was sure that Dave was interested in her and yet he just handed her off to Alan like a football. "Even if I say yes, how will I manage without bringing the proper clothes or toiletries? I simply can't do this, Alan. I'm not that spontaneous. Let's have lunch some place nearby and talk. Truthfully, we have serious matters between us. I'm not comfortable going anywhere with you now until they're settled."

"Marci, for God's sake, I said I was sorry about last night, and I am. You can't go on punishing me forever." His voice was steely cold and she noticed his palms on the leather steering wheel were beginning to sweat. "You're making a big deal about a lover's spat and frankly it's not at all becoming."

"I'm not punishing you," she sighed with frustration. "This is ridicu-lous. Please turn the car around. If you don't want to go to lunch locally, then please take me back to the shop. We had an argument, like all couples do. But that's no reason to act so irrationally and behave like a brat." She wanted to confront him about driving by her house last night, but given his foul mood, she didn't dare. She was afraid he was about to explode.

"Marci. You're being brainwashed. The Wrights don't like me, and don't think I can't tell. They've trying to turn you against me."

"That's simply not true. They've been nothing but kind to me and certainly aren't brainwashing me. They do believe that you and I are getting too serious too fast, that's true, but they've never said anything unkind about you. You're sounding paranoid, Alan. If anything's turning me against you, it's your possessiveness and lately your lousy temper. You're not the same kind, funny person I started dating almost a year ago. You're completely different now, dark and scary. And not only don't I love you, I don't even like you anymore."

She gazed at him intently and realized she had gone too far. Something in his facial demeanor and body language alarmed her. Suddenly all she wanted to do was get out of his car and away from him. *How had everything gone so wrong?*

"We need to take a break from each other," she spoke up bravely. "To give ourselves some time and space to figure out what this relationship is all about. I told you in the beginning that I was not interested in getting serious with any man. I've been burned badly and don't want that to happen ever again. I stupidly let my guard down and allowed myself to fall for you, and now look at the mess we're in. Please Alan, take me back to the shop or let me out here and I'll call an Uber."

CHAPTER 39

What do you mean Mrs. Trent doesn't have a grandson?" Dave was astonished by Savannah's revelation. "We've suspected something was off about Alan, but never that he wasn't who he said he was. Are you absolutely positive? Can you really trust what that nurse said? She may have misunderstood you. We need to verify that information. If he's not her grandson, then who is he and what's he doing living on Mrs. Trent's property and selling her jewelry?"

"I have no idea, but I intend to find out." Savannah was resolute. "Dad, shouldn't Marci be back by now? We have to tell her that she's fallen for a con man."

"Oh, God, what have I done? Marci's alone with him now because I urged her to go with him." He was so angry at himself and fought the urge to strike out at the nearest thing with his fist.

"I wanted you to have enough time to do your business at the estate, so I suggested Alan take her to lunch. I even gave him money to do it. How could I have been so dumb?" Dave's face turned pale. If anything happened to Marci, he had only himself to blame.

"Dad this is not your fault, but we have to think logically about what to do. Did Alan, or whoever he is, give you his social security number?"

"Yes. He wrote it on the form."

"Okay. That's a start." Savannah began to pace nervously around the room, trying to make sense of this latest development. "We can give the number to Sheldon's private detective. I'm sure he can track down the real name associated with that number. He seems to be able to find out just about everything, for a price."

"Yes, I'm sure he can." Dave was worried about Marci who should have been back from lunch by now. "Let me go get it. Why don't you call Marci on her cell and say we need her back here right away, but don't say anything about Alan."

He walked quickly into his office and came out with the paper.

"He signed as Alan A. Trent and listed his social security number as 215-555-5613."

"Okay. Give it to Sheldon right now." Savannah was insistent. "We have to find out who Alan really is and protect Marci. For all we know, she could be in real physical danger. He could be a serial killer or a true sociopath. There's no telling what he's up to."

Dave immediately called his attorney. After briefly explaining the situation to him, he implored him to tell the PI that their request was urgent. "We are very concerned about what's going on and are afraid Marci might be in real danger."

Sheldon was worried too, much more than he wanted his friend to know. If Alan was an imposter, then whose jewelry did *Wrights* take on consignment? And were the pieces his to sell or were they stolen? If the latter proved to be true, the police would have to be called and an investigation would follow. The reputation of *Wrights* and its owner, so stellar in the community until now, was definitely at risk. There were many loose ends to tie up. Confirming Alan's true identity was the first step.

"I'll get you answers as soon as possible," Sheldon assured his friend. "In the meantime, if you see Alan again, continue to act as if everything is normal. We don't want to scare him off. It might cause him to run or do something bad in retaliation."

Dave put down his phone, but fear was still visible on his face. "Honey, did you reach Marci?" He would give anything to see her smiling face walk into the store. He felt very protective of her and after last night he realized he wanted to see much more of her, and not just as friends.

"I called but her phone went right to Voicemail. I left a message."

"Keep trying," her father urged. "Please keep trying."

CHAPTER 40

Marci reached for the door handle. "I mean it Alan. Stop this car right now and let me out. You're frightening me."

"What's the matter with you? I don't understand you at all. I plan a beautiful weekend for us and you act like I've committed a crime. I don't like the change that's come over *you* recently. You used to be so sweet-natured and easygoing. Now you're always angry. It's you who's changed, not me."

"I am not always angry," she answered defensively, still fiddling with the door handle. "It's your behavior that's erratic, not mine. I feel like I have to walk on eggshells around you. You are in a bad mood most of the time and you want to control my every move. I'm an adult, for God's sake. I don't need to justify having to work late to you or grovel for permission to go to dinner with a friend. You're not my husband, Alan, and you never will be." Hot, angry tears began to stream from her eyes. She was furious at herself for allowing him to see how upset she was.

Alan was beginning to panic. His carefully thought-out plan was falling apart. Marci was not buying his apology. He had to do take control immediately and say whatever was necessary to win her over again.

"Marci, you're right," he tried to make his voice sound sincere. "I see that now. I didn't realize that I was being so overbearing. My only excuse is that I've been so lonely. Between taking care of Grandmother and all her needs, I had no personal life until I met you. Meeting you changed everything. Spending time with you has been a gift from God. Before you, I'd forgotten how much fun being in love could be. When you blew me off last night, I was afraid you were lying to me and had found another boyfriend. I panicked. Please forgive me."

"I didn't blow you off," she insisted. "I had to lie to you because I knew you'd go ballistic if I said my boss wanted to talk to me. It was one night away from you, Alan. For God's sake. One night!!!!"

"I know. I know. But I knew you were lying, Marci. You went out with Dave Wright and you weren't working late, as you pretended. I'm ashamed to admit it, but I followed you, so don't bother to deny it. Knowing how much I love you, how did you think I'd react?" He looked deeply into her eyes and appeared to be begging her to understand. "I know I was wrong. And, I swear I'll never again make you feel that you have to lie to me. Please give me another chance," he pleaded. "I don't want to lose <u>you</u>, to lose <u>us</u>."

He reached over and gently removed her hand from the door handle. Searching her face, hoping for a sign that she'd forgiven him, he continued to talk. "I've got an idea. Since you don't want to go away this weekend, let's spend it at my house, lying in the sun by the pool and making love all night. I really want to be alone with you Marci. It's the perfect time because no one will miss you. I confess that I told Mr. Wright I was taking you to Chicago as a surprise for a few days, and he'll surely tell Savannah that. For a while we'll be free as birds and won't be interrupted by anything or anybody. I won't even answer my phone. Grandmother's nurse can handle anything that comes up. It'll be a special time for just the two of us. We'll start over again. I'm going to arrange a special surprise for you too. Let's turn off our phones right now and just be together. What do you say?"

Marci wasn't sure what she should do. What Alan said made sense. Maybe he was right. She had lied to him, after all. Maybe feeling guilty about that, she'd overreacted. What they needed was time alone to figure everything out and decide where, if anywhere, they were heading. She knew now she was partly at fault. She'd placed too much importance on her date with Dave. And then, he'd practically forced her into Alan's arms earlier at the shop. She was confused. She truly didn't know whether she could forgive Alan, or if she could ever love him again. Maybe if she spent the weekend with him she would figure it out.

"All right," she said uneasily. She turned off her phone and handed it to him.

He smiled and muted his own.

CHAPTER 41

D ave was becoming more and more anxious about Marci. It had been four hours since she'd left the shop with Alan. Savannah had texted and called her cell phone repeatedly with no response. Marci was not answering.

"This is not like her." Savannah was worried. "She's so dependable. If she wasn't coming back to work, she would definitely have called. What should we do, Dad?"

"I don't know, but I agree with you. Marci's too reliable to simply take the afternoon off like this. Did you check the office answering machine, in case she left us a message that we missed?"

"Yes, and there's nothing from her. Do you know where Alan was taking her for lunch?"

"No, I didn't ask." Dave said. "I assumed it was some place on Las Olas. I just wanted to keep him occupied so that you could talk to Mrs. Trent and then get off the property undetected. Do you think Marci might have become ill and gone home?"

"I doubt it. Her car is still behind the shop in the parking lot. I've already checked. I suppose she could have asked Alan to drive her home if she suddenly felt ill and was unable to drive herself, but surely she would have called us."

Dave paced back and forth in the office trying to make sense of Marci's disappearance but he could think of nothing that would have prevented her from calling...unless she'd been in an automobile accident. Suddenly panicked at the idea that she'd been hurt, he shouted at Savannah. "Hang the 'shop closed' sign on the front door. We need to make some calls.

"I think we should contact all the hospitals in the area and see if she's been admitted. And I'll call the police department to see if Alan's Porsche was involved in any kind of a traffic accident this afternoon." Before Savannah could reply, he dialed 911 to ask about recent accidents.

Savannah took a seat at her desk and started calling the major local hospitals, Broward General, Holy Cross and Imperial point. None reported admitting anyone matching Marci's description. She was relieved that her friend had not been hospitalized, but it made Marci's disappearance even more troubling.

Dave hung up and told Savannah that the police confirmed there had been no accidents that afternoon in the entire Ft. Lauderdale metropolitan area involving a red Porsche. He was becoming more and more distressed and not knowing what else to do, asked if he could file a missing person report. The police informed him that he would have to wait 24 hours before he could legally report Marci missing. Dave was frustrated and growing more and more uneasy.

"I think I should walk down Las Olas and go into each restaurant to see if they're inside or if they had been there earlier today. Do you have a picture of Marci on your phone that you can text me? That will help identify her."

"Sure." Savannah immediately sent him two pictures of Marci taken in Las Vegas.

"Do you think Alan could have taken her to Miami or maybe to Boca?" Savannah asked, grasping at straws. "It seems pretty far to go for lunch, but then Alan's not a predictable person."

"I'm sure Marci would have told him that it was too far and reminded him that she had to be back at work in a reasonable amount of time. You could check with the Miami and Boca police, if you'd like, about accidents, but I think it's a waste of time."

"I don't know what else to do, Dad, so I'll make the calls. We have to keep trying to find her."

Dave walked to the front of the store and looked up and down the street, as if he expected to see her walking back apologetically after a lunch where she had lingered too long. *Where could she be?* He walked out of the store and began to canvass the dozen or so restaurants that lined the popular street. Savannah continued her phone calls to the other police departments but with the same results. No red Porsche had been in an accident and no one matching Marci's description had been admitted to any hospitals.

Dave marched back into the office and grabbed his car keys. "Honey, no one has seen them and I can't sit around here any longer. I'm going to Marci's townhouse. Maybe she's passed out or is too sick to call us. Close up here and go home. I'll call you later." He darted out the door before she could respond.

"But Dad," she ran after him. "Wait. You don't have her address. Let me get it for you."

"I know where she lives. I was there last night." He shouted back and kept moving.

"What do you mean, you were there?" But he was already in his car and speeding away.

She began turning off the lights and locking up. *Why would he have been at Marci's last night? And why had neither of them mentioned it to her this morning? What's going on?*

CHAPTER 41

Alan took Marci's phone and placed it in his car's glove compartment. He didn't want her to be able to use it until the weekend was over. She was now staring out the window, lost in her thoughts and not paying attention so he dropped his own phone in his pants pocket.

"Now no one will interrupt our weekend." He was ecstatic that he would be having Marci all to himself. No work, no Savannah or Dave Wright interfering. Just enough time to implement his plan. He'd been praying for an opportunity like this for a long time and ironically his apparent rival, Dave, had given it to him.

"You're about to make me a very happy man," he smiled. "I've been planning this surprise for several weeks."

She turned to him and smiled. "Now you're making me really curious. I can't imagine what it could be."

They drove to his grandmother's home and he guided his car into one of the main house's enclosed garage spaces. There were two other cars parked there. Alan explained that one belonged to Pedro the butler, and the other to Consuela, his grandmother's nurse.

"Since we won't be going anywhere this weekend, I might as well be smart and protect the new wax job on my car. I had it washed and detailed yesterday," he explained casually.

"It does look beautiful," she agreed. "You have a gorgeous car."

"It should be, for what it cost. Grandmother was appalled by the extravagance but, you know what they say. You can't take it with you. Might as well spend and enjoy it now."

"Well fortunately, in that regard you're lucky. When I was married, money was never an issue. But now that I'm a member of the working class, I have to be careful about how much I spend."

They walked outside and he closed the garage door with a remote.

"When do I get my surprise?" she asked eagerly.

"In a while. I still have some last-minute finishing touches to do. In the meantime, we can relax and enjoy the pool. But since we never got around to lunch, let's make some sandwiches first."

"Whatever you say," she said. "I guess you're in charge for the weekend. I'm putty in your capable hands." She was glad everything seemed to have returned to normal between them. Maybe a good argument now and then was good for a relationship, and wasn't make-up sex supposed to be the best? But they still had to talk. Everything felt different after last night. Alan's possessiveness would not go away on its own. And after the attraction she felt for Dave, Marci wasn't sure she and Alan could go back to where they were. She felt drawn to Dave and safe with him. She could not imagine him bullying her like Alan had. But why had Dave practically thrown her into Alan's arms?

They worked side by side in his kitchen assembling bacon, lettuce and tomato sandwiches, a fruit salad and making a pitcher of sweet tea. Taking their lunch out by the pool, they enjoyed the sunny afternoon. Marci closed her eyes contentedly and let the sun wash over and warm her face. She felt her body relax, muscle by muscle and she soon dozed off. She wasn't sure how long she had slept but when she awoke, Alan had cleared away the lunch dishes and was standing protectively over her smiling.

"Hi sleepy head. Did you have a good nap? You were sleeping like an angel. I couldn't keep my eyes off you."

"Please Alan," she whispered, "can I lie here just a little longer? I feel kind of woozy."

"Sure, my love. You go back to sleep and I'll tend to a few things in the guest house. But first, have some more tea. You'll get dehydrated lying in the sun. I'll be back in an hour or so. We'll play some tennis if you're up for it." He kissed her on her lips and watched with a knowing expression as she drifted off and began making little purring sounds.

This is going to work out just fine, he thought gleefully to himself as he entered the guest house. Humming the Broadway tune, *I'm getting married in the morning,* he grabbed his phone. "Consuela, I'm ready for your help. Marci's passed out by the pool, so you can come straight over. And bring the dress."

CHAPTER 42

Savannah had been home for two hours and had not heard a word from her dad. Marci had not called either. She was distraught that something awful had happened to her friend. She was convinced of it; after all, they had looked everywhere, called the hospitals and law enforcement. Dave had driven to Marci's place and she had passed by Alan's house. There was no red Porsche to be seen. Where were they? She paced restlessly around her living room carrying a glass of chardonnay, but her hand was shaking so severely that she kept spilling droplets of the wine on the carpet. She finally put the glass down when her landline rang. She ran to grab it.

"Hello," she gasped into the receiver. "Dad, is that you?"

"No, Savannah, It's Sheldon. I've been trying to reach your father all afternoon."

"I'm afraid he's not here, Sheldon. I've been expecting him to call, but he seems to have gone missing too. He's out looking for Marci."

"Why Marci and what do you mean gone missing *too*?"

"Oh, sorry. I can explain. I'm upset because Dad and I think something may have happened to Marci. She left the shop today for lunch with Alan but she never came back. It's absolutely not like her. I can't reach her by phone and her car's still in our lot. Marci is completely dependable and would never pull a disappearing act like this. I know something's very wrong and I'm at a loss about what I should do next. Dad is beside himself with worry too. He went to her place to see if she'd gone there, but he hasn't come back either. I'm beside myself with worry."

"Try to calm down, Savannah," Sheldon tried to comfort her. "There must be a logical explanation."

"Well, if there is, I don't know what it would be. First Marci and now Dad."

"Do you want me to come over and wait with you until you hear from one of them?" He was very fond of both Dave and Savannah and would be glad to help them in any way he could.

"That's very kind of you, Sheldon, but no, I'll be all right…once I hear from them." She walked back to the table where she'd put her glass and took a sip of wine. "By the way, why are you trying to reach Dad? Do you have any news for us?"

"Yes. That's why I'm calling. Dave asked me to trace a social security number. Apparently, Mr. Trent claimed it was his, but your father wasn't so sure. Do you know about this?"

"Yes. I was trying to access the Trent home yesterday and the nurse, Consuela, confessed that Mrs. Trent does not have a grandson. My questions seemed to agitate her, but I don't think she had any idea how startled I was by that news. So, if that's true, we're naturally wondering who the hell is Alan? We hoped you might find the answer by checking out that social security number."

"I had my sources look into it and it appears that Alan Trent is definitely a fake name. The social security number he gave you belongs to someone else...a man named Peter Scant. My PI checked the motor vehicles department and found that Alan's driver's license was also issued with that very same social security number and a fake name...Trent. My guy crosschecked the birthdate with the birth certificate registry for that year. He could find no records of an Alan Trent being born here and furthermore, Marjorie Trent, the woman he claims is his grandmother and the owner of the property in Coastal Beach, is childless. Meaning, there are no grandchildren. That's an irrefutable fact."

Savannah was stunned. "You mean Alan is really Peter Scant and he's been using a fake identity all this his time?"

"Precisely."

"Oh my God! Poor Marci. She's been taken in by a con man and Dad and I were duped by him too." She was suddenly sickened by the thought and its ramifications. "Sheldon," she asked in panic. "If it wasn't Mrs. Trent's jewelry we sold, then who did all those pieces belong to? What's going to happen to us now?" Her mind was spinning with possibilities -- her thoughts scattered all over the place. "I have to call the police and tell them about Alan. They have to help us find Marci."

"I'm a step ahead of you, Savannah. That's what I wanted to tell your Dad. When I realized Alan was not who he claimed to be, and that he had put you and *Wrights* in the middle of a stolen jewelry scam, I reported him to the local police. Using a fake social security number and fake driver's license is identity theft and fraud. It's definitely a serious crime. I made an official report, and the authorities very much want to have a serious conversation with Alan aka Peter Scant.

"The police believe that the jewelry he sold was most likely Mrs. Trent's and that he's been stealing it from her over a period of time. She never made a police report about anything being missing. Thank goodness you were smart enough to take pictures of each piece when you took them on consignment. The precious stones and diamonds in them are significant enough that other reputable jewelers would remember them and would have kept records of their resale. It will take some time, but most of the jewelry can probably be traced back to its original owner, which I believe will be Marjorie Trent. The sixty-four-thousand-dollar question is how did Alan get her to turn over her jewelry to him? What did she think he would do with it?"

Savannah interrupted him. "Do you know anything more about this Peter Scant? Who is he? Where did he come from? Does he have a criminal record? And how did he find his way to Marjorie Trent?" She had so many questions and so few answers.

"I've learned a little about him," Sheldon replied solemnly. "And I can tell you that he's not a nice guy."

"In what way? What do you mean?"

"For one thing, he has a criminal record in three other states. So far, he's clean in Florida, but apparently not for long. He's presently on probation from another state where he served time for grand theft. His paper trail then leads to Dallas where he was arrested for drug possession and suspicion of selling cocaine. He served three years in jail there. Then, he skipped town and resurfaced in New Orleans. There he was arrested for passing counterfeit checks. He's pretty slippery and is always a step or two ahead of the cops. Believe me, if the police catch him this time, he'll be in jail for a long, long time."

Savannah could not believe what she was hearing. She thanked Sheldon for his call and promised to keep him informed about her father and Marci, if either turned up. Then she lay down, on her bed and wondered what her hero, Nancy Drew, would do in this situation. An hour later, whether it was foolish or brilliant, she had formulated another plan.

CHAPTER 43

Dave parked his car in front of Marci's small townhouse complex. Hers was the end unit nearest the street. He walked up to her front door and rang the bell. He noticed a small pile of mail lying on the threshold. Leaning over, he picked it up, hoping to hand it to her when she opened the door. He rang the bell again, but still no reply.

The townhouse was in a nice neighborhood but was a very small one bedroom one bath unit. If she was home, it would only take her a minute to answer the door. Although the square footage of the place was sparse, Marci had decorated every inch beautifully. It felt cozy and inviting. He remembered from last night that originally, she'd been embarrassed to show the place to him. She'd laughed and confessed that the entire townhouse could fit in the living room of her DC home. He remembered seeing the clothing racks arranged along the wall. She laughed and said the closet space was almost nonexistent. He'd assured her that it wasn't her furniture that he was interested in.

Marci had poured them each a brandy and they sat side by side on the sofa talking about their childhoods and their favorite memories.

Marci shared the hurt and anger she suffered as her marriage ended, and Dave told her of the pain he'd endured while helplessly watching his wife battle cancer. He told Marci that he secretly feared Savannah's breast cancer would return, but so far, she was in complete remission and was the picture of health. The two commiserated and agreed that they had endured a lot but were both eager to see what the future had in store for them. Hours passed and it was after two when Dave finally looked at his watch and reluctantly decided it was time to leave. It had been a wonderful evening from beginning to end. He was sorry that it was over.

Now, still holding Marci's mail, he

walked slowly around the entire structure. There were no signs that anyone had tried to break in. He returned to his car before any neighbors spotted him lurking about and called the police. When he was about to start the engine, he realized he still had Marci's mail. He didn't feel right about leaving it on her doorway. Anyone could come along and take it, although as he randomly thumbed through it, there didn't seem to be anything worth stealing…a few circulars, a cellular phone bill, and two magazines. He placed Marci's mail on his back seat and drove away. He'd give it to her when he found her.

Where was she? Why hadn't she called?

The longer she was missing, the more anxious he became. For reasons he couldn't explain, she had become very important to him and he couldn't allow himself to think that anything bad had happened to her. He had to concentrate on thinking positively.

He decided to drive back to the store and see if she'd returned for her car. He didn't know what else to do.

CHAPTER 44

Savannah parked her car in front of the same house she had the last time she visited the Trent property. This time she wore a Marlins cap over her wig and looked nothing like herself. Her over-sized dark glasses hid most of her facial features. If she encountered Consuela again, she was sure the nurse would not recognize her as the census taker.

Savannah was determined to find Marci and get her away from Alan. Since she hadn't heard from her, she decided to do the next best thing… find Alant. Where he was, Marci was sure to be.

She had devised a plan to give her access to the main house. If she could only speak to Mrs. Trent, she could find out why she allowed Alan to live in the guest house and pass himself off as her grandson. Did she know his real name and his criminal background? Was he blackmailing or threatening her?

Approaching the mansion on foot, she walked casually past it for a few hundred feet, glancing in all directions, checking for anyone in plain sight. Seeing no one, she circled back and boldly walked up to the front door. There were no cars in the driveway. Alan's red Porsche was gone. That meant that he and Marci were not there either. Disappointed, she had no choice but to go ahead with Plan B… the second part of her scheme.

She tapped loudly on the brass door knocker and waited. This time Consuela did not block her way. Instead, a nice-looking man in a business suit opened the door. "May I help you?"

"Yes, please. I'm here to see Mrs. Trent. We have an appointment."

"I'm Mrs. Trent's attorney, Steven Framin. May I ask what this is about?"

"I'm sorry. It's a private matter. Mrs. Trent called me this morning and asked me to come see her. She said she had something very important to discuss." Savannah tried hard to keep her voice steady and her hands from shaking. She was not a good liar and the attorney was very tall and intimidating. He did not look like he believed her.

"And you are?" he asked matter-of-factly.

"My name…my name is Nancy Drew," she stuttered, taken off guard. It was the only name she could come up with so quickly. She was immediately mortified at her stupidity however; thankfully, the lawyer didn't seem to recognize the fictional sleuth's name. He must never have had sisters or a teenage daughter. She continued on. "May I see her please?"

"Come this way, Ms. Drew." He led her into an enormous living room and pointed to the sofa. "Take a seat." He suddenly looked very stern.

Savannah looked around the spacious room. The furniture was of the old-world style, with comfortable chenille sofas, over-stuffed arm-chairs, decorative floor lamps with fringed shades and numerous tables made from a rich variety of woods. The walls were painted a pale gold color and there were obvious marks where large paintings had previously hung. Mahogany plantation shutters covered an entire wall of windows facing the backyard. They were open to showcase the magnificent setting beyond and the enormous white yacht docked at the water's edge.

"When exactly did Mrs. Trent call you?" Mr. Framin asked, keeping his eyes on Savannah's face. "Today, you said?"

Savannah had not expected to run into anyone but Consuela. Her plan had not called for this encounter. "Yes. It was earlier this morning. Why does it matter?"

"Really? That's strange," he continued, his eyes now boring a hole through her with an unrelenting glare. "Mrs. Trent has been in a comatose state for the last ten days and she passed away two nights ago. Who," he demanded in a steely voice, "are you really, and what is it you want here?"

CHAPTER 45

Dave Wright drove quickly back to his store to check out the employees parking lot behind it. Marci's car was still there. Sighing, he opened the door to the shop using his personal code and went directly to the answering machine in the back office. He listened to several messages from clients and two from vendors, but there was nothing from Marci.

He relocked the store and got back into his car. *What's the old expression, if the mountain won't come to Mohammed, Mohammed must go to the mountain. In this case, if Marci won't come to me, then I'll have to go to her. And, the only place I can think to start looking for her is at Allen's place.*

He drove down Federal Highway, then over the 17th street bridge and a few minutes later was in the swanky Coastal Beach neighborhood. There was a small gatehouse at the entrance to the exclusive enclave that was designed to ward off intruders, but it wasn't manned. As he pulled up close to it, the automatic arm rose to admit him.

He had not been to the Trent property before so, he entered the address he had taken from Alan's paperwork in his GPS system and began slowly navigating through the winding streets until he found the house. Once he was sure that he was at the right place, he pulled into the deserted driveway. Alan's car was not there. *Shit,* he thought. *That means Marci isn't here either. Well, I'm not leaving. I'll just stay here and wait here for them to come back.* He needed to be patient. Marci was worth it.

After an hour, there was still no sign of Alan or Marci. Dave was restless and needed to stretch his legs. He decided to try to find the guest house but had no idea which direction to go. He noticed a pathway by the side of the main house and decided to follow it. He spotted the huge yacht, docked at the back of the property. He couldn't resist taking a closer look. It was a magnificent looking boat.

As he approached the mega yacht, he realized that he was trespassing on private property. If he got caught, it would not be good for his reputation or that of *Wrights*. What would his friends and uber wealthy customers think? His plan to find Alan had been rash and he needed to leave before he was detected. He was acting like his impulsive daughter.

It occurred to him that there were probably security cameras stationed around the property, so he ran up to the side of the house and crept as close to the building's walls as he could, hoping to blend into the shrubbery and escape detection. The cameras must not be functioning, he thought, or the police or someone would have spotted him by now. Relieved, he moved cautiously around the perimeter of the house, and jumped when he inadvertently stepped on some twigs. They barely crackled but to him, the noise sounded like an explosion, as loud as a canon. He froze and waited nervously to be sure no one had heard him. Only a few more feet and he would be back on the pathway and could make a run for his car. Enough of the private detective shenanigans. He'd leave that to Savannah. *What was a grown man doing creeping around a stranger's property anyway? Had he lost his mind?* It was only his concern for Marci that had made him act so irrationally.

As he passed along the side of the building, he found himself standing in front of a wall of windows. Bending lower so anyone who might be inside the room would not see him, he took a few more steps. He couldn't help taking a quick peek inside, however, and realized that he must be looking into the Trent's living room. The pure opulence of the space was stunning. In spite of himself, he leaned in closer, placing his nose firmly against the window for a better look. He could make out an enormous sofa facing him, and a woman was sitting on it. In an adjacent armchair, he spotted a man. The two were engrossed in conversation and had not noticed him spying on them. He was about to move away, to make his escape, when the person sitting on the sofa shifted positions slightly and glanced briefly in his direction. He got a full glimpse of her face. It was his daughter. She was wearing her favorite wig and a baseball cap, but he had no doubt that the woman was Savannah.

CHAPTER 46

"Aren't you the sleepy one," Alan grinned at Marci. "I'm glad you had a nice nap. Now let me do one more thing and then I'll show you the surprise." He didn't wait for her to answer but walked to the other end of the pool deck and using his cell phone, made a whispered call.

"Everything's all set," he smiled upon returning. "Take my hand and follow me."

"I feel funny," she slurred her words. "It's as if I'm tipsy."

"You can't be. You only drank iced tea with lunch."

Marci stumbled and almost tripped when Alan helped her up and led her towards the house.

"Well, what do you think?" he asked proudly, spinning her around. The lunch fixings were gone, obviously cleared away while Marci slept. "As you can see, I've turned the living room into a wedding chapel and my bedroom, soon to be ours, has been transformed into our honeymoon suite, complete with chilled champagne and caviar for after the ceremony."

"Ceremony?" She swayed back and forth holding onto Alan's arm for support. "I don't feel at all like myself. What are you talking about Alan? I never agreed to marry you."

"What? Are you kidding? You most certainly did. Why do you think I went to all this trouble? This is no time to joke around, Pretty Lady. I made everything here exactly the way you asked me to…down to the minutest details. Let me get you some water. Maybe it will help clear your head. You don't look so good."

He plopped her down on a kitchen stool and poured a tall glass of water from an open bottle sitting on the counter. "Here drink up. You'll feel better. I have to admit I'm a little dismayed by your reaction. I thought you'd be thrilled to death. I did exactly what you asked."

He walked to the hall closet and brought out a beautiful white Duchess satin wedding dress hanging on a padded hangar. It had hundreds of baby pearls and Swarovski crystals sewn around the v neck and circling the waist. This is the dress you picked out yourself, silly girl. Here," he showed her a page torn out of *Bride's Magazine*. "Marci's dress" was written in black magic marker across the top. "It's Vera Wang. Surely you remember asking me to order this for you in a size 6?"

Marci shook her head trying to shake the fog from her brain. *What was happening to her?* "I don't remember ever seeing that dress!" She was adamant. "This is all some terrible mistake."

"Marci, I don't like the way you're behaving. You're being very ungrateful. I went to considerable expense and took a great deal of time preparing this place for our ceremony. Look around this room. It's every bit as pretty as any wedding chapel you'd find any place in the world. There are over two hundred white lilies in here alone. You can't be so mentally fragile that you don't remember asking for them! Look at your ring finger, for God's sake," he demanded angrily. "That's the engagement ring

I bought you. It's 8 karats. You picked it out yourself from *Wrights*. Surely you remember that?"

Marci took another huge gulp of water before studying her ring finger closely. She saw an enormous pear-shaped diamond ring set in white platinum gold. She stared at it in astonishment. *What was going on? Was she losing her mind?* She had no memory of ever seeing that ring before. She knew all the inventory at *Wrights* and they had never carried that ring, or had they? She wasn't sure anymore. What was happening?

"Let me help you get dressed my love." He softened the tone of his voice and tried to hide his annoyance. "And I'll change too. I'll put on the Tom Ford tux we picked out together at Saks. Once we're married, you'll laugh at your forgetfulness. I assure you; no one ever forgets their wedding day. You must be very stressed, my darling, but this will be over soon and you'll have the rest of your life to relax and laugh at this."

He pulled her gently off the stool and began to undress her. Slowly, admiring every sensuous curve of her body, he replaced her work clothes with the wedding gown. Once she was dressed, he smiled admiringly and led her to a full-length mirror. "You are the most beautiful bride in the world." He took her in his arms and kissed her. "I will always be proud to call you my wife." He took out his phone and snapped pictures of her from several different angles. "For our album," he explained. "I didn't think to hire a professional photographer."

Grabbing the back of a stool for balance, she watched Alan as if in a dream. He meticulously dressed himself in the brand-new tuxedo, tied his bow tie and put on shiny new patten leather evening shoes. Even in her blurry state of mind, she had to admit that he looked very handsome. He approached her and drew her to him. "Are you feeling any better? I want everything to be perfect for our wedding."

"I don't know," Marci mumbled and swayed backwards. "I feel so strange. I honestly don't understand any of this...the ring, the dress, anything."

Alan caught her as she started to fall and propped her upright. "Maybe you have a touch of the flu." He sounded concerned as he gave her more water. "You'll be Mrs. Alan Trent within the hour." *And not soon enough*, he thought. *This is getting very tiresome.*

Marci started to protest again. She wanted to run away but she had no energy. She was weak and disoriented. Her legs felt wobbly and her eyes burned. She reached for her ring finger and tried to pull the offending diamond off, but she didn't have the strength. Her hands fell limply to her side. *Oh God. What's happening to me? This is a nightmare.*

The doorbell rang, startling her. She tried to say something but her tongue wouldn't work. She opened her mouth but no words came out. Feeling nauseous and about to faint, she leaned helplessly against the refrigerator. Alan went to open the door.

"That, my love, is the justice of the peace," he said smugly. "He's here to marry us."

CHAPTER 47

Sheldon Blake was frustrated because he had critical, new information to share with Dave and Savannah and hadn't been able to reach either of them. Incredibly, Savannah's Voice mailbox was full and Dave's just went to his Voicemail. His private detective had given him a full report on Alan, aka Peter Scant.

Sheldon continued to call Dave and Savannah repeatedly throughout the day and finally decided he had no choice but to leave a long urgent message on the store's answering machine. In the worst-case scenario, one or both of them would hear it first thing Monday morning when *Wrights* opened its door for business.

"Dave, Savannah, hi, it's Sheldon. I have very crucial news and would have preferred to share it with you in person, but you are both inexplicably off the radar this weekend, so I'm leaving my detective's findings in this message. Please call me ASAP.

"As you requested, I asked our PI to follow the money trail to see where Alan deposited the $779,000 you gave him for the jewelry. I did so. This is what I've learned.

"Marjorie Trent and her husband Hubert bought the Coastal Beach property in 1965 and they lived there together until his death fifteen years ago. After he passed, she remained in the home with the support of a huge staff. She continued to host numerous social galas and non-profit

fundraisers there. Marjorie was a well-liked, elderly philanthropic woman, but she has been in declining health and has become somewhat of a recluse. I've known her lawyer, Steven Framin from several legal organizations and will reach out to him and see what more I can find out. He's a good man and a fine lawyer. The long and short of this rambling message is that I have no idea how Peter Scant is getting away with pretending to be Alan Trent. He's an imposter and a dangerous con artist.

"As to the second part of this news… the money trail. That was harder for the PI to track down, but he's nothing if not persistent. He finally uncovered proof that Alan has, over the last year, been making frequent large deposits, including the $779,000 he got from you, into an account at the Wells Fargo Bank. And listen to this -- the names on that account are *Marci Morgan* Trent and Alan A. Trent. The address the bank has for them is an apartment on Collins Avenue in Miami.

"I'm sure you realize the serious implications here. Marci is either already secretly married to the guy or it's his intention to tie the knot with her very soon. I believe the marriage is a convenient way for him to cover his tracks while having unencumbered access to the account. If the money was illegally gained, Marci could be in big trouble. At some point she must have signed the signature cards to open the account. Anyway, it appears that she's an accessory to whatever he's been doing. I'm not suggesting she's a knowing partner in this scheme. I'm sure he set her up. But we'll have to prove that because right now, she looks as guilty as he does.

"I urge you to send her to an attorney right away. I can't help her because of my association with you and *Wrights*. It could be a conflict of interest. But it's clear your friend is smack dab in the middle of some dubious and most likely illegal activity.

"Sorry to lay all of this on you by a phone message, but you've left me no choice. Please call me immediately. You sure picked a hell of a time to disappear.

CHAPTER 48

Steven Framin got right to the point. "There's something sinister going on in this house and I'm trying to get to the bottom of it. I warn you; I'm going to call the police right now unless you explain your presence here and your part in all of this." He leaned forward and almost thrust his nose into hers. "Let's start over again, and this time I want to hear the full unvarnished truth. Understand?" He stood his ground and waited for her to speak.

"Okay," Savannah said weakly. "I'm sorry Mr. Framin. I did lie to you. My real name is Savannah Wright and I came here to try to speak to Mrs. Trent. I understand that she doesn't receive visitors anymore. That's why I had to bluff my way into the house. I agree with you that something sinister is going on around here, and I hoped she could shed some light on it for me." Savannah twisted nervously in her seat, imploring him to believe her.

"My best friend, Marci Morgan is romantically involved with her grandson, or so he claimed to be. I know now that Mrs. Trent had no children. But this man, Alan, who I've only recently learned is actually

Peter Scant, keeps bringing packets of Mrs. Trent's jewelry to our shop, *Wrights* and asking my father to sell it for him on consignment. He claims that Mrs. Trent's attorney…" she suddenly blinked with recognition. "Oh, forgive me, I guess that's you. Anyway, Alan said you ordered him to sell his grandmother's jewelry and some pieces of art to lower the estate's value for inheritance tax purposes. The whole thing doesn't seem right and I was hoping Mrs. Trent would enlighten me." She looked at the lawyer optimistically. Had she been candid enough with him so that he wouldn't call the police? She couldn't read his expression. Was he still angry at her deception?

Steven sat back in his chair to take it all in. "Well," he paused, the dual bombshells about Alan and the jewelry appeared to have shaken him. "I believe we have a lot to discuss. May I call you Savannah? And I'm Steven. There's so much to say. I don't know where to start."

"Please start by saying that you're not going to turn me into the police."

"No," he smiled. "Don't worry. I won't." He thought that she was actually very charming and he was interested in learning more about her and the man impersonating his client's grandson.

Savannah studied him subtly while pretending to look around the room. He was attractive in an English professor sort of way. But rather than wearing a tweed jacket and smoking a pipe, instead what she conjures the Floridian version to be. He was dressed in a linen sports jacket, Levi's and polished penny loafers. The effect was charming and a little eccentric.

"So, tell me," she said. "Did you instruct Alan to sell Mrs. Trent's jewelry? My dad and I wondered why you didn't recommend he contact an auction house instead of bringing the pieces to us piecemeal. It would be so much easier for everyone."

Steven sighed deeply. "I hardly know where to begin. Let me start with this. I don't know this Alan person and would never advocate selling off any of Marjorie's assets without her written approval. Mrs. Trent has been in declining health for some time. I was told by her nurse that she was losing her mental capacities, that she had a progressive form of dementia. Although, whenever I visited her, I came away feeling like there was something else wrong. She slurred her words and was often unsteady on her feet...more like she'd been drugged than was just being forgetful. I was never able to get her alone to ask if everything was okay. Her butler, Pedro was always hovering nearby. Every time I requested a private conversation, she would become agitated and tell him to make me leave. She seemed completely dependent, even mesmerized by the man. Frankly, it was a little eerie.

"Anyway," he continued soberly, "before we go any further, I must tell you the circumstances around Marjorie's passing. Something is suspicious. Pedro said she fell in the bathroom and hit her head on the marble floor. But remember, I said she'd been in a coma. How then would she have gotten to the bathroom? Before the coma, when she was awake, she was confined to a wheelchair. The medics and the police never found a wheelchair and Pedro claimed he had no idea what happened to it.

"The night of the accident Pedro called an ambulance and when it arrived, he told the authorities that Marjorie had accidentally fallen and hit her head. I'm told the medical examiner wasn't so sure. There was not enough blood on the floor from what was supposed to be a fatal blow to her head, so the medical examiner ordered an autopsy. We won't release the news of Marjorie's death until we know more."

"What does the coroner suspect?" Savannah was more than a little curious. "Does he think Pedro killed her? But why?"

"I'm not sure, but my bet is they're looking for some kind of drugs in her system as the cause of death. That would explain the slurring of her words that I mentioned. She may have been systematically poisoned over a period of time. In my recent interactions with her, she never seemed quite right in her head, although the change was hard to detect. For the longest time, she was sharp as a tack. And by the way, I am the estate's lawyer and I assure you there's no one named Alan in the family. As you said, Marjorie had no children and therefore no grandchildren."

Savannah could see the attorney was upset, but she had more questions and now was as good a time as any to ask them. "Steven, if not Alan, did you instruct anyone to sell off Mrs. Trent's jewelry for any reason? That's what I came to ask her. It's the reason for my subterfuge."

"I most certainly never instructed anyone to sell Marjorie's things. That's ridiculous. And if I were to ever recommend that action to a client, I would certainly suggest dealing with a reputable national auction house, not a local jeweler, no offense to you and your Dad. I'm familiar with *Wrights*. It's a lovely store."

"Thank you," Savannah smiled. "No offense taken. We *are* a reputable business and cherish our good standing in the community. That's what bothers me so much about all of this."

Steven stood up and began pacing around the room. "My first question to you is -- who the hell is Alan? And who is Peter Scant?"

Savannah sat forward and nervously rubbed her hands together. "As I said, Alan claims to be Mrs. Trent's loving grandson, but my father's attorney, Sheldon Blake, had his private investigator check into Alan's past and confirmed that Alan's real name is Peter Scant. They are one in the same."

"I've known Marjorie for years and have written her will and several codicils. She left all her assets to a favorite charity that addresses the needs of children. I can't say more at this time, but the fact that she was unable to conceive was one of her deepest sorrows. It is why she was so involved in the welfare of our young people."

"Well, where is this overbearing butler?" Savannah interrupted. "We need to talk to him. He would have to know who Alan really is and how he was able to get ahold of Marjorie's jewelry."

"That's a good point," Steven agreed. "But it's probably not going to be possible. Right after they took Marjorie's body away, Pedro packed his things from his room upstairs and disappeared. He has not been back since. Consuela has gone too, but I know how to reach her. She gave the police her home address."

"Wow, that leaves us at a dead end," Savannah sighed. "But no matter what, we have to find Alan. He's taken off with my best friend and I'm afraid she's in real danger. Please Steven, can you help me?" She looked at him and suddenly giggled. "I hope you don't mind, but I have to take this wig off. It's itching like crazy." She pulled it off quickly and tossed it into her shoulder bag. "This is the real me...a bleached blond."

He chuckled and studied her closely. "I must admit, I like the real you better. I never would have known you were wearing a wig, though."

"That's the point," she grinned. Before she could say anything else, there was a loud pounding on the front door. Savannah looked at the lawyer hopefully. "Maybe Pedro decided to come back."

CHAPTER 49

Alan flung open the door. Marci continued to lean against the refrigerator. The room was swimming. *What's wrong with me?*

"Mr. Trent? I'm Harrison Bates, the justice of the peace."

"Come in." Alan escorted the man into the living room. "My bride and I have been expecting you. Thank you for coming on such short notice. This is such a happy day for us."

"My, my, you have recreated a wedding chapel here. So many flowers," he said carefully, looking around in utter amazement, but not wanting to inhale the overpowering scent or offend the groom.

"Thank you," Alan smiled. "I went the extra mile to make my bride happy."

Alan had lined dozens of white lilies around the entire perimeter of the room. Shiny white satin ribbons hung down from the ceiling and were taped to the backs of the furniture, the oven and kitchen cabinet handles and even the dishwasher handle…every available surface. A small portable fan placed on the countertop stirred the air gently making the ribbons appear to be white shimmering waves. Real red rose pedals were strewn all over the floor and shifted around gently from the fan. The effect made the floor appear to be moving too. Two large white paper Mache bells were suspended from the hallway door jamb by the same kind of silver satin ribbons, similar to a trellis or a Jewish chuppah. A square piece of white carpet lay beneath the bells designating the area as an altar. Alan had gotten the idea for decorating the place from bridal magazines, but typically had ignored the maxim that "less is more" in favor of making *an impact*.

Mr. Bates walked over to Marci, who was now clutching onto one of the kitchen stools and looking miserable. He immediately noticed her extremely pale face and watery eyes. "You must be Mr. Trent's bride to be?" he stated as he stared at the willowy brunette who was clearly distressed. "I'm Harrison Bates, the local justice of the peace. Are you all right, Miss? Miss Morgan, isn't it? He referred to the notes he'd taken when Alan called him. You are a beautiful bride, surely the prettiest I've seen in ages; but if you don't mind me saying so. But you appear a little green around the gills. Are you feeling ill?"

Marci tried to focus and make the room stop moving. "Yes, I'm Marci Morgan," she managed to whisper. "And I certainly do feel a little queasy."

"She's just overcome with emotion about this happy occasion," Alan interjected and immediately came to stand by Marci's side, draping his arm protectively around her shoulders while holding her up from his grip on her waist. "Stand up straight, darling," he prodded her. "We'll be husband and wife soon, just as you've wanted."

She looked at him and wanted to protest but didn't have the strength.

"Come, Mr. Bates," Alan said. "Let's begin the ceremony and then Marci will feel much better. All she's talked about for days is getting married. I think the anticipation had been a little too much for her. I have the rings here." He handed the justice of the peace two matching white gold wedding rings which he'd placed on a square of white satin lying on a small Lucite plate.

"If you're sure," Mr. Bates said gently, looking to Marci for affirmation. He was not comfortable marrying a couple when the bride was in her condition. But she did not seem to object and had made no protest. He was paid to do a job, not judge the couples before him.

Marci tried to shake her head *no*. The word screamed in her head but she couldn't make the sound come out. Tears leaked from her eyes as the room continued to swim. The ribbons swaying and the rose petals moving along the floor like swarming termites were making her nauseous. She turned and threw up in the kitchen sink.

"Oh my," Mr. Bates said sympathetically. "I've seen some pretty nervous brides before but never anything quite like this. Are you sure you want to go through with this?"

"Of course, she does," Alan answered for Marci. "She's a fragile little thing, aren't you my darling?" He picked up a dish towel and wiped the vomit off her mouth. "Have some water Marci." He handed her an open bottle. "You need to keep hydrated."

"Well then," Mr. Bates sighed heavily and handed them the marriage certificate to sign. "As I told you on the phone, we'll need a witness."

From out of the back bedroom, an attractive woman appeared. She was dressed in an expensive beige silk suit and wore a small matching fascinator in her hair. Diamonds sparkled in her ears and on her fingers.

"I'm Marci's best friend and her maid of honor," she explained. She walked over to the bride and gave her a quick hug. "I'll be your witness."

She handed Marci a bridal bouquet of white lilies with more satin ribbons. Smiling seductively at the justice of the peace, she took her place next to Marci. "I'm Consuela. Shall we begin now?" She winked at Alan. She had played her part to perfection and had spoken in perfect English.

CHAPTER 50

The knocking on the door grew louder and more persistent. Steven sprang up to answer it, hoping, like Savannah, that it was the missing butler. Instead, an agitated stranger stood in front of him with an angry, confused expression on his face.

"My name is Dave Wright. What the hell are you doing in there with my daughter?"

"Dad?" Savannah heard her father's voice and ran to his side. "What in the world? How did you know I was here?"

"I didn't." Dave answered testily. "I came here looking for Alan. I figured that since we couldn't find Marci, I'd try to track him down instead. I assumed they'd be here together. I was searching around the grounds when I spotted the two of you through the living room window. Would you care to explain yourself, young lady?" He was relieved that she was all right, but furious with her at the same time. "How is it that you are here, in Mrs. Trent's living room? Did you finally get to talk to her?"

"If I might interrupt," Steve intervened between the father and daughter squabble. "I'm Mrs. Trent's attorney, Steven Framin. I think

I can clear a few things up. Like you, Savannah came here to find Alan and her friend Marci. She and I were simply getting acquainted and discussing all the strange things that have happened lately. She was telling me about pretending to be a Census taker earlier in the week and then about her attempt today to meet with Mrs. Trent."

"And Dad," Savannah tugged at his arm impatiently. "There's so much more to tell you. Steven told me that Mrs. Trent has died."

"Oh, my goodness," Dave gasped. "When? When did that happen?"

"Two nights ago, and I'm afraid it was under mysterious circumstances. The police are investigating." Steven said soberly. "They suspect a homicide."

Suddenly remembering his manners, he stuck out his hand to shake Dave's. "Mr. Wright, it's a pleasure to meet you. Please come in and join our discussion. We are only just getting started." He indicated they should return to the living room.

"I'll rummage through Marjorie's well-stocked bar and see if I can find her good scotch. I know she wouldn't mind. She always kept a Macallan Single Malt for me. Will that be all right? I think this conversation calls for a stiff drink."

Once the three were comfortably settled, Steve began to fill Dave in on all that he and Savannah had discussed. Dave was shocked to hear of Mrs. Trent's possible poisoning and that her fall may not have been accidental. Then Savannah told him about what she'd learned from Sheldon about Alan's real name being Peter Scant and about his criminal history.

"We were hoping you were the mysterious Pedro at the door," Steven said. "We really need to find him and get him to talk. He should be able to enlighten us about this dubious Alan character. I'm particularly interested in how he got access to this house and how he was able to walk off with some of Marjorie's most prominent paintings and her jewelry. He pointed to the empty spaces on some of the walls. I'd like to ask Consuela to come back here and speak to us too, but we'll need an interpreter. Her English is terrible."

"Tell me about it." Savannah rolled her eyes. She looked at her watch. It was only 4:30. "Maybe she can come over now while we're all here together. Dad's speaks Spanish pretty well. And we should call the police. They need to know that Alan has taken Marci and that Pedro has disappeared too." She shuttered.

"You're right," Steven agreed and dialed his office. "I'll ask my secretary to pick up Consuela and bring here. Her apartment is just on the other side of the bridge."

"While we're waiting, I have an idea." Savannah looked at the two men expectantly. "Dad and I both came here today looking for information about Alan and to find him. There's nothing more we can do here sitting around drinking Mrs. Trent's scotch until Consuela arrives, so how about we check out the guest house. That's where Alan pretended to live and where he spent all his time with Marci. Maybe we'll find a clue there that'll tell us what he's been up to and where he's taken her."

Steven and Dave gulped down the last of their drinks. "Let's go," they said practically in unison.

"No time like the present." Savannah leapt up and made her way to the front door.

CHAPTER 51

Mr. Bates took his place in front of Marci and Alan under the makeshift wedding canopy and read a passage about love from first Corinthian's 13: verses 4-5. Consuela stood next to Marci, smiling broadly.

"Love is patient, love is kind. It does not envy, it does not boast, it is not proud. It does not dishonor others, it is not easily angered, it keeps no record of wrongs."

"Can we skip right to the vows?" Alan asked impatiently. "I don't think Marci cares about that part."

Mr. Bates shrugged but did as he was instructed. He asked the bride and groom if they wished to exchange their own vows. Alan stepped forward and spoke for both of them. He explained that Marci was a divorcee and felt uncomfortable reciting the traditional ones. She wanted the simplest and shortest service possible as long as it was legal.

"But I've not been married before," he said slyly. "So, I'd like to say the words I've heard so often at my friend's weddings.

"Go ahead," Mr. Bates nodded his head. This was the strangest wedding ceremony he'd ever performed.

Alan turned to face Marci but his eyes homed in on the lovely Consuela and he spoke his words directly to her. "I, Alan, take thee Marci to be my wedded wife, to have and to hold from this day forward, for better, for worse, for richer, for poorer, in sickness and in health, to love and to cherish, till death do us part, according to God's holy ordinance and thereto I pledge thee my troth.

Marci's eyes remained tightly closed and she swayed precariously. Consuela had to move closer and hold her upright.

The Justice of the Peace turned to Marci. "And do you take Alan to be your husband?" When she didn't reply, he prompted her. "Just say I do."

Consuela poked Marci and viciously pinched her arm until she moaned in pain and mumbled something indiscernible. Mr. Bates assumed she had said "yes". He instructed Alan to place the wedding ring on the bride's finger, which he did, and then put on his own ring. Marci was starting to rock back and forth again. It took all of Consuela's strength to keep her standing.

The Justice of the Peace pronounced them man and wife. "You may kiss your bride."

Before Alan could do it, Marci bolted through the archway to the bathroom where she positioned her head over the toilet bowl and began retching.

"Oh dear, it seems that your bride is really quite ill. Do you want to call a doctor?" The justice of the peace looked at Alan with genuine concern. "

"No, no. I'll take her to Urgent Care right away." He walked over to a kitchen drawer and pulled out a small envelope. "For your services… and your discretion. Thank you again for coming on such short notice. Will you please see yourself out? I need to check on my wife."

Mr. Bates took the envelope and quickly let himself out, relieved that the whole ordeal was over. He checked the envelope and smiled. He was happy to make his escape.

Alan went up to Consuela and whispered, "Well done, Darling. Now go home and finish packing. I'll call you later." He kissed her gently on her cheek. "You look gorgeous, my love. Far lovelier than the bride."

He watched her leave and then walked into the master bathroom. Marci was kneeling over the toilet. He placed a cool, wet washcloth over her forehead and handed her a toothbrush and a toothpaste tube. "You'll feel better soon," he said soothingly. "Let's get you out of that dress and into something more comfortable. Then I'll take you to a doctor before we come back here for our wedding night."

Marci looked at him blankly and tried to rinse out her mouth. Then she carefully stepped into a pair of shorts and a tee shit that he handed her. Her balance was such that she needed to hold onto his arm for support as she dressed. "I'm sorry, Alan," she mumbled. "I don't know what's wrong with me. I've never felt like this. I *do* need to see a doctor."

He guided her into the kitchen and sat her down on a stool. Grabbing the large water bottle off the counter, he poured her another tall glass of the liquid. "Drink this down. Finish every drop, please, Marci, and then we'll leave."

She nodded gratefully and began to sip. Maybe the water would make her feel better. She felt disoriented and the last few hours were a blur.

She couldn't remember anything about them. "What's happened here?" She pointed to all the lilies, rose petals and the ribbons.

"We got married," he said calmly. "You are now Mrs. Alan Trent."

Stunned, Marci slid clumsily off the stool and fell to the floor in a dead faint.

CHAPTER 52

Steven led the newly formed trio around the side of the main house and down the winding pathway to the back of the property. They passed the tennis court and swimming pool before arriving at the guest house.

"Damn, I forgot to bring the key," Steven said in frustration when got to the doorway. "I'll run back to the main house and get it."

"No wait. Maybe the door's not locked," Dave suggested. "Let's see." He put his hand on the nob and pushed against the door. It swung open easily. "What the hell?" he shouted when he looked inside. "Come here everybody. Get a load of this place."

Steven and Savannah rushed behind him into the guest house.

"My God." Savannah took one look around the room and gulped. "What on earth is this supposed to be?"

"I'd say that with all the flowers and white froufrou, it's a wedding chapel of sorts," Steven answered as he moved more cautiously inside the room. "Be careful not to fall. The floor is full of slippery rose pedals and dozens of damn ribbons blowing around from everywhere. Can someone please turn that thing off?" He pointed to the kitchen countertop where a battery-operated fan was vibrating loudly.

The three stared in disbelief at the scene. "This is the most bizarre thing I've ever seen." Steven shook his head in wonder.

"I know this wasn't Marci's doing," Savannah grimaced. "She has too much class to arrange something as awful as this."

Dave was filled with so many conflicting emotions he could barely speak… anger, frustration, and dread. Had Marci really married Alan? It made no sense after the conversations they'd had last night. She'd been positive that she wanted to break things off with Alan. Something was really wrong. He could feel it in his bones.

"Look." Steven pointed to a business card lying on the counter beside the fan. "This belongs to Harrison Bates. It says he's the justice of the peace. He must have conducted the ceremony." He handed the card to Savannah.

"Alan, Marci," Savannah called out as she ran to the back of the house. "Are you here? Marci, are you okay?"

When there was no answer, she collapsed on the master bed trying to collect herself. This marriage, if that's what it was, had come completely out of the blue. Marci had never even mentioned the possibility of marrying Alan. As a matter of fact, in one of their last conversations she had told Savannah that she wanted to take a break from him…that he was too possessive. So why the hurry-up wedding?

Savannah spotted the duchess satin wedding gown thrown haphazardly over a chair. "Dad, Steven, come in here." She got up and continued to look around the room but could not find anything that would suggest where Alan and Marci might have gone.

"Am I seeing what I think I am?" Dave asked in shock. "Is that a wedding dress?"

"I'm afraid so. I think Alan must have somehow forced Marci to marry him," Savannah speculated. "She never would have done so on her own. And now he's taken her away." She fought back tears that threatened to spill from her eyes. "How could this have happened? Oh God. What should we do?"

Steven was the calmest of the three. "Maybe this Alan fellow threw a wedding for someone else, a friend perhaps?"

"That's really grasping at straws," Savannah observed. "First of all, he doesn't have any friends and look at this exquisite dress." She held it up for them to see. "It's Marci's size and her taste. And over there," she pointed to the bed. "Look at the man's tuxedo and shirt dumped in a pile. They must have been in one big hurry to leave here. Otherwise, I know Marci, who's neat as a pin, would have taken the time to hang up the dress and carefully put away Alan's outfit. She's compulsive about her clothes."

Dave tried to steady his emotions. The idea that Marci had married Alan devastated him. He had foolishly hoped that he and she might have a future together. Last night had been so special for him, and he thought it had been the same for her too. He truly cared about her; he knew that now. She was the first woman he'd had deep feelings for since his wife died. And now it appeared the evening had meant nothing to her. He felt despair and yet scared for Marci at the same time. Something wasn't adding up.

Savannah immediately noticed her father's reaction. "Dad, are you okay?" She worried and went over to him. "You're not having a heart attack, are you?"

"Good God no, Honey. Don't worry. I'm simply completely shocked. I haven't said anything to you about my feelings for Marci because I thought it was too soon and I wasn't sure how you'd react. She and I were together last night, just drinks and dinner and lots of conversation, but I had high hopes. I had the impression she was going to break off her relationship with Alan which would open the door for me. I guess I was wrong. Boy was I bloody wrong!"

"I'm not so sure," she said cautiously. "There's something really weird about all this. It might not be what it seems."

Suddenly he felt his phone vibrate in his pocket. "Damn," he said. "It was so late when I got home last night that I forgot to put it on the charger. I guess I was thinking about Marci, not the phone. Somehow the little sucker still has some juice left. He looked at it and saw that he had missed numerous messages and calls from Blake Sheldon. "Dave Wright speaking."

CHAPTER 53

t's Sheldon. Thank God you finally picked up. Dave, I've left messages for you everywhere, even at the shop. Where have you been? Did you get any of them?"

"No," Dave was agitated. "I didn't. Frankly, I've been a little busy. All hell's broken loose. What's so urgent?" He wasn't in the mood for a lecture.

"Have you talked to Savannah?"

"Yes, she's here with me now. Why?"

"Because I spoke to her earlier and told her that Alan Trent's a fraud. He's really a man named Peter Scant. He moved to Florida six years ago and is he's wanted by the police in several states for various crimes and misdemeanors."

"Oh Jesus," Dave moaned. "This day just keeps getting worse and worse. Savannah and I have been so busy trying to find Marci that we haven't had time to talk to each other."

"Well, the social security number Alan gave you belongs to this same

Peter Scant. And," he paused for effect. "The topper is that he's <u>not</u> Mrs. Trent's grandson. She never had any children."

"Yes, yes. I know that now. Savannah and I are here at Alan's house with Mrs. Trent's attorney, Steven Framin. He's already told us about that. But there's more. Did you know that Mrs. Trent died under mysterious circumstances two days ago?"

"Sadly no. I hadn't heard. Do you think Alan had anything to do with her death?"

"No. But we're thinking her butler, Pedro, was somehow involved. He's gone missing too, just like Alan and Marci."

"Hi, Sheldon. It's Savannah." She grabbed her father's phone and began talking. "There's been so much going on here that I haven't had a chance to tell Dad or Steven about Alan's checking account in Miami. I think it's significant in light of what we just discovered here."

"What do you mean?"

"This place is decked out like a wedding chapel, complete with rose petals and satin streamers. I think Marci married Alan here earlier today but they must have left in a big hurry because her wedding dress was all balled up and tossed on a chair. That's not at all like Marci." Savannah shook her head in disgust.

"Can you put Steven on the line, or push the speaker button?" Sheldon asked.

"Sure, you're on speaker now." Savannah answered.

"Steven, I don't know if you remember me, Sheldon Blake. We've met at several Bar Association functions over the years."

"Yes, of course," Steven answered. "Can you add any light to this bizarre situation?"

"I think so. My firm's private eye has been following the money trail and traced the funds Alan received from the sale of Mrs. Trent's jewelry to an account where the money eventually wound up."

"And?"

"And, those funds and other large amounts of money have been deposited over the last few months into a joint checking account at a Wells Fargo Bank branch in Miami. It belongs to Marci Morgan Trent and Alan A. Trent. Do you see the implications?"

"I certainly do. Sheldon. Let me explain the ramifications to Savannah and her father and I'm sure they'll be back in touch with you soon. Thanks for the information. It certainly adds clarification to the situation." He handed the phone back to Dave.

"Well, everyone," Steven said grimly. "I believe I know what's happened here. Although, how Alan managed to pull off this scam remains a mystery."

"Please explain," Savannah looked at Steven earnestly.

"Think about it," he said somberly, tapping his fingers nervously on the kitchen counter. "One day, a stranger comes into your store, represents himself as the grandson of a well-regarded Ft. Lauderdale socialite and spins a sad story to get you to sell the jewelry for him…jewelry, it seems, he's allegedly stole from her. Then he deposits the money in a bank in Miami instead of in Marjorie's account here in town. Clearly, he didn't have any intention of giving the money to her, so, he had to find a way to get his hands on it without directly implicating himself."

"I think I see where you're going," Savannah nodded.

"Well, I don't." Dave looked at his daughter in dismay. "What do you mean?"

"I'll answer for her." Steven jumped back in. "This is my theory. Let's suppose Alan withdraws the money that came from his illegal activities. If he's caught, he would be charged with theft and possession of stolen goods at a very minimum. If, however, he deposits the money in a joint account and the co-signer on the account, in this case, Marci, makes the withdrawal, she's the one who would be initially charged with grand theft. She would have to prove that she had no knowledge that the money was obtained illegally. By the time she did that, assuming she could, Alan may have fled the country."

Savannah had read about money laundering schemes like this in her detective stories so Steven's theory was plausible to her. "I believe that in Florida a wife can't be forced to testify against her husband. That's why Alan married Marci," she stated.

"But suppose she *wanted* to testify against him to clear her own name?" Dave said thinking out loud. "I know she would be appalled at what Alan has done and want to see him punished."

"Yes, and to keep her from testifying, he might threaten her or someone she cares about," Savannah worried.

"Exactly." Steven smiled. "You've got a logical mind Savannah. I'm glad we're on the same side." For the first time she noticed his sexy grin, strong jawline and twinkling milk chocolate eyes. *How had she not noticed before?*

She blushed at his flattering compliment. "Thank you."

"So, you think Alan married Marci to force her to retrieve the money?" Dave was appalled. "That bastard!"

"Yes, that's exactly what I think. I believe she's an innocent pawn. But I would further speculate that once he gets his hands on the cash, he'll have no more use for her …and then he'll kill her to keep her quiet."

"Oh my God! Your theory makes sense," Savannah said, devastated. "But how did he get Marci to go along with him in the first place? Why wouldn't she have simply refused to marry him?"

Dave stared into space for a few minutes, thinking. Then he turned to his daughter. "Alan must have threatened or maybe even drugged her to get her to go along with this crazy wedding." He looked around the room at Savannah and Steven. "We need to find her right away. If you're right, she's in terrible danger."

"We need to bring the police in on this now. We don't have the luxury of waiting to talk to Consuela first. The authorities need to know everything we do. Otherwise, we can be accused of withholding evidence. Enough of us all playing amateur detectives." Steven looked tense. "This is dangerous stuff and Marci is as much a victim of Alan's deceit as poor Marjorie."

"That's exactly what Sheldon and I will have to make the police understand. But we can't wait any longer. Think what we're keeping from them…Marjorie died under questionable circumstances and we suspect Pedro may have drugged or poisoned her. Her jewelry and art are missing and no report was ever filed or insurance claim made on her behalf. Alan or this Peter Scant has been masquerading as her grandson using fake identities and he probably coerced Marci to marry him. And to top it off, three people are missing now…Alan and Marci have gone off God knows where? And Pedro is in the wind. We have to report this."

Steven dialed 911. Minutes later he put his phone away and turned to Savannah and Dave. "The police are on the way. Let's go back to the main house and wait for them."

CHAPTER 54

Back at the main house, Savannah, her father and Steven waited impatiently for the police.

"I think we should set a trap for Alan," Savannah announced impulsively. "It's what Nancy Drew would do."

"Ah yes, the fake identity you tried to use with me," Steven said with a smile. "Sadly, for you, I was on to you because I grew up with three sisters and immediately recognized the name when you first used it. I wanted to see where you were going with it."

Dave smiled spontaneously at his impetuous daughter, the first real moment of levity he'd had all day. "What's your idea, Honey?"

"Well, it occurs to me that if Alan continues his pattern and frequently goes to Miami to collect his money from his apartment's mailbox, we should stake it out. We know where it is. And when he shows up, we'll be there waiting."

"What do you mean, we'll be waiting? Shouldn't we leave that to the police?" Dave didn't want Savannah involved with Alan any more than she already was. "Alan's a dangerous man, a possible murderer, and you're certainly not equipped to take him on."

The doorbell rang interrupting the conversation. Dave went to the front door expecting to find the police. Instead, an attractive dark haired woman stood there glaring at him, accompanied by to a shorter, stouter lady.

"We're here to see Steven Framin," the short woman explained. I'm his secretary, Laurie and I've brought Consuela with me as Mr. Framin requested."

"Come in Laurie." Steven called out to her from the living room, motioning for the two women to join him. "With all the excitement, I'd forgotten that I asked you two to come over. Hello Consuela."

"What now you want?" The nurse spoke in broken English. She was clearly not happy to have been summoned to the mansion. "Why you in *casa*? What wrong now? I not want be here. I miss Senorita Trent."

"Laurie, please ask Consuela to sit down and explain to her in Spanish that we have a few questions for her. Try to reassure her that she's not in any trouble," Steven said.

The secretary turned to Consuela and relayed the message. The nurse nodded a little too quickly, as if she had understood every word Steven had uttered.

Maybe her English was better than she's pretended? Savannah thought, remembering her earlier encounter with Consuela when the nurse supposedly couldn't understand anything Savannah said.

"A lot of Mrs. Trent's expensive jewelry and a few valuable paintings have disappeared from the main house," Steven explained to his secretary. "We'd like to know from Consuela if she knows anything about that and who might have taken them?"

Laurie translated again and listened to Consuela's rapid reply in Spanish.

"She says one day she came in to work and the pictures were gone. She doesn't know anything about the jewelry."

Consuela looked increasingly more uncomfortable, fidgeting and staring intently at her feet while the others talked. She appeared to be studying a spot on the carpet.

Steven had a sudden epiphany. "I think Pedro must be the one responsible for the missing items. That explains why no one reported their loss. Only he and Consuela would have known, so they must be in this together." He looked at Consuela. "But how did Alan end up with the jewelry?"

"Wait a minute!" Savannah practically leapt up from her seat. She was putting the puzzle pieces together in her mind. "Can you describe Pedro?" She turned to Steven. "Or would there be a picture of him around here? Please ask Consuela to describe him."

"He's a tall, nice looking man," Steven said. "Almost movie star handsome, but a little too slick for my taste."

Laurie questioned Consuela and the nurse told her that she thought Pedro was around forty and was a hard worker. She claimed that she couldn't remember the color of his eyes but his hair was blond and always messy. She did not think there were any pictures of him in the house. "Why would there be?" she asked Laurie. "Pedro is the butler, not family."

"Surely Mrs. Trent must have done a background check or made a copy of his driver's license before she hired him. That's standard practice now-a-days." Savannah said evenly, ignoring Consuela. "Steven, since you're her attorney, can you legally go through her files and see if you can find anything with Pedro's picture on it?"

"I can try," he answered. "Come with me to her office and we'll see what we can uncover."

Steve led Savannah to the back of the house where he opened the door to Marjorie's office. Inside was a dainty writing desk sitting in front of a wall of metal file cabinets, like you'd see in a busy doctor's office. The cabinets were labeled with brass plaques -- Personal, Taxes, Charities, Abandoned Kids, Household Expenses, *Pampered* and Employees.

"Bingo!" Savannah shouted, pointing to the employees' file.

Steven began by pulling out the top drawer and then the next and the next. He searched the folder headings looking for anything that had the word Pedro or household staff on it.

Savannah walked over to the room's built-in bookcase and began thumbing through the titles and photo albums on the lower shelf. Curious, she pulled out one that was leather-bound that had *Pampered* embossed in gold on the spine. She flipped through several pages and came to a page entitled "Crew of *Pampered*." There was a picture of the entire crew on the bow of the ship lined up for some kind of celebration. Everyone held champagne flutes. The names of all the crew were written under the photograph like a group shot in a yearbook. She looked at all the faces and tried to tie them to the names.

Suddenly she stopped short and screamed. "Steven, come here." She pointed to the crew picture and put her finger on one particular face. "Is this Pedro?" Her voice was quivering.

She pointed to a tall, handsome man standing in the back row wearing a *Pampered* crew tee shirt. He had an enormous grin on his face and a large red rose tattooed on his right forearm. "Is this Pedro?" she asked again anxiously.

"Let me see." He took the album and studied the photo carefully. "Yes, that's him. Why are you so upset?"

"Oh my gosh," Savannah choked on her words. "Now it makes perfect sense." She grabbed the album back from Steven and ran to the living room to find her father.

"Look Dad! Look at Pedro!" She pointed to the man in the last row. "What, or rather, <u>who</u> do you see?"

Dave studied the picture for just a second. "That's Alan Trent! So, Pedro and Alan are one and the same person," he shouted in disbelief. "And that means that Pedro is really Peter...the infamous Peter Scant."

"So, it would seem." Savannah barely dared to breathe. "All this time, Alan has been Mrs. Trent's butler. No wonder he had free access to the property and helped himself to her belongings. I wonder if she had any idea that he was going around town posing as her grandson?"

"I'm sure she did not." Steven said firmly in defense of his deceased client. "Marjorie is -- was -- a straight arrow and would never have allowed Pedro to do that. I mentioned to Savannah earlier that I thought Marjorie had been acting strangely, almost drug-like on several recent occasions when I visited here. Pedro never let me be alone with her, not even for a minute, so I could never ask her how she really was feeling or if anything was worrying her. I guess he was afraid of what she'd tell me." He paused for a moment gathering his thoughts. "If Pedro had been systematically drugging Marjorie, then he's probably drugging Marci too."

"That's the only way he'd get her to marry him." Savannah declared angrily. "Damn him!""I wish the police would get here." Dave paced around the room angrily. "Call them again."

Steven redialed 911 and the group kept talking. Laurie yawned and looked at her watch. She announced that if she wasn't needed for any-thing else, she'd like to go home. "I'll drive Consuela back to her place," she volunteered as she stood up to leave.

Savannah looked around the room and darted out into the foyer. The front door was wide open. Consuela was gone.

CHAPTER 55

Alan tapped in the combination and opened the safe in his closet. He withdrew all the cash, some papers and several passports issued in different names. Putting his arm around Marci to steady her, he led her to the door. "Let's go, Pretty Lady. I'm taking you to the doctor."

Marci rested her head heavily on his shoulder and allowed herself to be simultaneously pushed and dragged along the pathway past the main house and into the attached garage. Her head was throbbing viciously, and every time she moved it slightly, she had to fight off rolling waves of nausea. She'd do anything to avoid throwing up again. Her throat was raw and her ribs ached from the dry heaves. She wanted to crawl into the back seat of the car and sleep forever. She had never felt so awful in her entire life.

There were several cars parked in Mrs. Trent's driveway, which was unusual. Marci was too ill to pay any attention to them, but Alan did. As soon as he recognized Mrs. Trent's attorney's car and Savannah's, he knew there was no time to lose. He had to make a quick and silent escape.

He had no idea how many people were looking for him, but they had probably figured out by now what he'd done. He opened the side door into the garage, pushing and prodding Marci into the front seat of a blue Nissan. Then he pressed the garage door button on the wall and the enormous door began to silently roll up.

Jumping into the driver's seat, he released the emergency break and began to coast out of the garage and down the slight incline of the driveway. He was almost to the street before he dared turn on the engine. Looking in the rear-view mirror, he was relieved to see that his departure had not alerted anyone inside the main house. As he drove off the property and out of sight around the corner, he sighed with relief. If the wedding had happened a few minutes later, or Marci had thrown up one more time, he might have been caught. Luck had been on his side. Now all he needed was twenty-four hours to finish his plan and he and Consuela would be sailing off into the sunset. Finally, they would be living the carefree, luxurious life they'd dreamed about.

He glanced smugly over at Marci who was slumped against the passenger door and sound asleep with her head resting solidly against the window. She was snoring lightly.

At first, he had honestly enjoyed being with Marci. She was a very sensual woman and very exciting in bed. But from the moment he discovered her working at *Wrights*, and he realized how he could use her, she'd been nothing to him but a convenient means to an end…a way for him to pull off his jewelry scam.

This tiresome game of playing both Alan Trent and Pedro was almost over. After tomorrow, he would never have to see Marci again. He and Consuela could start their new life together in South America or anywhere they wanted. Money would never be a concern again. He planned to buy a yacht bigger and more luxurious than *Pampered* and live on it. This time he would not be a lowly crew member, washing down the decks and polishing the teak. He would be the wealthy owner, giving the orders and demanding that his needs be met. His days of working for others were over, thanks to his genius, Mrs. Trent's mounting dementia and Marci's gullibility.

He looked over at Marci's slumped body. Whether she lived or died would depend solely on what she did in the next twenty-four hours. It was all up to her. He didn't care one way or the other.

CHAPTER 56

'm Detective Burrata from the Fort Lauderdale Sherriff's department. And this is Detective Andrews. Are you Steven Framin – the man who called us?" The two detectives, dressed in street clothes, marched into the Trent foyer displaying their badges.

"Come in. We've been expecting you." Steven led them into the living room, where everyone else had gathered. "We think we've stumbled across several crimes, including a possible homicide and a kidnapping."

After introducing themselves to the two policemen, Dave and Savannah took seats and listened as Steven recounted the stories about Alan and Marci, their sudden disappearance and Alan's probable involvement in Marjorie Trent's death.

"That's quite a tale," Detective Burrata said after listening carefully and taking copious notes. During his ten years with the sheriff's department he'd heard a lot of stories, but this was one of the most unusual. He pulled out his phone, tapped some keys and spoke. "I just pulled up a recording of the original 911 call the butler made the night of

Mrs. Trent's death and a summary of her autopsy report here. I see it just came in."

"Does the report support our theory that Mrs. Trent was drugged or poisoned?" Steven was curious to see if his theory was right.

"Read it for yourself." The detective handed him his phone. "It's all in the toxicology findings."

Detective Burrata looked at Savannah and her father. "To put it in layman's terms, Mrs. Trent was found to have ingested large amounts of Xanax and Valium. It's a dangerous combination and can cause severe disorientation and hallucinations. The victim's actual cause of death was from a traumatic brain injury sustained from a fall. But did she fall or was she pushed? That's the question."

"If she was drugged and disorientated, that would explain why Alan was able to manipulate her into giving him her safe's combination so he could help himself to her jewelry whenever he wanted." Savannah said with disgust. "What a horrible, depraved man."

"Yes, he is," Dave agreed. "But, what should we do now?"

"You all do *nothing*," Detective Burrata said firmly. "This is a law enforcement matter now. We appreciate your help, but we'll take over from here. I'll keep you informed. But now leave the detective work to us."

He spoke crisply into a microphone clipped to his lapel and called for a backup team.

"We'll assign a case number to your complaints. My deputies will begin searching both the main and guest houses for clues. I know you've all been in there and touched things, so the crime scene has definitely been compromised. With any luck we can still find some evidence to implicate Alan and discover where he's taken your friend."

"Are we free to leave now?" Dave asked impatiently. He wasn't convinced that the police would do everything necessary to find Marci and he was anxious to continue the search for her himself. He felt foolish standing around doing nothing when she was in danger.

The detective stood up and approached Dave. "My partner will talk to each of you individually to take your statements, and then you can go. In the meantime, I'll put out an electronic APB out on Alan Trent and Marci Morgan. If we're lucky, they won't get far. Do you have any recent pictures of them?"

"Marci Morgan Trent," Dave corrected the officer stiffly. "I'm sure Marci thinks she's Mrs. Alan Trent now. But," he was thinking out loud. "If Alan married her using a fraudulent last name, wouldn't it nullify the marriage?"

"Yes, you're absolutely correct," Steven agreed. "And that's the good news. She's definitely not married, but unfortunately the bad news is she may not realize it."

"How about those pictures?" the detective asked again. "I'll need them."

"Here." Savannah pulled out her phone and texted several pictures of Marci from their recent Vegas trip to him. Then she pointed to the *Pampered* album on the coffee table and identified Alan/Pedro/ as the missing butler.

"I hope you catch the son of a bitch and hang him out to dry," Dave seethed. Savannah and Steven nodded in agreement.

CHAPTER 57

Detective Andrews questioned Steven first. "Why were you at the Trent house today?"

"I came to inventory the artwork and furniture. I'm the attorney for her estate."

"And were you expecting Mr. Wright and his daughter?"

"No. Not at all. Today is the first time I've met either one of them."

"Why were they here then?" The detective persisted.

Steven explained about Savannah's concerns about Alan and her earlier attempt to meet with Mrs. Trent to question her…when Savannah pretended to be a US Census taker. She had not been permitted to see Mrs. Trent at the time because Consuela prevented the meeting. Today Savannah made another attempt, but this time, she ran into me. I have to give her points for tenacity."

Detective Andrews's face was passive, but he was writing everything down.

"I informed Savannah that Mrs. Trent had passed away a few days ago and that I heard the circumstances of her death were suspicious.

One thing led to another and we just kept talking, trying to figure out what might have happened."

"Was Mr. Wright with her?"

"No, he arrived shortly after Savannah did. But he didn't know she was here. He came here hoping to find Marci and Alan. He had no luck and was about to leave when through the picture window he saw Savannah and I talking in the living room."

"Pretty coincidental," the detective murmured. "It seems a lot of people are playing 'NCIS' around here. Is there anything else you can tell me?"

"I don't think so, Detective Andrews. I believe you have all the facts as I know them. I will add though, that I think Mr. Wright and Savannah are honorable people and they're telling the truth. They are both terribly concerned about their friend Marci and aren't involved with Alan and his alleged illegal activities in any way. We all hope you're able to find her quickly. And another thing, *Wrights* has a good reputation in the community and any perceived involvement in anything untoward could ruin their business. It's imperative that they be exonerated from any wrongdoing."

"I hope they will be," he answered. "Thank you for your time. Will you ask Mr. Wright to come in please? And then you can go."

Dave walked into the room and quietly began answering Detective Andrews questions. He was frustrated by how much time was being wasted while Marci was in danger.

He glanced outside at the huge yacht sitting regally in the water and thought that it would be the perfect place for Alan to hide Marci. The police would be busy searching the main and guest houses. It would never occur to them to look for her on the boat. Everyone assumed Alan had taken her away with him and that the two were on the run. But Dave wasn't so sure. He had noticed Consuela's reaction to the picture of Pedro and that made him suspect that Alan and Consuela might be romantically involved and in this scam, together. It would be logical as they were the only ones on the property and were living in the house with Mrs. Trent. They controlled everything that was going on there. If Consuela was an innocent party, why had she run away? Had she gone to the boat to warn Alan that the police were on to his real identity? Dave needed answers. Then he'd let the police deal with Alan and Consuela -- but not before he'd taken Marci safely home with him.

Finally, it was Savannah's turn to answer questions. She stood anxiously on one foot and then the other, wanting to help the detective, but finding Marci was her only concern. She didn't care about Mrs. Trent's jewelry, just Marci's safety.

"Ms. Wright, do you have anything to add to what Mr. Framin or your father told us earlier?"

"Not really," Savannah said thoughtfully. "I think we've told you everything we know and what we suspect. But there's one thing that's always puzzled me."

"And that would be?"

"When Alan first came into my father's store, he bought an expensive brooch supposedly for his grandmother and paid for it in cash. He pulled out fifty-five thousand dollars, in one-hundred-dollar bills from his briefcase. The next day he came back and spent another twenty-three thousand on a matching ring, and again paid for it with one-hundred-dollar bills. I keep wondering why the cash? It was bound to raise eyebrows."

"Yes, but if he was hoping to pull your friend Marci into his plan, he would have taken the risk. Typically, behavior like that suggests a money laundering scheme of some sort. The perpetrator gets large amounts of cash from illegal sources and then hides the money by purchasing legitimate material goods like jewelry, real estate, boats and cars. Later, he'll sell those items and pocket the "clean" money. In my experience, the money eventually shows up in a foreign bank account, in places like Morocco or the Cayman Islands, for instance."

"Do you think that's what Alan did?" She was intrigued. Savannah certainly wouldn't put it past him.

"I can't say yet, but the first place to start looking is at his bank account here."

"Our family attorney, Sheldon Blake, can help you with that. He had his firm's private investigator check out Alan's finances. He discovered a new checking account at Wells Fargo Bank, titled in both his and Marci's names. I'll give you Sheldon's contact information."

"That would be helpful. Thank you for your time. I'll follow up with Mr. Blake."

Savannah shook hands with the detective and went to join her father and Steven. She was tired of the endless, repetitive questions and wanted answers instead.

"Are you ready to go?" Steven asked her. "It's been a long day and I've had enough excitement for a while."

"Yes, let's get out of here, but where's Dad?"

"Your father tore out of here as soon as Detective Andrews finished with him. He said he had an idea where Marci might be and he'd call you later. I tried to stop him but he was like a man possessed. I'm beginning to think that he cares for Marci on a personal level, more than a boss for his employee."

Savannah nodded in agreement. "Although it's hard for me to accept, especially given their age difference, I think you're right. And her disappearance has upset him greatly."

"Would you like to get a quick dinner with me? I'm starved and Marjorie's scotch is beginning to go to my head."

"Yes, I'd like that." Savannah smiled shyly. "My car is parked around the block. Where should we meet?"

CHAPTER 58

D ave didn't care what the police thought about him contaminating a possible crime scene. His only thought was to rescue Marci. He was determined to free her from that sociopath, Alan Trent or whatever his real name was.

After answering Detective Burrata questions he ran out of the main house and dashed across the lush back lawn to the dock. No one tried to stop him. Breathless and perspiring, adrenaline pumping through his body, he stopped in front of the gangplank and looked up and down the dock. It was deserted. He tossed off his loafers so he could move silently about the yacht and climbed aboard to the aft deck.

He was momentarily stunned by the sheer beauty of the boat. Every surface gleamed. He noticed a large dining table surrounded by twelve blue and white striped canvas chairs. A bowl of sumptuous fresh fruit sat in the middle of it next to a stack of blue and white appetizer plates and a pair of fruit shears. A bucket of champagne was on ice by the sideboard. Dave could easily imagine the extravagant meals that had been served to guests in this spectacular setting. And from appearances, it looked like *Pampered* was expecting guests once again...and very soon.

He moved to the sliding glass doors which opened automatically as he approached them. Stepping inside the luxurious main salon, he noted the tasteful décor, complete with several large sofas, four swivel chairs and a huge flat screen television. The walls were covered in expensive nautical artwork. On the port side, he saw an onyx step-down wet bar with eight leather bar stools. It was completely stocked and would provide guests with a variety of cocktails and beautiful scenic views once the boat was underway. Dave noticed that there were nuts, olives, maraschino cherries and little pearl onions set out in Waterford crystal bowls atop the bar. Someone was planning on taking a trip, fortified with lots of cocktails.

Dave moved cautiously through the salon and out to the spacious foyer at mid ship. A huge spiral glass and steel staircase and an elevator were visible on the left and on the right was an exit door to the wraparound main deck. Creeping forward cautiously, he came to the owner's cabin which was separated from the rest of the hallway by double frosted-glass doors. He gently turned the nob and the doors slid open silently.

Stepping into an office area, he saw a massive desk holding three computers, a printer, nautical maps and assorted files. He scanned the desktop, looking for anything that would help him figure out where Alan was planning to go. At the bottom of a pile of papers, he found a colorful brochure and began reading an advertisement for the Westin Grand Cayman Hotel. It showed the beautiful resort and bragged about its seven-mile beach and private spa. Dave shoved the pamphlet in his pocket. Was Alan planning to take Marci there on the boat?

He remembered from *The Firm,* an early John Grisham novel, that the Cayman Islands boasted of having no corporate taxes, no capital gains and no withholding taxes. It was a perfect place for Alan to deposit his money and hide out. Dave was feeling energized by his discovery and more hopeful that Marci was somewhere onboard *Pampered.*

He kept moving. On the right, there were three oversized windows overlooking the dock. He ducked down quickly and crawled forward on his knees so that he could not be seen by anyone standing on shore. Once past the windows, he stood up cautiously and entered into the large stateroom with its over-sized port holes facing away from the Trent house. The room contained a built-in king size bed with a heavy quilted bedspread, a leather headboard and dozens of decorative pillows. There was also an enormous sofa, a huge flatscreen television and twinkling lights mounted in the ceiling to give a starry night effect.

Much to Dave's disappointment, Marci was not in there. He sighed and continued into the bathroom with its own steam shower and hot rock sauna. But that was empty too. If Alan had hidden Marci onboard, she was not in the luxurious owner's accommodations. He realized he needed to go below and search the guest rooms and the crew quarters. Maybe Alan had locked her in one of them. As he was leaving, he saw a black thong lying on the floor in the corner. Did it belong to Consuela or to Marci? He didn't dare touch the skimpy underwear. It might be evidence. Also, he didn't know Marci well enough to know what kind of panties she preferred.

Putting the thong out of his mind, he dashed to the staircase in the foyer and taking the steps two at a time, barreled down them. He was no longer afraid of being seen or heard. He would handle whatever happened if he was discovered. He was desperate to find Marci.

CHAPTER 59

Savannah followed Steven to the Seasons 52 restaurant in the Galleria Mall. They both valet-parked their cars and went inside together.

"I'd like an iced tea to start," Savannah said to the waitress.

"Me too," Steven agreed. He's had enough scotch. "And can you bring us a margarita flatbread to start and your grilled artichokes?" he asked the server politely. "We're both starved."

Once they settled in with their drinks, Steven studied Savannah carefully. She was an extremely attractive woman. He felt lucky to be sitting across the table from her. His law practice kept him so busy that that he had little time for socializing. He was about to change that.

"I want to learn more about you and your family business," he began. "But first, what do you make of the nurse, Consuela? Did you get a sense she knows more about what's going on than she's admitted?"

"I do think she knows more than she's saying. She was awfully nervous when we started asking about Pedro. And what's with her English? When I first met her, she spoke in choppy broken phrases, but today she seemed to understand completely everything we said. I bet she's fluent in English."

"Yes, I noticed that. In my past dealings with her, language was always difficult. That's why I asked Laurie to interpret. Do you think it's possible she and Alan planned this scam together? That they're partners in crime...and maybe in real life?"

"Hmm. I guess it's possible. At least it's as good a theory as any at the moment. What I don't understand is why no one on Mrs. Trent's payroll ever called him out? I mean, it was a large staff. *No one* was ever suspicious of him? Sure, at the end, Pedro and Consuela were the only staff left, but what about the earlier years? How did he get away with stealing the artwork and jewelry, and no one alerted the police?"

Savannah put on her Nancy Drew hat and looked pensive. "If I was writing a story about this, I think I'd make the staff all undocumented workers. They would be paying Alan to keep quiet, to protect them, and Alan in turn would have exerted tremendous leverage over them. He could have reported them to Immigration with one phone call."

"That's a stretch," he laughed. "But I suppose it could be true."

She nibbled on a piece of flatbread and then speculated some more. "Wasn't Alan acting as Pedro in charge of hiring and supervising of the staff?"

"Yes, that's what I understand. Marjorie pretty much let him manage the whole estate," Steven said.

"Well, what if he deliberately hired only people without their green cards? That way he could force them to do his bidding. Like I said, he probably held the threat of deportation over their heads like a Herculean sword."

"It's entirely possible, especially in this town." Steven answered. "In my experience, numerous people in south Florida are here illegally. I'm sure unscrupulous people take advantage of them in untold ways...Alan probably being one."

"Well then, if my theory is even halfway correct, shouldn't I call Detective Burrata and tell him what I think?" Savannah asked.

"Not without some proof. He didn't seem too receptive to us getting further involved in his investigation. Let's put Alan/Pedro out of our minds for a while and enjoy our dinner. Can we do that?"

"Sure, but just one more thing." Once Savannah had an idea, she would not let it go. "I know this might sound farfetched, but suppose Alan was also working on another scam at the same time. Follow me here," she smiled. "Suppose Alan intentionally *only* hired undocumented workers to staff the house and then extracted money from each of them to keep immigration officials away. In the years he worked at the mansion, he could have accrued quite a vast sum to use as his own personal slush fund. For one thing, he drives a flashy red Porsche. That would explain the large amounts of cash he carried around...and he certainly could not afford a Porsche on his salary as a butler. Every time I saw him, he was always well-dressed and carried a very expensive briefcase. He had to get the money from someplace other than his salary.

"Think about it," Savannah continued, her eyes bright with excitement. "When the estate was running at its best, Mrs. Trent employed an enormous staff -- chefs, housekeepers, gardeners, handymen, etcetera. Let's imagine that if, when Pedro hired them, he demanded each one pay him even $75 a month from their wages, the amount would add up quickly. *Pampered* alone carried at crew of twenty until very recently.

If this blackmailing scheme has been operating for many years, Alan would have accumulated a small fortune -- on top of what he's stolen!"

Steven was impressed. "I have to admit, you really do have a detective's mindset or a very ripe imagination. Maybe you should quit the jewelry business and write crime novels. Either way, I find you charming and funny." He raised his iced tea. "To the next –" His cell phone rang before he could finish his toast.

"Hello," he sighed. "This is Steven Framin."

"It's Detective Burrata. I'm letting you know that we've finished our initial investigation of the premises and we found something very interesting. There was a large open bottle of drinking water sitting on the guest house kitchen counter."

"Yes, I remember seeing it in that God-awful wedding set-up."

"Well, it had a funny odor and unless I miss my guess, the lab will find some kind of drugs in the bottle. I bet they will match those found in Mrs. Trent's body at her autopsy."

"Thank you for letting me know, Detective." Steven disconnected the call and looked at Savannah with genuine concern. "I don't know how much water your friend drank at that 'wedding' of hers, but let's hope it wasn't a lethal amount."

"Why, what do you mean – a lethal amount?"

"That was Detective Burrata on the phone, "Steven explained. "And he thinks there was poison in the water bottle they found in the guest house. I hope Marci didn't drink too much of it, or she could get very sick." He didn't say 'or *she could die*,' but he was thinking it.

CHAPTER 60

Marci clutched the small, chipped bathroom sink and splashed cold water on her face. Reaching for the thin facecloth, she dried off and stared in the mirror, hardly recognizing her own reflection. Her normally sparkling green eyes were dull and underscored in brown and her skin had a grayish tone. She looked and felt like she had a terrible case of the flu. Her entire body ached, even her tongue seemed swollen. She was unbelievably tired. Every movement took enormous effort. Slowly turning away from the mirror, she gingerly made her way back to the safety of the sagging bed and collapsed onto the thin mattress, pulling the cheap bedspread over herself. She was freezing and shaking violently. Reaching her hand up to feel her forehead for a fever, she noticed a wedding band. *What the hell? Where did that come from?*

Her memory was foggy. She had no idea where she was. Looking around the dingy, unfamiliar motel room she struggled to recall how she'd gotten there. Fighting to remain awake, she tried to remember the events of the last few hours. She knew that Alan had driven her to this run-down motel and then left her. But why?

Falling in and out of consciousness, she vaguely recalled flower pedals lying over the floor of a chapel, the sickening odor from dozens of flowers and white satin ribbons. Where would she have seen that? She pinched herself to stay awake and remember more details. Her mind wandered. She couldn't focus. Her head throbbed. Her eyeballs felt like they had been scratched with sandpaper. What was the matter with her? How had she gotten so sick?

She pressed her hands against her eyes and remembered leaving the guest house and getting into a car with Alan. Not the Porsche but something else. He had promised to take her to a doctor, but instead he'd driven to this motel. She thought she'd seen the Miami Airport tower in the distance from the car window. As if to prove her memory was correct, a loud jet flew low over the motel room, vibrating the walls and shaking the furniture. And a few seconds later there was another, and then another. She was obviously somewhere in the airport's final approach pattern. *What was she doing at the Miami airport? And where on earth was Alan?* She was still so disoriented. Nothing seemed real…except for the damn wedding band on her ring finger.

Marci knew she needed to get away from this place before Alan came back. She looked again with disgust at the wedding ring and tried to yank it off, but the chore required too much of effort. She started to cry.

Finally, drying her eyes, she looked wearily around the dismally furnished room and saw the door. It was only a few feet away from the foot of the bed. If she could make it to the outside, she could find someone to help her. The chore seemed daunting but she had to try. Using all her energy, she rolled to the side of the bed and forced herself to stand up. Dizzy at first, she took a few deep breaths and was able to make her feet work. Taking one tiny step at a time, she moved ever so slowly toward freedom. Her hand finally touched the door handle. She gratefully began to twist it.

Alan pushed his way into the room. "Where do you think you're going?" He hissed angrily at her. "I told you to stay in bed and wait for me."

"I. I," Marci hesitated. She was frightened by the cruelty in his voice and the anger she saw on his face. "I wanted to get some fresh air. This room is so stuffy. I'm feeling sick in here."

He softened a little. "Yes, I admit, the AC here is not great." He took her by the hand and led her back to the bed. "Marci, you need to rest. You've been very sick. I went to the motel office to buy us some drinks from the soda machine. You need to keep hydrated. This dump doesn't have room service." He handed her an open Coke bottle and took a sip from his own.

"Alan," she whined. "I want to go home. I don't like it here."

"We'll go soon, my love. Drink up and take a nap first. When you're feeling better, we'll leave. Remember the doctor said you had to rest and drink lots of liquids."

The doctor? She thought anxiously. She didn't remember seeing a doctor.

Marci didn't have the strength to argue with him. She was too tired and very thirsty, but some inner alarm went off. The coke bottle he'd handed her had already been opened. She faintly remembered all the water he'd made her drink at the guest house and how awful she'd felt afterwards. Instinctively, she turned her back to him and pretended to take a few sips.

"I'm really tired," she said wearily as she lay down and feigned falling asleep.

Alan was furious at himself for leaving the drugged water bottle back in the guest house. He needed it now to keep Marci quiet and compliant until it was time to go to the bank. Luckily, he had some Ambien stashed in the glove compartment of his car. He'd been able to dissolve a few of the potent sleeping pills in Marci's soda. She would sleep until the morning. That would give him time to pick up Consuela and finish up the arrangements he'd made for their escape.

When Marci awoke, he would take her to the bank, get her to withdraw all the money in their account and wire it out of the country. Then he'd be on his way to the Caymans with Consuela and Marci would be left in Fort Lauderdale to deal with the police.

Believing her to be asleep, he gathered up the few things he'd brought into the room earlier, carefully wiped off the door handle and the bedside lamp, removing his fingerprints with his handkerchief. He picked up the two coke bottles. Without a backward glance at his sleeping bride, he headed to his car. He was 24 hours from paradise.

CHAPTER 61

D ave searched every inch of every room and cabin on the boat. He even went into the engine room in hopes of finding Marci. There was no sign she had been there.

He finally realized he was alone on the yacht. But if his theory was right… that Alan was planning to take Marci away, then he had to stash her somewhere else until he was ready to leave. From what he saw, it was obvious the boat had been stocked and provisioned for a long trip soon. The fruit would rot and the champagne would get warm if not consumed soon.

Dave was thirsty and opened the galley refrigerator looking for a water bottle or a soda. He noticed shelves full of fresh vegetables and produce. The freezer was likewise stocked handsomely with roasts, steaks and chops. There was enough food there to cater a banquet. Whoever was traveling on this yacht would be well wined and dined

Discouraged that he had not found Marci, he got ready to leave the boat when he heard voices coming from outside on the deck. Alarmed, he looked for a way to escape. The gangplank was situated aft and he'd be in clear sight of anyone standing on that side of the deck. He was trapped in the main salon. Scrunching down behind one of the sofas, he hoped the men would move to the front of the boat so he could escape unseen out the back.

In a few minutes he heard one of the voices say. "Captain, Pedro told me to go to Miami and bring the crew back here. They'll sleep onboard tonight and tomorrow afternoon, we'll take off. Will you be bunking on board tonight too?"

"Yes, I have all the charting and docking arrangements to do. I'll be in my quarters. When the head stew arrives, send her to my cabin. I'll go over the cruise details with her."

The other man said something, but Dave couldn't make out the words. He went to the gangplank and left the boat. The captain walked forward to inspect some lines and then went up to the bridge.

It was Dave's chance to escape. He dashed to the aft deck and hurled himself down the gangplank, not stopping to retrieve his shoes from the dock. He glanced around apprehensively. Apparently, everyone including the police had left. He dashed across the yard to his car. Disappointed that he had not found Marci, he was nonetheless confident that he knew where Alan was taking her. In as many days as it took for *Pampered* to make the voyage, she'd be at the Westin Hotel in the Grand Caymans. He planned to be there waiting.

CHAPTER 62

Savannah had been serious about staking out the apartment building's lobby in Miami. She knew that at some point Alan would have to show up there to get his money. Detective Burrata had emphatically told her to leave the investigation up to the police, but inaction was not in her genes. She wanted to catch the lying bastard herself and see that he got punished for what he'd done to Marci and to Mrs. Trent. The only question was… should she go on the stakeout alone, take her dad or ask Steven to come along?

The next morning, after a restless night, Dave stood morosely by the office door surveying the empty showroom. It was ten o'clock. Savannah had not come in, and there had been no customers. Was it possible that rumors of *Wrights* illegal involvement in selling Mrs. Trent's jewelry had already reached the Fort Lauderdale gossip mill? But how could anyone possibly know about it yet? The police had not released any statements and no reporters had picked up on the story. Marjorie Trent's death had not even been announced, for now.

But much more important to him was Marci's continued absence. He wanted to alert the police to his theory that Alan would soon be taking off on the yacht with Marci, but he had no real proof to back up his claim. All he had was the brochure he'd found in the office of the master stateroom – and he'd have a hard time explaining *that* without also admitting to trespassing on the yacht. The police had warned all of them yesterday about staying out of the investigation. Still, an anonymous call to the precinct couldn't hurt. He started to dial the number but stopped, thinking he should ask Savannah to go with him back to the yacht and wait for Alan and Marci there. In case that didn't work out, he'd book a flight to the Caymans for himself.

Sheldon Blake slammed down his desk phone in frustration. He'd just finished talking with Steven Framin, caught him up on all the bizarre happenings at the Trent house. He was infuriated about Alan/Pedro's criminal behavior and worried about Dave Wright's angry reaction. He sensed his old friend had strong feelings for Marci. He said as much on the phone. Dave had waited a long time since losing his beloved wife to feel so strongly about someone else. It would be grossly unfair if he then lost her too. Where was the justice in this world?

Detective Burrata accidentally dripped some coffee on the police report he was reading and tried to mop it up with his tie. He had hoped to have developed some solid leads by now as to Peter Scants whereabouts. An APB had gone out hours ago, but no one had reported seeing him or Marci. The usually active anonymous tip line on the nearby desk had remained mostly silent. A few people had called in citing a person of Marci's description snorkeling in the Keys, browsing in a book shop in Boca Raton and shopping on Worth Avenue in Palm Beach. None of the tips had proven to be valid.

The detective continued to stare at the phone, willing it to ring. A little while later came a whispered and obviously disguised voice. "There's a woman in room #9 at the Seaside Motel off I95 in Miami. I think she's the one you're looking for. She came with a dude earlier this evening but he's gone now. How much is the reward? Where can I get it?"

"There's no reward at this time. I'm sorry, but thank you for the information. Please keep your eye on that lady. The police are on their way. You may have saved her life. That should be reward enough."

———————

Steven paced nervously around his office wondering whether or not to call Savannah. He had been very taken with her yesterday and intrigued with her theories about Alan. He wanted to see her again, but knew she was overwhelmed by the disappearance of her best friend. After going back and forth about it for another ten minutes, he thought, *what the hell* and decided to call her. However, he didn't get the chance. His secretary's voice came over the intercom. "Mr. Framin a miss Savannah Wright is on line one and asking to speak to you. Are you in, Sir?"

"Hell, yes," he answered a bit too quickly. "I most certainly am."

———————

Marci lay perfectly still on the bed, afraid to move in case Alan returned and found her awake. He would know instantly that she had tricked him, and not drunk the soda. She didn't dare move a muscle for a full ten minutes. When she finally felt it was safe, she carefully stood up again and slowly, on wobbly legs, made her way to the dingy motel window. She sighed with relief. There were no automobiles in the parking lot. Alan had evidently gone left. To her left she noticed the blinking neon "Vacancy" sign, and behind it, a small shack-like structure that looked like the motel's office. Surely if she could make it to there, someone inside would help her.

———————

Alan sped along the airport access road happily congratulating himself on the cleverness of his scheme and for getting away with robbery and murder. He thought about everything he and Consuela had done over the last few years to get to this place. They were so close to the end. He could taste victory.

Marjorie Trent had been a perfect target for them…a wealthy grand dame, lonely and in desperate need of attention. He had filled that need and pretended to be devoted to her. At first, he was hired as her butler, but he soon maneuvered his way into her affections and she appointed him as the estate manager. He soon became her confident and best friend.

She allowed him free rein to run the place. She had been an easy person to control. *Not like Marci*, he thought bitterly.

Over the seven years that he'd worked at the mansion, he'd been able to successfully isolate Mrs. Trent from her friends and made her completely dependent on Consuela and himself. With the help of daily doses of valium stirred into her food every day, she became groggy and forgetful. The more disoriented she became, the more she trusted and needed him…and the more he and Consuela took advantage of her possessions and checkbook. Early into his employment, he had hired his girlfriend, Consuela, as Mrs. Trent's nurse. The two ran the estate together and controlled every aspect of their employer's life. Alan hired only undocumented workers and devised a plan to regularly collect money from every one of them in return for promising to keep their immigration status a secret. That was only the beginning of building his fortune. He cemented their loyalty by rewarding them with lighter work schedules, extra days off, and interceding on their behalf with Mrs. Trent, if there was ever a problem. They worshiped him. But what he worshipped was the old lady's money…very single dime of it.

Alan hummed to himself. Everything had gone perfectly. Now all he had to do was circle back for Consuela and retrieve the latest batch of money from his illegal sales at his Collins Avenue mailbox. Renting that apartment had been a stroke of genius. By renting the small unit in a high-rise building in a nice section of town, he would appear legitimate to any of the jewelry or art brokers doing business with him. After he signed the lease, he never spent a night in the apartment. It had stayed empty all this time. He went to the mailbox regularly to collect his checks, usually late at night or early in the morning before the building's concierge arrived for duty.

Alan looked at the dashboard clock. It was time to pick up Consuela and then return to the motel for Marci. He'd put enough Ambien in her coke to keep her asleep for many hours. When he was ready, he would get her sobered up quickly to complete the transactions at the bank. Her pretty face would be caught on the video cameras and her signature would be on all the paperwork. By the time the police figured everything out, he and Consuela would be long gone, *Wrights* reputation would be ruined and Marci would be stuck with all the blame.

CHAPTER 63

Savannah and Steven drove to Miami. They chatted amiably, enjoying each other's company and discovering that they liked many of the same things. They exchanged their stories --Savannah told him about her Fort Lauderdale childhood, her brief early marriage, about joining the family business at *Wrights*.

Steve shared stories about his teenage years in a tough area of Brooklyn and how he'd learned to protect himself from street thugs that terrorized the neighborhood. He showed her a scar on his left arm where he'd been slashed with a knife by someone trying to rob him. He'd left New York for college, where he had excelled and attended Harvard Law School. After graduation he'd been recruited by his present firm, one of the largest law practices in South Florida and never regretted leaving the northeast climate behind. They were having such a good time that they almost forgot about the seriousness of their mission.

"I'm all for adventures," Steven said once the conversation refocused. The tiny lines around his brown eyes crinkled when he concentrated.

"But I don't think we've really thought this stake-out business through carefully enough. What we're doing is pretty impulsive and maybe down-right dangerous. Alan's a wanted man now, remember, and I'm sure he won't hesitate to hurt us if he feels trapped. If he did murder Marjorie, he'll have nothing to lose by killing us too."

"I know, but I don't plan on confronting him. I only want to snap a good picture of him emptying out his mailbox. Since that's the end of the money trail, the photo should be evidence of his guilt and if the police can prove the box contains money from the sale of stolen goods, that should nail him."

"That's a big if. How do you plan to take his picture without Alan seeing you?" He looked skeptical. "I think we should take Detective Burrata's advice and leave the police work to the cops."

"What fun is that?" She frowned and tapped him playfully on his arm. "I'm hoping that we can hide so he won't even know we're there. If we're lucky we can go in and check out the place before he arrives. My idea might not work, but for Marci's sake, I feel I have to try. Seriously, Steven, I was the one who brought her into the store to work and that's where she met Alan, so I feel this whole thing is my fault."

"That's ridiculous. You're not responsible for the corrupt morals of the customers who come into *Wrights*. That's absurd."

"I know. Logically you're right, but I feel responsible, nonetheless. I have to do something to help catch Alan. Besides, I'm hoping he'll bring Marci with him. If he does, we can snatch her."

"No. I think we have to avoid personally confronting him. That's the cops' job. I'm not sure how you think this will play out, but I've put Detective Burrata's number in my speed dial, just in case we need back up."

She sighed. "Whatever it takes to put Alan behind bars."

They pulled into the apartment building's parking circle and looked around. Diagonally across the street there was a small strip mall. Savannah could make out signs for a Chinese restaurant, a pet groomer and a dry cleaner. It was early enough that the dry cleaner was open.

"Let's park over there," she suggested. "I don't see Alan's car. We can go inside and see if there's any place to hide and still have an unobstructed view of the tenants' mailboxes."

He pushed open the car door and watched in amusement as Savannah pulled her wig out of her purse. "Very fetching," he kidded dryly. "So now you're a red head? Did you get that in a Nancy Drew spy kit?"

"Never mind," she snickered. "You can make fun of me if you want, but this wig and I go back a long way. I'm empowered by it, like some *men* are by Superman capes."

"Well, I don't need a cape to confess that I think that you're quite an amazing woman and I'm very glad that we met, even under these unusual circumstances." He gently took her hand and led her across the street to the apartment's front door entrance.

They walked inside and found themselves in a small but tasteful lobby. A concierge desk was directly ahead. On the far left side was a wall holding about sixty mail boxes.

Savannah nudged Steven. "Go kneel behind the desk and see if you can see me? I'll go to the boxes. Will you be able to get a clear camera shot from there?"

"I think so, as long as the concierge doesn't appear and want his desk." He crouched down and called out to her. "Savannah, I can see you. Alan is much taller than you, so we should be able to get a full head shot of him from here if we do it quickly."

She looked outside through the door and instantly rushed to his side. "I saw a man getting out of a car in the parking lot," she whispered. "And he looks like Alan! There's someone with him but I can't tell if it's Marci. I guess we're about to find out. Do you have your camera ready?"

"All set." He pulled out his cell phone and pushed the camera app. They crouched down behind the concierge desk. Steven dialed Detective Burrata.

"It's Steven Framin," he whispered hastily. "Savannah and I are inside the lobby of the Cannaught apartment building on Collins Avenue that Alan uses as his address. It looks like he's about to come inside and someone's sitting in his car in the parking lot out front. We can't tell if it's Marci. We're trying to get a picture of him emptying his mailbox."

"Shit," the detective stammered. "I told you to leave this to the police. I'm on my way. Don't do anything stupid. And for God's sake, don't try to apprehend him yourself."

Amateurs, Steven thought he heard Burrata swear angrily to himself. *Why can't they let us do our jobs?*

CHAPTER 64

Marci left the motel room and inched slowly along the building's concrete block wall, leaning against it for support. She felt a bit stronger than earlier in the day, but feared that any strong gust of wind would blow her over. At least her head had stopped throbbing and the relentless waves of nausea had slowed. Her muscles still ached ferociously. She was very thirsty but hadn't dared take a drink from the soda bottle Alan had given her. Once she entered the motel office, she'd ask for some water. Keeping her eyes focused on the office she slowly made her way there.

She was about to push open the door, when she several police cars came flying down the street with flashing lights and sirens blaring. Something bad must be happening somewhere, she thought. Normally she would be curious, but not today; she had her own problems.

"Excuse me," Marci said softly as she pushed open the door and entered the motel office. "I'm so thirsty. Could I trouble you for some water, please?" She collapsed in a metal chair by the registration counter. "I'm sorry to intrude. I'm not feeling well."

The young clerk looked at her with concern and handed her a plastic bottle of cold water. "Here drink this. It'll make you feel better. You're staying here, aren't you? I registered you and your husband last night."

"My husband?" Marci was confused and tried to shake the cobwebs from her brain. Then she looked at her finger and the sparkling diamond engagement ring and matching wedding band. The sight jolted her back to reality. *Did I really marry Alan? And why didn't he take me to the doctor as he promised, instead of bringing me to this seedy airport motel?* She shook her head trying to make sense of it.

"I don't know where my husband is," Marci said forlornly. "I think he may have changed his mind about our marriage and abandoned me here." Then she remembered the coke bottle and her fear that he'd drugged her. "I'm so confused. Can I use your phone? I must have misplaced mine." She did not remember giving it to Alan back at the Trent house.

The clerk handed her his phone and she hastily dialed Savannah's number. The call went straight to voicemail. Frustrated, she tried to think of someone else she could call. *Dave, she should call Dave,* but she didn't know his number. She did the next best thing and dialed the shop.

He answered on the second ring. "Wrights Jewelry. Dave Wright speaking."

"Dave, it's Marci. I'm in trouble and I need you," she began to sob, barely able to enunciate her words. "Please help me."

"Marci, is that really you? My god, the whole town's been looking for you. Are you all right? Where are you?" His mind was full of questions. He was so relieved to hear her voice. "Tell me where you are and I'll come get you."

She looked around the office and back onto the street." Nothing looked familiar. "I don't know where I am," she cried. "Somewhere near the Miami airport, I think…in a motel. Here," she handed the phone back to the clerk. "Please tell my friend where I am and give him the address."

CHAPTER 65

Alan reached into his pants pocket and retrieved his key. Looking around the apartment building's parking lot he saw nothing unusual. A few cars were parked in the small shopping mall across the street, but otherwise the sleepy lot was deserted.

"Stay put, Darling," he said to Consuela. "I'll back in a minute. If you see any police, hit the horn." He made his way quickly to the front door and disappeared inside.

The lobby was empty as he knew it would be at this early hour of the morning. Tugging a baseball cap lower on his head to hide his face, he approached box # 113 and inserted the key.

Savannah and Steven were squatting behind the concierge desk and had a clear view of him, if they dared to stand up. Nodding at each other, they silently mouthed one, two, three and stood up together. Each rapidly clicked the cameras on their phones before squatting back down again. The whole thing had only taken seconds, and Alan, intent on pulling envelopes out of the box, had not noticed a thing.

With his baseball cap in place, the image of Alan's face was not clear.

The pictures showed him from the back and a little on his side. His body, however, was clearly recognizable. Savannah had managed to capture his arm reaching into the box and his rose tattoo was visible. She smiled at Steven. They remained squatting in their hiding place. Savannah prayed that Detective Burrata would arrive before Alan left.

Alan worked quickly, pulling envelope after envelope out of the box. When the box was empty, he threw the key on the floor and bolted out of the door.

"Damn! He's getting away! Where are the cops? How can we get Marci out of the car?" Savannah wailed. "Damn, damn, damn."

"I'm sure they're on their way, but we'd better follow Alan ourselves or he may disappear permanently. Come on," he urged. "Let's get to the car and hope he doesn't see us."

"Wait," Savannah urged. "Let me pick up the key. It's more evidence. Do you have a handkerchief?"

Steven handed his to her and she scooped up the key, careful not to get her fingerprints on it.

They sprinted out of the building and ran across the street to Steven's car, just as Alan drove out of the parking lot and made a right turn. Steven gunned his engine and with tires squealing they started the pursuit.

"I don't think he saw us," Savannah said, keeping her eyes on the tail-lights of Alan's car. "He's too busy thinking about all his money, I guess."

"We can't be sure. He's pretty crafty. Look, he's turning on to the highway. I'm going to come up on his right to see if Marci's with him. Then I'll pull back and follow from behind. We can try to figure out where they're going and call Burrata."

As he pulled closer, Savannah looked past Steven to get a glimpse into the car beside them.

"I don't know," she said nervously after their car dropped back. "But from the quick glance I had of the passenger, the person in the car has long blond hair and Marci's a brunette.

CHAPTER 66

Marci continued to sit in the motel office waiting for Dave. The clerk made a few phone calls and busied himself with paperwork, but he kept his eyes on her. When she suggested she should get out of his hair and go back to her room, he insisted she stay with him. "You're not well Miss, and I don't feel right about you being alone in the room. Wait here with me for your friend. I'm sure he'll be here soon."

She'd been too tired to argue, so she curled into a ball on the uncomfortable chair and tried to sleep. It was not possible. She was too agitated and scared. She knew it would take Dave at least forty minutes to reach her. She prayed he got there before Alan returned.

Dave drove thirty miles per hour over the speed limit and raced down the highway towards the motel. He didn't care if he drew police attention. He hoped they'd see him. There was never a cop around when you wanted one.

When he'd heard Marci's frightened voice, bile rose in his throat and adrenaline surged through his body. He wanted to kill Alan for what he'd done to her and swore to see Alan punished, no matter what it took. He would do anything to keep Marci safe and would not let her out of his sight until Alan was locked up behind bars. The thought of his beautiful Marci, drugged, alone and scared horrified him. He was afraid of what else Alan may have done to her, but he wouldn't let his mind go there. He reached for his cell and called Detective Burrata.

———————————

Detective Burrata, his partner Detective Andrews and two other squad cars were racing towards the Miami address in response to Steven Framin's call. Alan Trent was there. They were less than five minutes away. He would be arrested, caught red-handed with money from his illegal sale of jewelry, and hopefully the missing woman, Marci was with him.

When Dave Wright called him, he was forced to change his plans. He ordered the other two squad cars to continue to the apartment building to arrest Alan and he made an immediate u turn, heading west and sped toward the Seaside Motel.

———————————

Alan saw speeding cop cars coming towards him, lights flashing and sirens wailing. He momentarily panicked. *Were they after him?* He didn't know if he should slow down and hope the cops flew past him or speed up and attempt to evade arrest. His heart raced. When they sped past him, he relaxed and slowed his car down, not wanting to draw any attention to himself.

The motel was only fifteen minutes away. He'd be there soon to wake up Marci and take her to the bank. Then, if his luck held, in a few hours, he and Consuela would be together on *Pampered,* sipping cocktails and enjoying every luxury as they sailed toward the Caymans. Poor gullible Marci would be left behind to clean up his mess and rot in jail as his accomplice. Reaching into his glove compartment, he pulled out two cans of Red Bull and a box of No Doze. "Keep these handy," he smiled conspiratorially at Consuela and suggestively rubbed her thigh. "God, you're sexy. I can't wait to fuck you on the boat."

———————

"Where do you suppose he's going?" Savannah asked Steven. "It looks like he's heading to the airport. The ramp is just ahead."

"I'm not sure, but if we're right about his plan to use Marci to get his money out of the Wells Fargo account, he'll have to meet up with her soon. Once she empties it out, she'll be of no more use to him. Either he'll let her go, or." He didn't finish his sentence because he saw Savannah was beginning to tremble. "It'll be all right," he reassured her tenderly, taking her hand in his. "I'll call the detective back now and tell him that we think Alan and Marci will eventually be heading back to Miami Beach and Wells Fargo. I hope the police get to the bank before he does."

CHAPTER 67

Alan pulled into the motel parking lot and stopped his car in front of room # 9. He glanced quickly around.

"Bring the Red Bull," he told Consuela. "We need to wake up Marci." He reached into his pocket for the room key and pushed his way into the room, yelling, "Marci, get the fuck up. It's time to go."

He looked around the dark grimy room and turned on the overhead light. The bed was empty. The small grimy bathroom was empty. He pulled back the shower curtain. Nothing. She wasn't there. "Dammit!" he shouted. *How did she wake up? How did she get out? In her weakened state, where could she have gone?*

He had no time to waste. The cops would be looking for Marci by now. The crew he'd hired would be waiting on *Pampered* with a late afternoon departure time. Frustrated, he told Consuela he'd be right back while he ran to the motel office to see if she was there.

Bursting through the office door, he startled the desk clerk and Marci. "I'm looking for my wife. She was in room nine. She's not in there and I've got to get her to the doctor. She's sick. Have you seen her?"

The clerk nodded towards Marci who was wrapped into a fetal position on the chair next to the counter. She struggled to sit up and looked frightened when she saw Alan. "What are you doing here?" she asked. "I thought you deserted me. I called Dave Wright to come get me."

"You moron," he seethed. But he had no time to waste berating her. He had to get her out of the motel before Dave and his sanctimonious cavalry arrived. "We're leaving right now. Follow me."

He grabbed her arm, squeezing it so hard that she shrieked in pain. Then he brutally dragged her out of the office. She fought him as best she could, but she was in no condition to put up much resistance.

It all happened so fast that the clerk had no time to think. "Leave her alone," he shouted and ran out the door trying to help her. Alan released Marci for a second and punched the clerk in the face. He fell to the ground and Alan kicked him in the ribs to finish him off. The clerk writhed in agony. Alan grabbed Marci again and shoved her towards the car, swearing at her the whole time.

The parking lot was still deserted but Alan noticed one automobile slowly pulling into the lot from the side street. He didn't take the time to see whether the car was carrying that jerk Dave coming to Marci's rescue. Alan flung the car door open and with Consuela's help shoved Marci into the passenger seat. Consuela then jumped nimbly into the back seat and they sped off.

Marci twisted around and saw a woman in the back seat. She didn't recognize Mrs. Trent's nurse. "What's going on Alan?"

"I'll tell you everything in good time, Marci," Alan smiled smugly. "For now, just keep your damn mouth shut and if you do as you're told, I may let you live. Don't give me any trouble. Understand?"

Marci nodded her head, but she did not understand anything. What did he mean? He'd let her live? And who was the blond in the back seat?

"Alan, please tell me what's going on," she begged. "You owe me that."

"He doesn't owe you anything, stupid bitch," Consuela snarled at her. "He's my man and he doesn't give a damn about you."

———————

A police cruiser pulled up to the motel office and came to an abrupt halt. Seconds later Dave Wright appeared. "Is Marci inside?" Dave shouted when he recognized Detective Burrata. "Are we in time?"

"I don't know. Let's go inside." The detective drew his gun as the two men barged into the office, startling the clerk who was just limping back to the front desk. "Where is she? Where's Marci?" Dave demanded.

The clerk was still in pain and barely able to speak. "Her husband came and dragged her away. I tried to stop him," he said haltingly, "but he punched and kicked me… and threw her into his car. They left a few minutes ago."

"Was she Okay?" Dave was crushed. "Did she seem all right?"

"She said she was sick and she looked pretty terrible," the clerk answered nervously. "She didn't want to go with him. He had to drag her to his car." He rubbed his aching jaw before continuing. "She was here waiting for someone she'd called to come get her, but he never showed up."

"Oh my God," Dave slumped dejectedly into the chair where Marci had been only minutes before. "That's me. I should have driven faster."

CHAPTER 68

Steven and Savannah jumped out of their car and ran into the motel office.

"Dad, what are you doing here!" she cried. "Is Marci okay?"

"I'm afraid not," he replied. "I was too late. Alan got here first."

Steven looked at Detective Burrata. "When I called, you told me that you were only minutes away from the motel. What took you so long?"

"Please calm down Mr. Framin. And everyone." He looked sternly at Savannah and her father. "For God's sake. Do you clowns see how ridiculous you are? You're all running all over town playing amateur detectives. I didn't request a posse. As a matter of fact, I specifically asked you to butt out and let the police do their work. This time I am not asking, I'm telling you. Go home and stay out of this. Right <u>now</u>, Alan is getting away while I have to spend precious time scolding you. Any more interference from any of you and I'll arrest you for hampering a police investigation. Do you understand?"

Savannah could not contain herself. "You would not have even known Alan was at the apartment building if Steven hadn't called you.

We have every right to look for our friend and if that bothers you, too bad." She put her hands on her hips and stared right back at him, holding her ground.

"And," Dave interjected angrily, "I resent your implication that I'm getting in your way. I'm only here because Marci called and asked me to pick her up. My daughter and I are not trying to interfere. We're only trying to help."

Steven did not want to add to the tension but he had a question. "I know why Dave is here. Marci called him. And I know that Savannah and I followed Alan here, so that's why we landed at this God-forsaken motel. But, why are you here Detective? What or who tipped you off that Marci was here?"

"I did," the beleaguered clerk announced. "I called the anonymous tip line hoping for a reward and told the police the name of this motel and that I thought the woman they were looking for was in room number 9. I wish I'd kept my damn mouth shut." He looked nervously at the detective's gun. "Can you all please leave? I need to lie down myself."

"Come on Dad," Savannah knew her father was about to lose his temper with Detective Burrata. "He is right about one thing. We are wasting time. Let's go somewhere and regroup."

"Okay, Honey." Dave followed Savannah and Steven towards the door.

"I'll let you all know when we find Mr. Trent and your friend, Marci," the detective called to Savannah. He used his walkie talkie and asked for his police back up to take the clerk's statement and search room # 9.

"And I'll let you know when we find Marci," Savannah barked before marching out of the office in a huff.

"Come. Let's go back to my place and calm down," Dave said smoothly.

"Not so fast," Savannah broke away. There's one more thing I have to tell that arrogant detective. She ran back inside the office and confronted him.

"Yes," he turned to face her. "I thought you had left."

"I almost forgot," she said breathlessly. "I know exactly where you can find Alan and Marci, but you'll have to hurry. Would you like me to tell you or would I be interfering too much?"

The policeman glared at her with exasperation. He knew enough not to disregard what she had to say. "And where exactly would that be?"

"At the Wells Fargo bank branch on Miami Beach. He'll be bringing Marci there to close out their joint account. Our lawyer's PI discovered that a joint account had been opened in Alan and Marci's names. That's where the money trail ends."

"And I suppose that you and your merry group of sleuths will be going here too?"

"Damn right."

CHAPTER 69

Alan took Marci's hand trying to calm her down, but she remained angry and confused. She had no idea what was happening and why Alan had suddenly turned on her. He had gone from being a devoted lover to becoming a total stranger. She doubted she had ever known the real man. The drugs he'd given her had almost worn off but she didn't want him to know. She pretended to still be disoriented. She would be safe as long as he believed she was under his control. All that remained from her symptoms was a dull headache, a heaviness in her chest and an ache in her heart for what might have been.

Over the last twenty-four hours, she had come to understand that Alan had never loved her as he'd pretended. But then, why had he bothered buying her an expensive dress and ring? Why go through the charade of a wedding ceremony? Why the hoax of the marriage?

Alan pulled his car into the back of a Wendy's parking lot and shut off the engine.

Marci finally got the courage to speak up. "What is it you want from me?"

"I want you to help me with one small errand," he said as he reached over to the glove compartment and pulled out the Red Bull cans. "But first, I want you to drink both of these and swallow some No Doze pills. You have to be completely alert and wide awake."

He turned to Consuela. "Give her the stuff and see that she drinks it all." He got out of the car, locked the doors and went behind the dumpster. "I have to take a piss."

"I'm not drinking anything," Marci glared at Consuela defiantly and clenched her teeth together. "Alan's been drugging me. I don't trust him."

"Here bitch," Consuela hissed. She took a swig from the can. "See it's perfectly safe, and if you want us to let you go in one piece, I suggest you drink every last drop and take the pills NOW."

Marci was scared. She took the can and cautiously began to sip. "What do you have to do with all of this?"

"You really have no idea what's going on, do you? How can you be so stupid?"

"I guess God made me that way. Why don't you enlighten me?"

"I'll do just that for her," Alan bellowed as he got back into the car and bragged. "It's really quite simple. When I got the job as Mrs. Trent's butler, 'Pedro', I saw an opportunity to make a lot of money on the side. I gradually made myself indispensable to her thanks to my charm and competence. I ran the household, hired the staff, and oversead her finances. I brought Consuela in as her nurse. Working together, she and I gradually took control of the old lady's life and her estate. Once we started giving her daily doses of valium, it was all very easy."

"But what do I have to do with any of this? And why that strange wedding?"

"It was part of the plan…to get you to marry me. I have already cashed out most of the old lady's money and jewels. Now I need to get my hands on it and leave the country. Consuela is my real wife and the only woman I love. She and I will be fucking millionaires as soon as you help us complete the final phase. As my loving bride, the government can't make you to testify against me. That's why the hurry up marriage, fake wifey dear."

"But I don't understand. Why do you need me at the bank?"

"I think I've explained enough. That's all you're getting until this is over and I let you go. In a way, I'm sorry that I involved you in this. You're a nice person, but Jesus, you are so naïve. You were as easy a target as Mrs. Trent. I needed someone to help fence the stolen jewelry and what better than a shop girl at the local jewelers?

His cruel words stung Marci and she recoiled against the car door.

"I won't hurt you if you cooperate. But as insurance that you will do what I tell you, while you were out cold, I abducted your dear friend Savannah. And make no mistake. If you cross me, I won't hesitate to kill her like I did dear old Grandmother. I suggest you do as you're told and, in a few hours, you and Savannah will be free to resume your boring lives and Consuela and I will be gone. How this plays out is up to you? Your life -- and Savannah's depend on it."

Marci was dumbfounded. How could she have misjudged Alan so badly. He was evil and deranged. And poor Savannah had been right when she warned her about Alan. Marci had stubbornly refused to listen. Now Savannah's life was in danger and it was all Marci's fault.

CHAPTER 70

Detective Burrata and seven other Ft. Lauderdale policemen arrived at the Wells Fargo Bank in unmarked cars. They parked in various spaces around the three-story brick building and, wearing casual street clothing, walked separately into the lobby pretending to be customers. Detective Burrata asked to see the manager. There were two people standing in line for the teller. He waited for them to finish their transactions and leave. Then he disappeared with the manager inside the closed door of his office. He emerged ten minutes later and told his fellow officers to take their places in the several glass enclosed cubicles situated around the lobby. They would appear to be working and wait for Alan to arrive.

The regular bank employees, except one, were herded together into the bank's cafeteria on the third floor. They were told that the bank would be providing them with free lunches and instructed to stay there until they were notified that it was safe to return to their jobs. Detective Burrata asked each one to turn in their cell phones so they couldn't communicate with anyone outside the bank. A few grumbled but they followed instructions without resistance.

The Detective took a seat in the manager's chair, leaving the door open, while he pretended to study paperwork on the desk. A legitimate bank employee was positioned at her desk in the next cubicle. She would be needed to perform the transfer of funds when Alan requested it. The other police officers stationed themselves in the cubicles around the perimeter of the lobby and two posed as customers in the teller line. Detective Andrews took his post behind the one teller cage that would remain open. One officer went into the electrical room behind the manager's office and manned the computer which showed all the live security camera feeds, both inside and outside of the branch. When Alan and Marci arrived, he would know in advance and alert everyone with a whistle.

A line of large wall clocks showed several different time zones. Detective Burrata noted that it was now 1:30 p.m. Eastern Standard time. He made some notes and jotted down the time for the commencement of "Operation Imposter".

CHAPTER 71

'm hungry," Consuela whined. "Can't we stay here and get something to eat before we go to the bank? I can run in, grab us something and we'll be on our way."

Alan glanced at his watch. He was in a hurry to get to the bank but he knew Consuela could be a handful when she was hungry. It was better to give in to her than put up with her bad temper.

"Okay, go get whatever you want. But hurry. Bring me a burger and a chocolate shake. How about you Marci? The culinary experience here won't match my cooking expertise though." He sneered. "Think of it as our wedding meal."

Marci shook her head in disgust. Alan really was crazy. One-minute he was threatening to harm Savannah and herself and the next, he was offering to buy her lunch.

"I don't want anything from you except my freedom." She slid as far away from him as she could and reached for the door handle. Before she could open it, he slapped her hard across her face and grabbed her shoulder to shake her.

"You're not going anywhere, Marci. Behave yourself or you'll make me hurt you."

Stunned by his sudden violence, she gently rubbed her cheek which was already starting to bruise. "Don't you ever touch me again Alan Trent," she screamed. "Let me out of this car right now!" She attempted to push open the door again, but this time he slammed his fist into her ribs. She fell back against the door and momentarily blacked out.

"What the hell's going on here?" Consuela slid into the back seat with their burgers. "I could hear Marci screaming from inside Wendy's. A few people inside heard it too and ran to the door to look. You'd better get out of here fast before one of them calls the police and claims he witnessed domestic abuse."

"Shit." Alan slammed his fist on the steering wheel. "It seems Marci suddenly developed a backbone and tried to get away. But I think she understands the situation now, don't you wifey dear?" He glared angrily at her as she struggled to catch her breath. "Don't you, bitch? Answer me when I talk to you. You do exactly what I tell you and stop making so much noise or you won't live another day."

Marci was much too scared to rebel again. She nodded her head and closed her eyes in defeat.

Alan started the engine and began pulling out of the parking lot as someone from inside the restaurant came running out while talking on his phone.

"Shit, shit, shit," Alan bellowed. "That guy's probably giving the cops our license number. We have to ditch this car."

He peeled out of the parking area and onto the highway watching for the police in his rear-view mirror. After traveling for a few blocks, he saw a Best Buy store and swerved into its lot.

"Forget the food and help me get Marci out," he ordered Consuela. "I'm going to hot wire a car."

CHAPTER 73

Savannah took over her father's kitchen and made sandwiches for the three of them. She set plates on the kitchen table and poured a beer for her dad and Steven, and lemonade for herself.

"I can't just sit here and pretend that everything's all right," she sighed. "But I don't know what to do. Poor Marci, she must be scared to death. Any illusions she had about being in love with Alan must be shattered by now."

"I don't think there's anything we can do," Dave replied. "Believe me, I want to rescue her too, but Detective Burrata made it clear enough he doesn't want us involved and I haven't got the faintest idea how we could help."

"I think we've done all we can," Steven said, sipping his beer. "We gave the police the Wells Fargo information and I'm sure they're planning to capture Alan there when he attempts to get his money. Which we know he will."

"You mean when *Marci* gets the money. Remember, that's the reason for this whole farce." Savannah took a bite of her sandwich and looked at her father. "Marci's smart. When she realizes what Alan wants her to do and why, she'll come up with some way to thwart him. She's not going to go along with his plan."

"Not unless he threatens her," Dave said soberly. "I wouldn't put it past him. That's the only way he'd get her to do something illegal. I swear on my life that if that man lays a hand on her, he'll answer to me."

Steven was also worried about Marci, very worried, but he didn't want to say anything that might further upset Savannah. He excused himself, saying he needed to check in with his office and called Sheldon Blake instead. After updating his legal colleague on the apartment mailbox incident and the situation at the motel, he got to the real reason for his call and asked if Alan's police records showed any arrests for physical violence or assault and battery charges.

"As you now know, Alan's real name is Peter Scant." Sheldon answered. "But he's gone by many other aliases including Pedro. He's got a lengthy police record and has served time for selling drugs and passing counterfeit checks. There's an outstanding warrant for his arrest in Georgia for allegedly beating a woman. Why do you ask now?"

"Because the police are determined to arrest Alan, or whoever he's pretending to be, for stealing money and jewelry. I think that's the least of the danger he presents. They should be more concerned with trying to find and protect Marci from that sociopath. I'm pretty sure he killed Marjorie Trent, and if he did, he won't hesitate to kill again."

"I don't disagree, but why are you calling me?"

"Because I have an idea but I wanted to run it by you before I mentioned it to Savannah and her father. I hope it doesn't sound too crazy."

"Tell me," Sheldon said.

———————

After Steven finished his conversation with Sheldon, he explained his idea to Savannah and Dave. Savannah laughed. She had threatened detective Burrata with doing the same thing back at the motel but thought better of it. Now that Steven had suggested it, it seemed like a good plan and she was all in. Without wasting another second, the three ran to Steven's car and sped to the Wells Fargo Bank on Miami Beach.

"I don't know how we did it, but I think we beat him here, unless Alan's driving a different car," Savannah observed. "I'll go inside and check to be sure." She reached inside her purse and pulled out her red traveling companion. She placed the wig on her head and disappeared through the bank's front door.

Dave and Steven waited inside the car. Savannah walked up to the counter when it was her turn. "Has a tall brunette woman come in here in the last few minutes asking to close an account?" She asked. There was something familiar about the teller's face, but she couldn't remember where she might have seen him before.

"No, Ma'am. Not that I know of, but she wouldn't come to me for that. You can check with the manager. His office is over there in the corner."

She thanked the teller and walked towards the manager's office. Glancing inside, she was shocked to see Detective Burrata sitting pompously behind the desk. Now she remembered. She turned back to the teller and realized instantly that he was Detective Andrews. She had inadvertently walked right into the trap they'd set for Alan. If Detective Burrata saw her, he'd arrest her -- he'd threatened as much before. Turning around quickly, she hastily left the lobby and ran back to Steven's car.

"Marci's not in there," she reported, "but Detectives Burrata and Andrews are, and they're posing as bank employees. They must have heeded our advice and they're expecting Alan to show up any minute. We can't let him see us or we'll all be going to jail."

"Look," Dave almost shouted with relief. He pointed to a tall woman coming from around the back of the bank building and moving slowly towards the bank's front door. "That's Marci. Thank God! I think she got out of the green Audi parked around the corner. I noticed that car when we drove into the lot because all the windows and the doors were open. There were three people inside but I never thought to look more closely. I was looking for the red Porsche."

Savannah took a few steps forward, craning her neck, but couldn't clearly see the faces of the people in the car.

"I see Pedro," Steven whispered. "He's in the driver's seat. He must have coerced Marci into going inside the bank by herself and do his dirty work. And wait! I think that's Consuela next to him in the passenger seat?"

Savannah muffled a shriek of happiness. "I've an idea. Steven, can you pull your car around to the side and use your car to block the Audi and Alan's view of the sidewalk…just for a minute or so? When his view is blinded, I'll run up and grab Marci."

Steven nodded and slowly drove around the side of the building and paused in front of the green Audi's front fender. His car completely blocked Alan's sightline.

Savannah jumped out of the car and ran to catch up with her friend. "Marci, Marci come here! It's me, Savannah," she screamed at her friend, pulling off her red wig so Marci would recognize her. "Come here now!"

Marci was so happy to see that Savannah was okay that she began to cry.

"There's no time to talk," Savannah took her arm. "Follow me."

"What are you doing here? It's not safe. Alan's in the car waiting for me. He'll kill us both if I don't come back with his money." She controlled her tears but her voice was shaking. "Run away, Savannah please. He's a terrible man and he said if I didn't do what he wanted; he'd kill you. Believe me, I know he will."

For the first time Savannah had a good look at Marci's bruised face. "My God, he hit you?" She was indignant.

"Yes." Marci stammered, looking around nervously. "And Alan will be wondering what's keeping me. Leave me here. Go away Savannah, please. He's seriously deranged." She suddenly looked again at Savannah and didn't understand how she could be standing there. "But wait." Marci shook her head and wondered if the drugs were still clouding her thinking. How could this be? "Savannah, he said he'd kidnapped you and would kill you if I didn't cooperate with him! How did you escape?"

"That was just a ploy to get you to do his bidding. He never got anywhere near me. I'm fine, Marci, really," Savannah coaxed, "but we have to get out of here right now."

Suddenly Dave was by her side. "Savannah's right. We have to get out of here now."

Between Savannah and Dave, they quickly, but gently maneuvered Marci into Steven's back seat. Dave jumped in besides her while Savannah launched herself into the front seat. It all happened so fast that Alan and Consuela never saw Savannah or had time to realize what had happened. Alan began honking his horn trying to get the car blocking his to move. He had not recognized either Steven or his car.

Dave gently wrapped his arms around Marci before he helped her fasten her seatbelt. "Everything's going to be all right," he soothed. "You're safe with me now and I'm not letting you out of my sight."

"For heaven's sake, Steven, let's get out of here." Savannah said impatiently. "Step on it."

"Wait, wait." Consuela jumped out of her car screaming at them as soon as she saw what had happened. She ran toward Steven's car, but her stiletto heels hampered her speed and she was too late. Marci was safely inside that vehicle and Steven's car lurched forward and out onto the street.

"What the fuck?" Alan shouted at Consuela. "What the hell just happened?"

"That bitch Savannah and her friends grabbed Marci." She looked like she was going to explode in anger. "Now what will we do? How will we get our money?"

"I don't know," Alan moaned. "I thought I had it all figured out."

"You did. I assure you, but you never expected the bitch's damn friends to rescue her. Aren't we going to chase after them? What are you waiting for?"

"What good would that do? We'll never get her back here. I'm sure the sanctimonious *Wrights* have already called the police. If I take just one step inside this bank, I'll be arrested for kidnapping on top of everything else. Damnation! We need to get out of here and get to the boat. Then we'll figure out what to do next."

CHAPTER 74

W hat the hell?" Detective Burrata slammed his fist on the desk and stared at the security camera footage. "Marci never came into the bank."

The officer in charge of the security cameras tried to calm the detective down. "The suspect was driving a green Audi, so I didn't immediately recognize him. He must have changed cars after someone reported him being involved in a domestic disturbance at Wendy's." He studied the camera footage for another minute and then looked up. "Looks like he parked the new vehicle around the back of the building, by the driveway entrance, presumedly so he could make a quick exit. Then as you can see, he shoved the lady around to the side of the building and pushed her forward. I can't tell from the camera angle, but from the way he's holding his right arm, it appears he had a gun aimed at her. Then he said something to her, and returned to his car."

"But she never came into the lobby." The detective shook his head. "What the hell happened?"

"I'll show you." A female detective fast-forwarded the tape to a view from another outside camera. "You can see that Ms. Morgan was alone when another man and a woman sprang our of a car and grabbed her."

"Can you show me a close up of them?" Detective Burrata had a sickening feeling he knew precisely who had interrupted his "Operation Imposter."

"Damn," he shouted when Savannah's picture came up standing with her father and Marci. "I've warned them to stay out of this! I'm sick of their interference. Call Judge Carmichael and get a warrant for their arrest."

"But there's more," the female detective persisted. "Another woman was there too."

"Show me." Detective Burrata was as angry as he had ever been in his life. He did not like to look like a fool and especially not before his squad. He knew this fiasco would have career ramifications for him and they would not be good.

"Starting here," she pointed. "See the woman in those heels running after the car? Of course, she couldn't catch them, but at least she tried."

"And where was Alan during all of this?"

"He was sitting in the car waiting for Marci to return. In the next frame, you'll see him shout at the other woman and then they speed off in the Audi."

Detective Burrata sat down heavily on the bank manager's chair. "You might as well give the employees back their phones and tell them to come down to work," he said in a steely voice. "The suspect will not be coming back here, I guarantee you. This sting has been a colossal bust."

He was furious at Savannah and Dave Wright. They were

single-handedly responsible for Alan's escape. On one hand, he was glad their friend Marci was safe, but her freedom would cost him in the eyes of his superiors. Heads would roll for his inability to stop amateurs from screwing up his operation and the complete waste of money and manpower. Instead of receiving a flattering citation from the Chief of Police, he and his team would be the laughing stock of the department.

CHAPTER 75

Dave kept a tight hold on Marci as he helped her from the car. He was careful not to touch her ribs which were still hurt from Alan's fist punch. The side of her face had started to turn black and blue. She leaned heavily on him as she walked uncertainly inside Dave's house. She was so relieved to be away from Alan and Consuela, but the ordeal of the last twenty-four hours had taken a physical toll. She was exhausted and while happy to be with Savannah and Dave, she needed to sleep. There were still drug remnants in her system.

"Lie down, Darling," he gently urged, helping her onto the sofa. "No one's going to hurt you ever again. I'll be right here with you until Alan is behind bars, and long afterwards if you'll have me." He gave her a tender kiss on her forehead and sat down beside her.

Marci's eyelids fluttered and she fell into a well-deserved sleep with a smile on her face.

"Let's go into the kitchen," Savannah whispered. "We can keep an eye on her from there but won't disturb her with our chatter.

"Sure," Steven agreed and went over to the table where only hours before they'd eaten lunch. Their half-consumed sandwiches were still on the plates in fact. At Steven's suggestion, they had left the house in such a hurry to intercept Marci at the bank that they'd left their dishes and uneaten food on the table. "I'll clean this mess up."

"I'll join you soon," Dave whispered. "I want to stay here with Marci until I'm sure she won't wake up suddenly and be afraid."

"Sure Dad," Savannah said suddenly understanding how much her father cared for Marci.

"Just because we have Marci here with us doesn't mean she's out of danger. Alan's so desperate that he may still try to kidnap her again. If he can't get into his accounts, he may try to hold her to get safe passage away from here." Steven looked at Savannah intently. "I think we should demand police protection for her."

Savannah grinned in spite of the seriousness of what Steven just said. "Oh my gosh. Can you imagine detective Burrata's reaction if I asked him to do that? He's already furious at us. What will he do when he finds out we foiled his plan at the bank and saved Marci ourselves?"

"I suppose he'll be very annoyed, but on the other hand, Marci is safe now. He should at least be grateful for that."

"I don't know." She shrugged. "But I agree, it's possible Alan may come after Marci again. What should we do about that?"

Dave walked into his kitchen, looking emotionally drained. He had come so close to losing Marci and didn't want to think about what Alan might have done to her. He opened the refrigerator and handed out beers to everyone. "I heard what Savannah said. I also think the detective will be ticked off at our interference again. I'd feel better if we hired our own security to protect Marci until Alan is apprehended. I'll call Sheldon and get him to arrange it. I have a very sophisticated alarm system throughout the house and perimeter cameras too. I installed them because I used to keep a lot of expensive jewelry here for the shop. I also have a carry permit and a gun by my bedside. Alan won't get anywhere near Marci. I promise you that." He went into another room and called Sheldon to arrange for private guards and then went upstairs to retrieve his gun. He was taking no chances with Marci's life.

"I've never seen Dad so protective," Savannah smiled. "It's kind of cute. I guess I'm going to have to put my reservations aside and support them as a couple. Although my dad and my best friend together…that's weird, but maybe good weird. I'll get used to it."

"I don't think you have a choice. Because you love your dad, you want him to be happy. Apparently, Marci's the person to make that happen," Steven said seriously. "But to change the subject, Alan's a very dangerous man and I don't want anything to happen to you either." He pulled her into his arms and gave her a passionate kiss. "I'm going to keep you safe too, Ms. Nancy Savannah Drew."

"Well, well," Dave laughed when he entered the room, gun in hand. "Romance is definitely in the air around here." Savannah blushed and backed away from Steven. She still tasted his lips on hers and had not expected the day to end romantically. Life was full of surprises.

CHAPTER 76

Alan and Consuela were furious that their plans had been thwarted. By this time, they had expected to be celebrating on the yacht with millions of dollars waiting for them in a Cayman Islands account. Instead, they found themselves aimlessly driving around town in a stolen car with no idea of where to go or what to do.

"What are we going to do?" Consuela worried. "We needed Marci for the plan to work."

"I know. That's why I 'married' the bitch after all. Now we'll have to come up with a new way to wire the money to the Caymans."

"Why not just go to the Caymans anyway and make the transfer from there?"

"I think you may have just hit on an idea, my love! The whole point was that I don't want any paper trail connecting the money from the sale of jewelry and art to me. Right now, our priority has to be getting out of Fort Lauderdale and away from the Florida police's jurisdiction. But, how's this for a Plan B? Once we get to the Cayman's, we'll fly someplace that doesn't have an extradition treaty with the United States. Maybe Morocco, or Qatar. Once we're set up there, I'll just withdraw the funds electronically and the US government won't be able to touch me."

"Sound like a plan." Consuela smiled for the first time since the fiasco at the bank. "Call the boat's captain and let him know we're on our way. I need a drink."

CHAPTER 77

Savannah was thoughtful. "Even if Detective Burrata hates us, I think we must let him know that Dad thinks *Pampered* is provisioned to take off soon, probably with Alan and Consuela on board and quite likely planning to flee the US."

"Right," Steven said. "I know we screwed up the police's bank sting, but maybe they can get to the boat and arrest Alan before he leaves and the boat reaches international waters."

"Good idea," Marci walked into the kitchen smiling. "God, it's great to see you all here together. Thanks for rescuing me."

Dave jumped up and put his arm around her. "Are you feeling better? You have no idea how much we worried about you. Seeing you walk into my kitchen is like, well, the best Christmas gift ever!"

"Well then. I won't have to spend any money on your presents when the real holiday comes. I'll just walk in and out of here a few times and call it a day." Her eyes twinkled with love as she hugged him.

"We'll all have an amazing Christmas this year, thanks to Dad and Steven. " Savannah said earnestly. "By the way Marci, meet Steven Framin,

Mrs. Trent's lawyer. He's been a tremendous help in rescuing you. I want you to know that he and we did everything to get you safely away from Alan." She jumped up and went over to give her girlfriend a hug. "Welcome home and apparently, welcome to the family."

"Glad to be here," Marci smiled and hugged Savannah back, Then she went over to Steven and hugged him too. "Thank you so much."

Marci looked happily around the room at all her friends. "Do you have a beer for me?"

"Sure," Dave handed her a cold one and pulled out a chair indicating she should sit down. "We were just saying that we think Alan may be planning to flee the country on *Pampered*. We have to believe he's still somehow at large, that he took off after we grabbed Marci from him. We would have heard from Burrata if they got him, don't you think? And we think we should tip off the detective that Alan's probably planning to escape on the boat. Maybe he can beat Alan there and nab him before he boards her."

"Alan always told me how much he loved that boat and how his grandmother would host extravagant parties with gambling once the yacht made it to international waters. The police have no jurisdiction there, so he said the gambling was legal."

"That's right, and I think the demarcation line is only about 3 miles out," Steven explained. "If they sail down the intercoastal to Port Everglades and out to the ocean from there, the boat could be safe in international waters within an hour, depending on the bridges. The captain will have to go slowly in the intercoastal because of the 'no wake' laws. Once he's in the open seas, he can go as fast as the engines will take him."

"Who has a phone?" Marci looked around the table. "Let's do it.

We have to stop him. What are we waiting for? Go ahead and call the cops."

Dave still had detective Burrata's number in his contacts. He dialed the detective and winked at Marci.

"This is Dave Wright," he began. "I want to advise you that I have Marci Morgan safely with me here at my home. I thought you should know that I have reason to believe Alan will be taking Marjorie Trent's yacht, *Pampered*, to the Cayman Islands *today*. And that he probably has a reservation at the Westin there but I don't know under what name. The boat is tied up behind the Trent property now. If you hurry, you might be able to catch Alan as he tries to board the yacht."

"And you know this how?" The detective was perturbed, if his day hadn't been bad enough. How did this bunch of neighborhood sleuths always seem to be a step ahead of him?

"I'll explain another time," Dave said. "But trust me, I believe my information is accurate."

"And I suppose you are with your little group of NCIS fans?" the detective said sarcastically.

"Yes." Dave smiled. "The gang's all here and we're happy to be reunited with Ms. Morgan." He was having a little fun at the detective's expense.

"Do you think you all could act like good citizens for once, and stay put there? And just let me do my job."

Dave could not keep from smiling. He could imagine the detective's face. Signaling for everyone at the table to get up, he replied. "Sorry. I don't think so. We're on our way. We'll meet you there."

"I was afraid of that," Detective Burrata choked.

CHAPTER 78

Detectives Burrata and Andrews, followed by six squad cars traveled in formation along heavily congested I95. The late afternoon hour signaled the start of rush hour. That forced the entourage to dodge in and out of lanes, driving as much as possible in the express lanes. They made it back to Ft. Lauderdale in record time -- forty minutes. Still, with local traffic heavy, the last few miles driving through the city streets to the Trent estate took almost as long as the entire trip had from Miami to Fort Lauderdale. Turning onto 17th Street and crossing over the bridge, they were almost within shouting distance of the mansion. They slowed down as they approached the entrance to Coastal Beach and went past the bogus guardhouse. If Alan was already on the yacht, they didn't want to announce their presence and give him time to flee. And if he was still on his way, they didn't want to scare him off.

"Do you think he's here?" Detective Andrews asked his colleague.

"I don't know," Detective Burrata answered. "Alan had to travel the same route as we did but I think we had a head start, so we're probably a few minutes ahead of him. Dave Wright and his band may already be here as they didn't have as far to travel. We should park our cars around the corner, so Alan doesn't see any unusual activity by the house when he arrives."

They parked a block away and sprinted to the mansion on foot. When they arrived, there were no cars in the driveway, so they made their way quickly to the boat...guns drawn.

The captain was standing in position at the bottom of the gangplank with a steward and the first mate. Detective Burrata showed his badge. "Is Alan Trent on board?"

"No sir. Not yet. He called a while ago to say he's on his way." The captain looked mystified at the detective and at all the police. "What's going on? Is Mr. Trent in trouble?"

"Yes, he is. My men and I will go on board now and wait inside the salon. When he arrives, escort him inside immediately but *do not* say a word about us being here. We don't want anyone to get hurt and don't want to use our guns unless necessary. Do you understand?"

"Yes, Sir," the captain answered nervously. "I take it we're not leaving the dock today?"

"That's absolutely correct. We'll arrest Alan and his girlfriend as soon as they step inside and take them downtown. Once we've done that, you can dismiss the crew or do whatever you want. Alan Trent won't be using this boat any time soon. He's going nowhere except to prison."

The police officers boarded the yacht and made themselves comfortable in the main salon. It was the first time for all of them on a yacht this size and they were impressed. Detective Burrata took a standing position by one of the large windows overlooking the dock. From there, he would be able to see Alan and Consuela as they approached. It was a little before five p.m.

The police were getting restless and kept looking at their watches. One by one they got up from their seats and walked around the main salon, occasionally joining Detective Burrata at the window. Even he knew that unless Alan had car trouble, he should have been here by now, even given the traffic. And where were Savannah and Dave Wright? They should have been here even before the police.

At 5:30 Detective Burrata picked up his I phone and pressed Dave Wright's number. "We're at *Pampered*," he said, gritting his teeth. "Alan hasn't shown up. Are you positive he planned to leave town by boat?"

"Yes, when I was onboard earlier, everything was set for a late afternoon departure. I heard the captain come on board while I was there. Did you speak to him?"

"Yes, and he confirmed that Alan called to say he was in route to the boat." The detective started to hang up but then said, "And, where are you and your squad of junior detectives? I thought you were meeting me here."

"We were, but then we had changed our plans. We decided to follow your advice and let you do your job. Do me a favor. When Alan finally shows up and you have him in custody, please give me a call. None of us will sleep peacefully until we know he's been arrested. Ms. Morgan deserves as much."

"Sure, sure, but I thought you were hell bent on catching Alan. What could be more important than you being here for his capture?"

"I can think of a lot of things," Dave chuckled, kissing Marci tenderly. "But to answer your question, we're making sure that Alan can never get his hands-on Mrs. Trent's money again. We're taking care of that right now. Good luck at your end." He hung up before Detective Burrata could question him further.

CHAPTER 79

'm glad we decided to this," Marci said proudly. "While I would have loved to be there and see Alan's face when he's arrested, this is more important. I'm sure he's already planning another way to escape. But now, after we do this, he won't have a dime to live on. Consuela won't want to stay with a poor man and live a life on the run."

"No, I'm sure he promised her a future of yachts and private jets and God knows what else." Savannah said bitterly. "Now he's going to find out what it feels like to be on the other end of a scam."

"Are you ready?" Dave asked Marci. "And are you sure you want to do this on your own? I'm happy to go in with you."

"Yes, I'm sure," she answered firmly. "Doing this will give me a lot of satisfaction. And I love that it's you who will be waiting for me just outside the doors instead of Alan."

"Always," Dave grinned. "I'll always be where you want me to be."

"Good luck," Savannah and Steven said and each hugged her.

Marci walked determinately to the main entrance of the Wells Fargo bank. It was just an hour before closing, but there was still plenty of time to complete the transaction. She strolled inside and headed to the manager's office.

"I'm Marci Trent," she said wearing a bright smile. "I'm here to close out my account and have you wire all the funds to my attorney's account for safekeeping." She handed him the number of her joint account with Alan and her identification. My license is still in my maiden name," she apologized sweetly. "Because I was only recently married." She pulled out the marriage certificate Alan had given her earlier. I think you'll find everything's in order."

"Have a seat please," the manager said as he looked up the account on his computer. "I see you have quite a large balance, multiple millions." He was visibly saddened that she was withdrawing it all from his bank. "Are you sure you want to wire the whole amount?"

"Yes, I'm sure and here are the instructions." She handed him Steven's firm's account number and routing numbers. She and Steven had discussed that a portion of the funds would be returned to the Trent's estate to pay expenses and the rest distributed to anyone else making a substantiated claim. The remainder would go to Abandoned Kids, just as Marjorie Trent had wanted. Steven promised to handle the legal details as a way to honor his former client.

The manager carefully filled out the necessary forms and asked Marci to sign them. Then he worked on his computer for a few minutes before handing her several pieces of paper. "Here's the closing statement on your account here. Note it now shows a zero balance. And here's another showing the wire transfer, and finally here's a copy of the wire transfer instructions you gave me. The funds will be in your attorney's account before you leave here today. You can check with him later. If there's any problem, here's the tracking information. Wells Fargo is sorry to lose your business, Mrs. Trent. Thank you and good luck in your new marriage."

Marci merely smiled and shook the manager's hand. She was grateful that Steven and Dave had both explained that her wedding to Alan was not legal because Alan Trent was a fictitious person. Peter Scant had married her and his name was not on the account or the marriage certificate.

Walking out into the golden Florida sunshine, she saw Dave waiting for her and went running into his arms. That's done," she smiled happily. "Alan is as poor as a church mouse now, or whatever that expression is."

CHAPTER 80

Alan and Consuela were almost to the entrance to Coastal Beach when he suddenly made a sharp u turn and swung the car around without warning.

"What the hell?" Consuela fell against the passenger side door with a thud. "What are you doing?"

"I have a premonition," Alan sputtered. "The police and that damn group of vigilantes always seem to be a step ahead of us. You saw how they've all been snooping around the Trent property. Suppose they figured out that we've been planning to sail out of the country on *Pampered?* What would they do?"

"Call the cops and warn them, I suppose."

"Yes, but you know, they seem to show up everywhere I go. I bet they're all onboard the yacht right now, waiting to nab us. We can't let that happen."

"Okay, genius, so what are we going to do?" She started chewing her fingernails nervously. "How can we get away? We can't drive to the Caymans."

"They're waiting for us to leave by sea, so we'll leave instead by air. We'll take the first flight out of Fort Lauderdale to anywhere. Then we'll change planes and fly somewhere to safety."

"But what about the money?"

"When we get to a safe place, I'll call Wells Fargo and initiate the wire transfer. Once we're in a place with no extradition, I'm certain that the cops can't prevent us from claiming the money."

"Are you sure you're not over-reacting? I really wanted to spend time on *Pampered*. Flying is such a hassle."

"I'll miss the boat too, but we'll buy a bigger yacht wherever we end up. I promise, darling. Be patient a little longer. We'll live the life of millionaires once we leave the USA."

Consuela slunk down in her seat. She was not convinced.

Alan drove at a normal speed to the airport. The last thing he needed was to get pulled over for a traffic violation. Once they arrived, he parked the car in the short-term lot, locked the doors and tossed the keys in the nearest garbage receptacle.

"Let's check out United and American and see which has the earliest flight out of here to anywhere."

"You don't have to go to the counter. You can check on that with your phone," Consuela said irritably. "You don't have to run from airline to airline. I think you're being ridiculous. We should have stuck with the *Pampered* plan."

"Grow up Consuela. We have to adapt and I'd rather take a few flights around the country to avoid the police than wind up in prison. You don't have to come if you prefer to stay here. You can always find another job as someone's maid or health care worker. It's your choice." He was angry now and started to walk away. Sometimes she was a pain in his butt.

"Wait, wait," she quickly relented. "Of course, I'm coming with you. Wait for me."

CHAPTER 81

Detective Burrata and his men drove back to the precinct to report their activities to their superiors.

"I'd say the whole day was a bust from start to finish," the police sergeant said testily. "I think you relied too much on information from dubious sources and forgot to follow regular police procedures. I suggest you regroup and check with the port authorities to see what private yachts left or are leaving today from Port Everglades or from the Port of Miami. Find out their destinations and who's onboard. You don't need to bother with the commercial cruise lines because no regularly scheduled itineraries leave again until Saturday. Then contact Amtrak and ask for passenger lists of today's trains. Check out all the commercial and private flights to anywhere leaving from Miami, Fort Lauderdale and West Palm in the late afternoon today. Do you think you and your men can remember how to do that?" He looked stern and unforgiving.

"Alan and his girlfriend could not have simply disappeared. Someone has to have sold them a ticket or seen them." Detective Burrata said bitterly. "Recirculate the APB picture of him. Do we have a photo of the person who's traveling with him?"

"No, but I'll get one. Her name is Consuela Lopez and she worked for Mrs. Trent for years. I'm sure there's a picture of her somewhere. I'll check the DMV. She must have a driver's license," Detective Andrews answered defensively.

"We have to apprehend them before they leave the country," Detective Burrata reminded his men. "Get on it, NOW."

———————

The men were standing by the Webber grill with steaks and fresh corn in hand. Savannah and Marci were in Dave's kitchen preparing a salad.

"We deserve to celebrate your freedom and Alan's arrest," Savannah suggested. "What would you think about taking a trip, just the two of us? Like Vegas, but with no business."

"Really, do you think Dave would let us both off work at the same time?" Marci looked up from the chopping block, her eyes wide with excitement.

"I think you have a lot of influence over him now a days," Savannah laughed.

"I must admit I'd love a girl's trip, but I hate the thought of leaving your father just when we're getting so close."

"I've heard that distance makes the heart grow fonder." Savannah said mischievously and filled two wine glasses. "Where would you like to go?"

"Paris," Marci said without hesitation. "I was there years ago, with Stan, but the trip was terrible. He was there for business and I was alone most of the time. It was pretty joyless. How much more fun the museums and cafes would be with a pal."

"Okay. Paris it is. Let's look at flights and hotels tomorrow. I think Dad will agree to hire temporary help for a week or so as long as we're back before the holiday rush begins."

"Do you really think so?" Marci was thrilled at the prospect of taking long walks and exploring the world's most beautiful city again with her best friend beside her. She yearned to re-visit the Louvre and Eiffel Tower, and to see what was left of the historic Notre Dame Cathedral after the devasting fire. The more she thought about the trip, the more excited she became.

"Do you have a current passport?" Savannah was always practical.

"Sure do. It's back in the desk in my apartment."

"Let's strike while the iron's literally hot." Savannah pulled Marci gently by her arm and they approached Dave and Steven at the grill.

"Dad, what would you think about Marci and I taking a little time off? A girl's trip for a week, maybe two? I think we both deserve a break. We could arrange for someone to cover the shop. We'd like to go to Paris." Savannah's eyes pleaded with her father. She hoped he would say Yes.

"Paris? What brought that on?" Dave looked at Marci. "Is that what you'd really like, a trip to Paris?"

"Oh yes, but I don't want to leave you and *Wrights* high and dry."

"Let me think about it for a minute." He smiled and pulled Steven away from the grill, out of earshot from the women. "What would you say to you and I joining them?"

Steven didn't hesitate. "I'd love to and I think I could take two weeks off without the firm falling apart. What about you and the shop?"

"I've never taken more than a week's vacation before because I've never had the motivation. But now I do." He looked lovingly over his shoulder at Marci. "August is a notoriously slow time in the jewelry business. I could simply close the shop for two weeks. I'd lose very little, if any, business. And follow up on internet orders every morning on my laptop before we go touring. I say let's do it."

The two men returned to the grill and casually turned the steaks over. They were both grinning.

Dave looked at Marci. "I can't stand the thought of being separated from you, even for just two days. I think I'll have to say 'no' to the trip. Unless...

Marci's face showed her disappointment but she was understanding. Small businesses required lots of attention. "That's all right." She lowered her eyes. "Thank you for considering it though."

"You didn't let me finish," Dave smiled at her affectionately. "I was about to say unless you let me and Steven come along."

Marci grinned and jumped with excitement. "Ouch." She clutched her bruised ribs. "Savannah, would that be all right with you? Can the guys come along?"

Savannah looked hesitantly at Steven. They barely knew each other but their attraction had been immediate and strong. She really wanted him to come. Paris was just the place for their romance to blossom. "Would you be interested in taking the trip with me," she asked shyly. "We hardly know each other."

"Yes. I'd like to make it a foursome," Steven winked at her. "When do we leave?" He walked over and twirled her around in the air. "*Mousse au chocolat*, anyone?"

CHAPTER 82

Alan and Consuela sat at a United Airline's gate in terminal One. Their flight to New Orleans was scheduled to depart in an hour and ten minutes.

"Once we land, we'll spend the night at a nearby hotel and catch our flight to London in the morning." Alan said, studying his ticket. "Then we'll change planes to Morocco."

"I'm exhausted thinking about so many hours in the air. You know I hate to fly."

"I know, but luckily I've got Ambien with me. When we get onboard, you can put yourself into a coma." He patted her knee, reassuringly. "Don't worry."

Consuela looked at him dubiously but had little choice. There was no way for them to get to Morocco except by air.

"We have time, do you want to get a drink? They won't board us for another thirty-five minutes." He thought she needed fortification to brave the trip.

Consuela immediately stood up and grabbed her purse. "Lead the way."

The two held hands and walked down the concourse, taking seats at the nearest bar. "Two Grey Goose on the rocks," he told the server. "And some nuts if you have them."

"Sorry Sir, because so many people have peanut allergies the airport won't allow us to serve any nuts. I can bring you some pretzels though."

"That'll be fine." Consuela flirted with the bartender. "And make mine a double." She was still dreading the long hours on a plane.

They sat at the bar enjoying their drinks and did some people watching for a while before returning to their gate. Alan was anxious to board and escape to the friendly skies. "Damn," he said angrily, pointing to the board above the attendant's desk. "Look, it says our flight is delayed an hour because of a mechanical issue."

"Go get a magazine or a book," Consuela said unconcerned. The longer she was on the ground the better she felt. "We'll just get into New Orleans a little later tonight but we won't miss our morning connection."

"I know. It's just that I won't feel good until we're out of Florida and on our way to our new life." He sat down with a thud and checked his watch again. The minute hand had barely moved.

Thirty-five minutes later the attendant spoke over the microphone, first in English and then in Spanish. "Passengers on United Flight 8212 to New Orleans, we have a gate change. We are taking this aircraft out of service but we are flying in another piece of equipment for you today from Orlando. Take your time and all your possessions and move to gate A33. We are expecting a departure time of 9:30 p.m. Sorry for the inconvenience."

Alan looked at his watch again. 7:10. "Shit, that's almost two and a half hours from now."

"Well, unless we switch airlines and destinations, we have no choice but to wait. How about grabbing something to eat and another drink?" Consuela was trying to keep Alan calm. He often acted irrationally when he was provoked. She could see he was tense and close to losing his temper.

"I don't want any dinner," he shouted and glared at the hapless airline employee. "I just want to get the fuck out of here." He marched up to the gate agent. "I have important business in New Orleans. Can't you get another fucking plane here sooner than 9:30?"

"I'm sorry, Sir," she apologized sweetly. "We were fortunate to find suitable equipment at all on such short notice. Otherwise, we would have had to cancel the flight and fly you out to your destination in the morning. But there's some good news. I have vouchers for everyone to have a free meal here."

Consuela came up and stood by his side. The attendant handed him two vouchers and smiled. "Enjoy dinner on us. There are several restaurants in this concourse, but please be back at the new gate at 9:00 p.m. to begin the boarding process."

Alan was seething but there was nothing he could do. "Come on," he snarled at Consuela. "I guess you're going to get your damn dinner after all." He pulled her away from the desk and began dragging her down the concourse. He almost knocked over an elderly man with a cane as he did so. Luckily, another passenger grabbed the frightened man and steadied him before he fell.

"Watch it jerk," the man shouted. "Ever heard of manners?"

Alan started to push the man. "Fuck off." He bellowed.

Consuela got in between the two men. "Come on, Darling," she urged Alan. "Don't call attention to yourself."

Alan's face was bright red and it took all of his control not to slug the meddling man. He turned away in a huff and started barreling down the concourse. Consuela, in her stiletto heels, fought to keep up with him. As he moved farther and farther ahead, she finally removed her shoes and jogged barefoot after him yelling, "Wait Alan. Wait for me!"

They were causing a mild disturbance in the concourse. Passengers turned to gawk at them. A nearby TSA agent watched the scene unfolding and captured it on his cellphone, taking a video.

Consuela finally caught up to Alan at the Burger Fi restaurant. They ordered cheeseburgers and sweet potato fries. Alan kept checking his watch. He gulped down his food and order a beer with a tequila chaser. And then another.

"Slow down," Consuela begged. "You'll be too drunk to board the plane."

"Quit the nagging," he ordered. "Let's go see if the new plane's here." He stood up a bit unsteadily and started to move away. Consuela put her shoes back on and followed discreetly behind him, not wanting to say or do anything to set Alan off. She had always been afraid of his bad moods and because of their long, unsuccessful day and now this delay, he was in one tonight. When they arrived at the gate Alan marched up to the beleaguered gate attendant. "What's the story on our plane? Has it arrived from Orlando?" he demanded angrily.

"I'm sorry Sir," she said hesitantly. She remembered him and his temper from the earlier gate. "There were thunderstorms in the Orlando area and the plane's departure was delayed. It's now scheduled to depart in an hour. It's a quick flight over to Miami however."

"Another hour?" He looked at her, shaking with fury. "I hate the fucking Friendly skies."

Several TSA agents were standing at the security checkpoint with three members of the Sherriff's department. They were laughing about the odd ball things that had happened that day.

"It must be a full moon," one TSA agent joked. "All the crazies have come out today. One lady left her baby in the stroller at security and went right to her gate. The woman finally realized what she'd done and came running back, practically hysterical and blaming me for not bringing the baby to her. Someone else came through the line trying to smuggle bottles of Cannabis Oil in her purse. She'd put the CBD oil in a few travel size shampoo bottles. When I found them and said she'd have to discard them, she bit me. No kidding. I had to get a tetanus shot." He raised his sleeve and showed them the red teeth marks. "Needless to say, I saw to it that she didn't make her flight." Then he pulled out his phone. "And a few minutes ago, I shot a video of a man storming down the concourse with a barefoot woman, someone straight out of *Playboy* bunny casting, screaming and running to catch him from behind. It was quite a sight. The lady, whose boobs were falling out of her blouse, was waving her shoes and pocketbook frantically in the air. It was like a scene out of a movie."

He handed the deputy his phone so he could watch the video. "Wait a minute," the deputy said. "That man looks very familiar."

CHAPTER 83

Marci jumped into Dave's arms. "Are you serious? You'd really come with me to Paris?"

"Not only will I come with you, but I'll have my travel agent make all the arrangements first thing tomorrow." He looked at his daughter with uncertainty. "As long as you feel comfortable double dating with your old man?"

"I am, I really am." Savannah reassured him. "I'm truly happy you and Marci have found each other."

"Me too," he grinned. "I'm a slow mover but I finally got it right."

Savannah pulled Steven to the side. "Speaking of moving, this thing between us is moving pretty fast. Are you sure you're up for this trip with me?"

"You bet I am." He picked her up and swung her around in the air. "My life was pretty staid until we met. Now it's a whirlwind adventure every minute."

"Let's talk about what we want to do during our two weeks in Paris, if we want to take any side trips, to Giverny and Normandy? Or maybe spend one of our weeks in wine country? And, when you all think you can leave. Then I'll take care of the tickets and reservations," Dave said, leading them back inside.

"I don't want to put a damper on this trip, but I think we should wait a week or two," Steven said. "I want to be sure Alan's caught and doesn't get bail. I also need time to put Marjorie's house on the market and take care of some estate details."

"Sure, that's fine," Savannah agreed. "That will give us time to get everything squared away in the shop, pay some bills in advance and notify customers that *Wrights* will be closed for vacation."

"Okay. I'll take care of it," Dave said. "By the way, has anyone heard from Detective Burrata? I thought he'd text us by now to say they've got Alan."

"I gave my phone to Alan back at the house," Marci remembered. "He must still have it. My first order of business is to get a new one. I feel lost without it."

"He wouldn't have texted you anyway," Savannah explained gently. "He doesn't know your number. But it's strange we haven't heard anything. Why don't we call him? We're certainly entitled to an update, and Marci will probably have to go to the police station to press charges against Alan in the morning."

Marci was worried about having to confront Alan in court. She would like never to lay eyes on him again, but she'd do whatever was necessary to see him punished.

The congenial group continued talking about their ideas for the Paris trip and agreed that they all wanted to spend a full week in the city with a day trip to Versailles and Giverny, and then spend time touring the Loire Valley and Bordeaux for wine tastings.

"I'd love to spend a night or two in one of the famous castles," Marci suggested sheepishly. "A haunted one, if possible."

Everyone laughed but they agreed it would be fun.

"I'll be sure to put that on the itinerary." Dave smiled warmly at her. "And I'll protect you from the ghosts."

"I've been to France several times over the years," Steven said. "And the landscapes are

spectacular and the wines are superb. But I have to be honest, I still prefer California grapes. However, I'm more than happy to give French wines another try."

"How noble of you," Savannah laughed. "Are you some kind of wine snob? And speaking of that. Does anyone want a glass now?"

"Good idea. We have to toast to Marci's freedom and to our Paris trip." Dave opened a bottle of sauvignon blanc and handed everyone a glass. "To Marci's return and to our upcoming trip to France."

The doorbell rang.

CHAPTER 84

He's the guy on the APB today," the sheriff's deputy said looking at the video. "Holy crap. Where did you say you took it?"

"On Concourse One at the beginning of the United gates," the TSA agent answered. "About fifteen minutes ago. I'll double back there. Hopefully he hasn't already boarded his flight. The rest of you take positions around the other gates until we determine where he's at. Then we'll move in together. We have to take him quickly and not endanger any other passengers. I don't know whether he smuggled a weapon past security, but we'd better be prepared."

The TSA agent who had taken the video turned around and sprinted back to the United Airlines gate area. At the beginning of them, he carefully checked out all the passengers in the waiting area. Not finding the suspect, he continued down the line of adjacent departure gates. At the fifth one, he recognized Alan sitting with the same woman he'd seen in the video, but this time her shoes were on her feet and her blouse was properly done up.

He strolled casually up to the gate agent and had a brief, whispered conversation with her. He never looked in Alan's directions. Then he left.

A minute later the agent picked up her microphone. "Ladies and Gentlemen, thank you for your patience. We are now ready to board Flight # 1812 to New Orleans. We apologize for the delay. We will board from the back of the plane forward to expedite the procedure and get you all off the ground as fast as possible. Would you please line up by rows starting with row 34? We'll board first class passengers last." She began collecting the boarding passes.

She continued to call the rows, two and three at a time. The waiting area emptied quickly. "Rows 10 and 9," she announced. Then she called for rows 8, 7 and 6. Finally only the five rows of first-class passengers remained. Alan checked his boarding pass for the hundredth time. He and Consuela were in the bulkhead, seats 1A and 1B. "Rows, 5, 4 may board," she said, deliberately not looking at Alan and his traveling companion. "Now row 2."

Suddenly Alan was alarmed. He and Consuela were the only passengers left in the gate area. He noticed the desk attendant picking up her belongings and beginning to walk away.

"Hey Miss," Alan shouted and ran after her. "You haven't called our row. We've been waiting here all this fucking time. You forgot row 1."

The clerk did not turn around but began to run down the concourse in the opposite direction. Suddenly a wall of police officers, TSA Agents and sheriff's deputies, standing with their arms linked together, moved in unison to surround the two.

"You won't be taking any flights tonight," a sheriff's deputy said loudly. "You are both under arrest."

CHAPTER 85

Detective Burrata smiling broadly, marched proudly into Dave's home. "I thought you would like to know that we arrested Alan and his wife at the airport a little while ago."

"The airport?" Savannah was surprised. "I thought they were taking the yacht to escape."

"Apparently they changed their minds. We got a tip from a sheriff's deputy that they were taking a United flight to New Orleans. We arrested them as they were about to board the plane."

"Did they put up any resistance?" Marci was curious.

"No," the detective answered smugly. "We had them completely surrounded. There was no way they could escape. They're being processed now and will be spending the night in the jail."

"I assume there will be no bail. Those two are definite flight risks," Steven said soberly.

"That's not up to me," Detective Burrata said. "You can attend his first appearance before a judge tomorrow. I just came by to tell you that we did our job...and without your help. Imagine that?"

"I'm sorry if we got in your way," Savannah said softly. "We were only trying to help."

"I'm sure your intentions were honorable, but civilians usually slow down investigations rather than helping. Anyway, what's done is done and now we have to tie up all the loose ends. We will need to take your individual statements again and file additional charges of kidnapping against Alan. Marci, you will need to come to the precinct tomorrow to take care of that."

"Yes, of course I will," Marci answered meekly. "I just want this whole thing to be over."

Dave put his arm around her. "If there's nothing else, we are all exhausted and need to get some rest."

"Yes, please do that. I'll meet with you all tomorrow. I still have to sort out the bank situation at Wells Fargo. The department will confiscate the funds in the morning and hold onto them until the court determines their rightful owners. Goodnight now." He left immediately and closed the door behind him.

Marci collapsed on the sofa. "OMG. We didn't tell him that I'd transferred the funds to Steven's office account. Will I be in trouble?" She looked at Dave in a panic.

CHAPTER 86

The next morning Savannah went to the police station to give her statement to Detective Burrata. Marci had an appointment an hour later. Dave and Steven were scheduled to meet with him later that morning.

Savannah was taken to an interview room where everything she said was recorded. Detective Burrata produced the previous statement that she'd given Detective Andrews at the Trent home. He asked her to read it and if it was accurate, to sign it again. Then he began another round of questions which were more intense and very specific. She tried her best to answer everything honestly and stick to the facts, although her dislike of Alan was obvious in her remarks.

She described when Alan first came into the shop and purchased the ugly pumpkin brooch from Marci. She expressed her surprise when he paid for it with hundred-dollar bills and the next day came back for the matching ring…again paying all cash. She continued to chronicle everything that happened when Alan brought Mrs. Trent's jewelry to Marci and asked her to have *Wrights* sell it for him.

"And how did you come to represent yourself as a Census worker and attempt entrance to the Trent estate?" he persisted. "Were you suspicious of Alan at that time?"

"Yes, very," she answered quickly. "I thought it was strange that he would be purchasing such expensive jewelry in cash. I even took some of the cash to our bank to be sure it wasn't counterfeit. The teller assured me that the money was okay, so Dad and I went to our family attorney, Sheldon Blake, and asked him to have his private investigator check out Alan. We were both worried that he was using Marci and our shop to promote illegal activities."

"And it turns out that you were right," Detective Burrata said. "But back to why you pretended to be a Census taker."

"Oh that." Savannah had gotten ahead of herself. "I wanted to talk to Mrs. Trent to be sure she knew Alan was selling her jewelry and to ask her if she still had the pumpkin brooch. That's because one just like it coincidentally showed up at a previously owned booth at the Las Vegas International Jewelry Convention. And we happened to know that brooch was one of a kind."

"Whoa, you've lost me. Slow down Savannah and start from the beginning." He looked at his watch. "I guess this is going to take longer than I'd expected. I'll order in some sandwiches."

CHAPTER 87

A s soon as Alan was arrested, he used his one call to hire a local criminal defense lawyer, who he found though an internet ad, to represent him and Consuela. While he waited anxiously in a holding cell for the attorney to arrive, he became more and more anxious about his legal predicament. And after his initial meeting with the lawyer, Alan grasped the full impact of his crimes and their consequences. He was in deep shit.

The lawyer, Grant McLean, pointed out that if convicted on all counts, Alan would spend the rest of his life in prison, but there was one strong ray of hope. He explained that the police would have a hard time making a case for murder. The evidence was purely circumstantial. No one could prove that Mrs. Trent hadn't taken the pills herself, or that she hadn't willingly given her jewelry to Alan. There were no witnesses to the contrary. Consuela would back him up with her testimony, although it wouldn't count for much given her personal involvement in the scam and her relationship with Alan. Mr. McLean bragged that he would use his considerable legal talents and expertise to refute the homicide charges and make a strong case that the prosecution had not proved its allegations beyond any reasonable doubt.

The fact that Alan might escape the death penalty did little to make him happy. To the contrary, he'd been in jail before, and dreaded the thought of spending the rest of his days locked up. He wished he'd been smart enough to have his Ambien with him now. He'd gladly overdose to avoid a life sentence.

Mr. McLean also explained that Alan's previous run-ins with the law were a huge problem. The real cause for concern, however, was the kidnapping of Marci Morgan. At a minimum Alan was looking at charges for kidnapping, identity theft, wire fraud, bank fraud, assault & battery and grand larceny. Marci would be called as a witness against him and would not be granted spousal immunity because she wasn't his legal wife. He had kidnapped her, drugged her, married her under a false name and held her against her will. Then he had blackmailed her to assist him in his scheme to defraud the bank by threatening to harm her best friend.

"The charge of kidnapping is tricky," the lawyer further explained, "and a conviction would stand or fall on a "he said, she said" defense. It all depends on how Marci testifies. She could exonerate you completely by stating that she went willingly with you to the bank, although that is of course unlikely. A judge or jury would take into consideration the reputations of each of you and clearly would be swayed in her favor. On your side though is the fact that you never made any ransom demands and in the long run, you did not significantly endanger or harm her. Let's not worry about what charges might be filed against you for the moment."

"*Easy for you to say, Asshole,*" Alan thought angrily but he kept his mouth shut. At the moment, Mr. McLean and his legal expertise was his only hope.

The more the lawyer talked, the more desperate and upset Alan became.

"Let's take one thing at a time," Mr. McLean stated. "The first order of business is to try to get you and Consuela out on bail and then we'll have plenty of time to strategize about your defense."

"Do you think they'll let us out?" Alan didn't think so after listening to the lawyer recite the list of possible charges.

"Consuela maybe, but I'm not so certain about you. The prosecution will claim you're a flight risk. I will counter that by saying you've been a dependable, hard-working employee at the Trent estate for many years. We can get some of the former staff to be character witnesses and speak on your behalf. It might work, but honestly, I don't have to remind you. You were arrested while trying to flee the country.

Alan started to shake and really needed a drink. His whole life had fallen apart in the last twenty-four hours, all his dreams dashed. Once he calmed down a bit, Mr. McLean continued. "I also will need to recommend that Consuela secure her own counsel. If the prosecution is smart, they'll get your girlfriend to turn state's evidence. She's your accomplice any way you look at it. If you go down, so will she…she may want to avoid all of that and make a clean break from you."

"Damn, this day just keeps getting better and better," Alan fumed.

CHAPTER 88

Marci sat erectly behind a metal desk across from Detective Burrata and patiently answered his questions.

"Start from the beginning and explain how you got involved with Alan Trent aka Peter Scant and tell me everything's that's happened between you two since." He turned on the video camera and began to take notes.

Marci explained that she met Alan when he came into shop to buy a gift for his grandmother's birthday and then went on to chart the short sordid story of his courtship and their "wedding". An hour and a half later, Marci finished by painstakingly describing how sick she'd been during the ceremony and that she believed that Alan had drugged her and taken her to a motel by the airport.

"May I have something to drink please?" she asked, on the edge of exhaustion. The recounting had taken an emotional and physical toll and she was visibly upset. She was eager to be done and get out of there, and run to the safety of Dave's arms.

The detective handed Marci a bottle of water and continued his relentless questions. "We're going to stay here until I have the full story," he said firmly. "I want to know everything that happened after you left the guest house, about your stay in the motel and when and why Consuela joined you. And, most importantly, why you closed out the joint bank account yesterday and didn't think to mention it to me before now."

The detective's tone was strained. Marci feared that now he saw her as a suspect, instead of as a victim.

"Yes, well, I'm terribly sorry. When you came over last night, we were all so excited that you arrested Alan and Consuela that I completely forgot to mention going to the bank. Am I in trouble? Do I need to call a lawyer? You are making me uncomfortable." She was trying so hard to be honest, but she could see that her interrogator was dubious about some parts of her story and she was suddenly afraid she might incriminate herself.

"It's your right to have an attorney present," he replied. "But it's not necessary and will just prolong this procedure. Attorneys always muck things up. Just tell me the truth and you'll be fine."

"I don't think I should say anything else," Marci said, her composure returning. "I have heard that a lot of innocent people are sent to jail and I don't want to be one of them. I'm not saying another word without my lawyer present."

The detective grunted and stood up abruptly, pushing a button on the desk intercom. "The lady wants a lawyer."

"Who is your attorney?" Detective Burrata asked, realizing he had lost the battle. "Do you have his phone number?"

"Actually, I don't have one, but I'm friends with Steven Framin. He's a lawyer. Can I speak to him please?"

"I'm afraid not. He's a witness in this case, so that would be a conflict."

"How about Dave Wright then? He's my friend. Can I ask him for a recommendation?"

"You could, but by the time you call him and he makes his calls, it'll have taken much more time. Why don't you sit tight and I'll see if I can find a court appointed lawyer for you?" He left the room abruptly to find one.

CHAPTER 89

Dave and Steven took their turns being interviewed by other detectives. Their questioning was routine. Dave confessed that he had given Sheldon Blake the pumpkin brooch for safekeeping and would hand it over to the police as evidence. Steven explained how he'd gotten involved in the case as Marjorie Trent's lawyer. Both men were quickly excused, but told they'd need to be available to testify at Alan's trial. When they were done, they asked about Savannah and Marci. They were told that Savannah had already left the police station for the courthouse and Alan's arraignment and that Marci was still in the interview room.

"I don't know why they're keeping her for so long," Dave worried. "Let's find Savannah and see if Alan got bail. Then we'll come back here for Marci."

The courthouse was directly across the street, so they did not have far to walk. They arrived in time to see both Consuela, who was sobbing and Alan, who maintained a blank facial expression and avoided eye contact with anyone, being led away in handcuffs.

"Dad, Steven," Savannah shouted. "Over here." She was standing against the wall looking pleased. "I'm sorry you missed it. The judge was not at all sympathetic and refused to let either Consuela or Alan out on bail. He said that they had been arrested in the act of fleeing the state of Florida and were therefore flight risks. They have to stay locked up until their trials."

"Well, I'm glad that part of this is behind us at least. I know that we're all going to be called as witnesses eventually, but the way the legal system works, that could be months or even years from now." Dave hugged his daughter in relief. "Let's go back and find Marci. I don't know what more Detective Burrata wants with her. She's innocent. Period!"

———————

When the three arrived back at the police station, Dave went up to the desk sergeant and asked if Marci was through with her interview.

"No, Sir," the officer replied politely. "She asked for a lawyer and she's been huddled inside talking to him. Lawyers always complicate things."

"A lawyer?" Dave asked. "Why would Marci need a lawyer?"

"You can ask him yourself." He pointed to a man in a dark, three-piece suit walking down the hall.

"Are you Marci Morgan's friends?" the lawyer asked.

"Yes, we are." Steven introduced everyone.

"I'm Robert Paine, her temporary court appointed lawyer until she can secure her own representation."

"Why would she need you or anyone?" Savannah was alarmed. "She's the victim in all this. I don't understand."

"You're correct," Mr. Paine said. "But the police have to verify her story. There's the problem of her wiring money that did not belong to her to some attorney's escrow account. She had no right to do that. The authorities need to verify that the funds went there and that she had no ulterior motive in moving the money. It's purely a technicality but has to be resolved before she can leave."

"That would be my account," Steven spoke up loudly. "She only did it to keep Alan from moving the money out of the country. I know. I was with her and I suggested she send the money to my firm's escrow account for safe keeping. My firm represents the state of Marjorie Trent."

"There!" Savannah snorted. "Don't you see? This is ridiculous. She's completely innocent."

"I agree," Mr. Paine said sincerely. "This is a misunderstanding and I assured Marci that it will all get straightened out in time. Justice moves slowly and right now she is being held in custody until the facts of her story can be verified. From the State's perspective, she's an accomplice until proven otherwise."

"Held?" Dave erupted. "Held where? This is unconscionable! We've all told you the same story. What more proof do you need?"

"I think the police want to investigate this and substantiate Marci's claim she was only trying to be a good Samaritan and keep Alan from moving it out of the country. He of course is claiming something else entirely. He has told police Marci was involved in all this from the get-go, and in fact, the whole scheme was her idea."

"That's the stupidest thing," Savannah cried in frustration. "Absolutely ludicrous. I want to see Marci."

———————

Minutes later, Savannah stood outside the Fort Lauderdale court-house with her father and Steven. She watched in dismay as a deputy from the Sheriff's department led her best friend away. Marci turned and smiled forlornly, bravely trying not to cry. Only hours before, they had been planning a celebratory late summer trip to Paris; now, the only place Marci would be visiting was a 6-by-8 foot holding cell in the local Broward County jail until she could clear her name -- or if charged with a crime, post bail and await her trial.

CHAPTER 90

We have to do something," Dave said frantically. "We can't let them keep Marci locked up. She's been through enough."

"I'm sure the police will straighten this out quickly," Steven said sympathetically. "She hasn't actually been charged with anything. The authorities are just detaining her until her story can be substantiated by someone, anyone other than her best friends." He looked directly at Dave and Savannah. "I'm sure you understand that you both may be considered a little prejudiced."

"Yes, but surely there's someone who can verify that Marci knew nothing about the money until Alan forced her to go to the bank on his behalf. As a matter of fact, I'm positive that she didn't even know she had a joint account with him. That's what we have to prove." Savannah's mind was already spinning with the possibilities.

"I'll leave that to you and the experts for now," Dave said. "I'm going over to the jail and see if they'll let me see Marci. She must be scared to death."

"Okay Dad. If you get to see her, give her my love and tell her that

Steven and I are working on a way to clear this up." Savannah looked at Steven begging for his help and he nodded his approval.

Dave walked toward the jail while Steven and Savannah huddled on the sidewalk, trying to decide what to do. "Should we hire a criminal attorney to represent Marci?" Savannah asked.

———————

Detective Burrata did not feel good about Marci being held. He had been with the FBI for twenty years before joining the Fort Lauderdale police department and had an intuitive sense of human nature. He would bet his life that she was an innocent pawn in Alan's diabolical scheme. Innocent people often went to prison and some spent their whole lives there in a tragic miscarriage of justice. He was bound and determined to make sure that didn't happen in this case. In spite of the aggravation Savannah and her friends had caused him, they were nice people sincerely trying to help their friend in her hour of need. He wished more citizens would try to help and support the police instead of protesting and defaming their reputation. After all his years in law enforcement, he knew just what to do. He called his former partner who still worked at FBI in DC and asked for a favor.

"Mike, it's me," he began. "How the hell are you?"

His former partner knew him so well and chuckled. "This is not a friendly catch-up call, is it? You must need something. What can I do for your sorry ass?"

"Guilty, as charged," Detective Burrata laughed. "I need a huge favor. Can you get me the name of an accredited handwriting expert in Florida?"

"Sure, but why? Do you actually have real crimes in that sleepy Fort

Lauderdale town?" he joked. "Besides jaywalking and littering, I mean."

"Yes, from time to time." Detective Burrata snickered. "I'll explain later, but I need that name ASAP."

"Hold on. I've got my rolodex right here on my desk."

Detective Burrata paced nervously around his office. Jail was not a safe place for a beautiful young woman. Marci would be okay in the holding area, but he didn't want to see her taken to an actual cell. And besides, he couldn't imagine what Savannah and her group of amateur sleuths would do to him if anything happened to her.

"I've got a name," Mike said. "but he's in Palm Beach. Is that too far?"

"No, no. That'll be fine. Can you text me his contact info? And thanks. I owe you one. We'll talk soon."

———————————

Savannah and Steven brainstormed on the sidewalk until the afternoon sun made them uncomfortable and they went inside a local diner to have a cold drink and cool off.

"How does one open a checking account?" Savannah asked.

"Normally by filling out a signature card." Steven answered. "I think you know that, but I see where you're going."

"Good." She smiled at him. "If Marci never signed a signature card, then that's the proof we need that she didn't know her name was on the account until she was kidnapped. If we can prove that, it will clear her."

Steven slapped a ten-dollar bill down on the table and they hurried to his car. Forty minutes later they entered the Wells Fargo Bank and asked to speak to the manager.

Savannah introduced herself and Steven, and she explained that they wanted to make a copy of the signature cards for Alan Trent's joint account. She told him about Marci's detainment and that they were there hoping to find proof that she had not signed the signature cards.

"I've been expecting you," the manager grinned. "Detective Burrata warned me that you'd probably show up."

"What?" Savannah gasped in amazement.

"He called a while ago and filled me in on everything about the Ms. Morgan's case and of course, I already knew about "Operation Imposter" that was foiled by some do-good civilians. I presume that was you?"

"Yes." Savannah looked embarrassed. "But tell us about Detective Burrata."

"Why did he call you?" Steve asked impatiently.

"The detective needed my help. He said he'd hired a handwriting expert and asked for copies of the signature cards for Alan Trent's account. I believe he is determined to prove your friend is innocent. I've already scanned and sent the cards to his handwriting expert in Palm Beach."

"Well, what do you know," Savannah grinned. "It looks like we underestimated the good detective. Can you believe it?" She was overwhelmed with gratitude. She turned to Steven. "He's a big softy just like Columbo!"

"You know, even if I had wanted to, I could not have given you access to those signature cards," the bank manager explained. "That's privileged information, so that's even more reason to be grateful that the detective took the initiative."

"I thought you'd have to turn us away." Steven looked sheepish. "But we had to try."

"Thank you for sending the cards to Detective Burrata's expert. I'm sure he will prove our friend is innocent." Savannah shook his hand.

"Glad to be of service," the manager smiled. "And Detective Burrata asked me to pass along this message if you showed up here."

"Oh Lord," Savannah held her breath. "Are we in trouble again?"

The manager smiled and began to read his notes. "Tell those boy and girl detectives that in spite of all their shenanigans, I wish all citizens were as conscientious. He said to tell you that his handwriting expert has already compared Marci's signature on her police statement with that on the bank's signature card. They were definitely <u>not</u> a match, absolutely not written by the same person. He's arranged for Marci Morgan's immediate release."

Savannah broke into happy tears and spontaneously hugged Steven, and then the surprised bank manager.

EPILOGUE

One Year Later

Marci and Dave gazed lovingly into each other's eyes and held hands. They were sipping café au lait in a small bistro with a view of the Eiffel Tower. The two were married in a simple church service in Fort Lauderdale five days earlier. The intimate ceremony was followed by a small reception at the Coral Ridge Country Club. Now they were enjoying their honeymoon in Paris. Savannah had been Marci's maid of honor and Steven served as Dave's best man.

With the newlyweds' permission, Savannah and Steven accompanied them on the trip that the four of them had planned to take a year ago. Savannah and Steven were celebrating their own engagement and planning a wedding in the Fall.

"A year ago, I would not have thought this trip possible...that we'd all be in Paris together," Savannah smiled. "At the time, it looked like at least one of us would be going to jail."

"Stop it," Marci warned. "That's nothing to joke about."

The previous year had been filled with depositions, court appearances and finally the trial of Alan and Consuela who, as an accessory to Marjorie Trent's murder, had not gotten an offer to turn's state's evidence after all. But it was also a time of love and many happy times. The four friends had become inseparable. After much consideration and serious discussions with Savannah, Dave sold his beloved store, *Wrights,* and retired completely. He and Marci spent weeks house hunting and they finally bought a beautiful home on the intracoastal waterway. Marci decorated and furnished it, with Savannah's help. She also took daily golf lessons so she could play competitively with Dave.

Savannah at first was a little lost without her job at *Wrights,* but with Steven's urging and support, she decided to spend her time doing what she loved the best, figuring out crimes. She took a basic course in policework at the local university and decided to begin her own series of detective novels for young adults. She didn't expect to compete with Nancy Drew and her followers, but there was enough room in the genre for other books on the same subject for a new generation.

Detective Burrata became a good friend and readily agreed to serve as Savannah'sa criminal and police consultant. He was full of good ideas and suggestions. She was almost finished revising her first manuscript and looking for a publisher.

The year had finally brought resolution to the Alan Trent situation. After a trial by jury, he was found guilty of murder as well as the lesser charges and sentenced to life in prison without parole. Consuela was found guilty as his accomplice. After serving her sentence of twenty years in prison, she would be deported back to Mexico.

"It's been quite a year," Savannah sighed happily. "But fabulous!"

"Yes, it has," Marci smiled mysteriously at her best friend. "The best year of my life."

"So how are we going to top it?" Steven asked. "It doesn't get much better than this." He looked around at the beautiful city, his heart filled with love for Savannah.

"I wouldn't be too sure," Dave grinned. "I know it's against the odds, and I never thought it would happen but Savannah, you my darling daughter, are going to have a baby sister or brother in a few months."

Savannah and Steven were momentarily stunned.

"But Dad," she quickly did the math in her head. "When your baby turns sixteen, you'll be seventy-six."

"I know, honey. Believe me, Marci and I have given this baby thing a lot of thought. But first of all, seventy is the new fifty. And think about how many men about my age have become fathers and started second families. Richard Gere was seventy when he welcomed his second son into the world. Rod Stewart was sixty-six when he had his seventh child and Clint Eastwood was also sixty-six when his child was born. If those men can do it, so can I."

"Wow, I guess you have done your homework." Savannah was impressed but still floored by the news. She never entertained the idea that Marci and her dad would have a child. This would take a little getting used to.

Marci looked at Savannah and squeezed her hand, trying to reassure her. "Don't worry. Your Dad and I will be stay-at-home parents. Our child will not go to daycare or be left with sitters while we go to work or travel for business. Think about it, our baby will have 24-7 hands on parents, except when we play golf." She winked at her husband. "But we have that figured out too. Dave has ordered a custom golf cart with a child's car seat installed in a specially designed rear seat.

"I guess you two have everything covered after all," Steven grinned. "Congratulations."

"Okay then." Savannah smiled and blew her father a kiss. "How about a group hug? This news calls for a celebratory drink. Steven, as our wine expert, would you recommend a French or a California one?"

"Under the circumstances, one of each would be appropriate," Steven laughed. "And some ginger ale for the mother-to-be."

ACKNOWLEDGMENTS

My deepest gratitude goes to Shandee Chernow and Richard Poczulp, without whose help this novel would never have made it to the publisher. They were "on call" for all kinds of computer emergencies and with patience and good humor always fixed the problems.

Additionally, I want to thank my outstanding editor, Susan Leon, for her creative ideas, her organizational abilities and her command of the English language. This is a far better novel because of her expertise and input.